FALLEN
ANGEL

BOOKS BY D.K. HOOD

Detectives Kane and Alton Series

D.K. HOOD

FALLEN ANGEL

bookouture

Published by Bookouture in 2021

An imprint of Storyfire Ltd.
Carmelite House
50 Victoria Embankment
London EC4Y 0DZ

www.bookouture.com

ISBN: 978-1-80019-336-9
eBook ISBN: 978-1-80019-335-2

This book is a work of fiction. Names, characters, businesses, organizations, places and events other than those clearly in the public domain, are either the product of the author's imagination or are used fictitiously. Any resemblance to actual persons, living or dead, events or locales is entirely coincidental.

To my family. You're always in my heart.

PROLOGUE

TUESDAY

An icy blast of wind hit Dakota Storm the second she stepped into the night from the warmth of the Glacial Heights Ski Resort. The two sets of doors, set up like an airlock to ease the patrons into the cold from the cozy inner sanctum, hadn't worked, although she had to admit she'd dallied far too long before the massive log fire. The tumbling overnight temperatures on the mountain usually had most people tucked up in their rooms well before midnight. Now, she understood why. Apprehension gripped her as she stared around getting her bearings. The resort appeared very creepy at night and, having no sense of direction, if she made one wrong step, she'd be lost.

Ahead, dark shadows fell across a winding pathway that broke into a spiderweb of trails leading through a thick wooded area to the numerous chalets. A shiver of uncertainty crept up her spine and she hesitated before making her way to the main pathway. The track was lit by a line of small lampposts with round globes. They resembled a string of miniature moons and offered a muted glow over the snow. Along each side of the pathway the blackened trunks of tall pines appeared to guard an eerie, endless mass of black spreading out into nothingness.

Pushing her fears of dark confined places to one side, Dakota peered at the signpost directing her to the chalets and looked all around, before taking a few hesitant steps into the tunnel of gloom. Snowflakes brushed her cheeks as she hurried through a wooded area, her boots sliding on the icy layer beneath the snow. Ahead, she spotted another signpost and slipped and slid in the direction of her *chalet*, a fancy name for a cabin in the woods. On arrival that morning, the scene had resembled a Christmas card from Switzerland. Her chalet was a gingerbread house sitting in a small clearing beside a partly frozen pool, fed by a trickle of water running from one of the many falls in the area. As she passed the small stream running alongside the pathway, the ice-packed banks and black ice-covered water sent chills down her spine. Falling in there would mean instant death.

A noise in the darkness stopped her midstride, and heart pounding, she turned in a circle, seeing nothing in the inky blackness between the trees. Did animals hunt at night? A loud crack came close by and she pressed one hand to her chest, sure her heart would break out of her ribs. All around her the dark pines creaked as their limbs froze, sounding like a wild beast crashing through the forest. Breathing so hard her chest hurt, she left the main path and headed for her chalet. The next moment the light outside her cabin exploded in a shower of glass, plunging her into darkness. Panic gripped her and she madly searched her pockets for her phone. With trembling fingers, she accessed the flashlight and, taking a steadying breath, headed for the door.

Before she had time to pull out her key, the muffled scrape of boots came from behind her. Her eyesight blanked out from a blow to the back of her head. Dakota stumbled forward, turned, and aimed her flashlight, but the blow to her wrist sent her phone tumbling to the ground. Sheer terror gripped her as a shadowy figure loomed over her. She scrambled back, slipping in the snow and falling to her knees. Fear had her by the throat and her scream came out in a husky whine. It was her worst nightmare and, struggling to her feet, she tried to gasp out a few words but hardly recognized her own strangled voice. "What do you want?"

No answer came in the night, only pain.

ONE

Black Rock Falls, Montana

Sheriff Jenna Alton headed for the shower after a grueling workout with Dave Kane, her second-in-command at the Black Rock Falls Sheriff's Office. So many things had changed since she'd left DEA Agent Avril Parker and the FBI behind, and entered witness protection as Jenna Alton. She should be safe, but the drug cartel she'd given evidence against was never far from her mind. Although all had been killed in a shootout with the police, being undercover for so long, Jenna understood just how far the families of the cartel stretched. Even with extensive plastic surgery to disguise her and hiding in plain sight in a backwoods town in Montana, she never really relaxed. Especially now that her once sleepy town had become the center of attention of late and, it seemed, a magnet for every type of murdering psychopath. Since the homicides, a series of novels had been written about Black Rock Falls and throughout the week a book convention was being held at the ski resort at Glacial Heights. Authors, agents, publishers, and readers from all over had descended on the town. The fact it was snowing hadn't deterred the inquisitive visitors, and a variety of tours to the gruesome scenes of murder and mayhem had been booked out for months.

After showering, she dressed in warm clothes and headed toward the smell of fresh coffee and bacon. As usual, Kane had gotten ready before her and was busying himself with breakfast. As Jenna heated the maple syrup in the microwave and placed the fixings on the table for the coffee, her black cat, Pumpkin, weaved in and out of her legs, waiting for a tasty morsel from her plate. Jenna smiled at Kane as he flipped the hotcakes. He made such delicious hotcakes from scratch and liked them with crispy strips of bacon and floating in maple syrup. She took the maple syrup from the microwave and heated two plates. "The bacon smells so good."

"Yeah, it's smoked. I had some at Aunt Betty's Café the other day and asked for the name of their supplier. The order came in yesterday with the other supplies. If we get snowed in, we can survive the winter." Kane looked over one shoulder at her. "Ready to eat?"

Jenna smiled at him. Since moving into her house, he'd taken over the laborious chore of ordering supplies. He was the most organized person she'd ever met and knew exactly what they needed for themselves or the animals at any given time. "Yeah, let's get at it. The snowplow guy just went through and, by the way it's snowing up a storm out there, the roads will be blocked before we make it to town."

"I'll attach the snowplow to the Beast in case we run into trouble." Kane slid hotcakes onto plates and added a stack of bacon. "Remind me to grab another coat for Duke as well. He got wet yesterday and his teeth were chattering like castanets on the way home."

Jenna nodded. The snowplow attachment Kane had purchased for his tricked-out black truck, affectionately known as the Beast, had been worth its weight in gold during the long winter months. "Sure." She poured the coffee. "I guess we should wander up to the convention and make sure everyone is behaving themselves."

"Ha." Kane poured cream into his coffee. "You just want to meet the authors." He grinned at her. "You've had your head in a book for the last few weeks."

Jenna nodded. "They're kind of addictive, you know, reading about our town and the crimes we solved. I'd love to get my copies autographed and there's a book signing this morning."

"Uh-huh." Kane tossed a strip of bacon to Duke, his bloodhound. "Personally, I like to forget the murders once we have the killer in jail, but I'm a sucker for a good thriller or a historical novel. They'll have books for sale there as well, I assume?"

Jenna nodded. "Yeah, from the flyer, a group of publishers are promoting a ton of authors." She cleared her throat. "I hope Rowley and Rio can handle the office for a couple of hours. Although nothing has come in on the 911 line overnight."

"I'm sure they can handle any accidents caused by the weather." Kane ate slowly. "We have snow every year and yet people still drive unprepared. It's hard to fathom." He gave her a long thoughtful look. "Although, with all the visitors in town just now, anything is possible."

Shaking her head, Jenna swallowed a mouthful of food and then sipped her coffee. "I figure the roads in town will be fine unless we have an unexpected weather event. A blizzard is always in the cards, but because the ski resort brings so much revenue to the town, this year the mayor purchased a ton of snowplows and salt spreaders. He's hired more drivers and has them working practically around the clock to keep the roads clear for the tourists. Most visitors are flying in for the convention and staying for a couple of weeks. The ski lodge is almost full and so are most of the cabins."

"Those chalets are growing like a small city up there." Kane leaned back in his chair and sighed. "The building is nonstop. I figure finding your way around there now will be like negotiating a maze." He took a long drink from his cup and eyed her over the rim. "I wonder if we could sneak a couple of days up there? Two days skiing and staying one night would be a nice break." He grinned at her. "But I so want to go to Hawaii next summer or maybe Florida. Somewhere hot."

"Oh yeah." Jenna chuckled. She enjoyed being in a relationship with Kane. It had been a long time coming. "Somewhere hot with a beach and palm trees is my dream vacation, but with our luck, something will happen to keep us tied to town." She sighed. "It's been ages since we last hit the beach." She finished her coffee and stretched.

"You done eating?" Kane stood, collected the plates, and stacked them in the dishwasher. "We'd better head off or we'll never make it to work on time. The roads might be okay in town but we still have to get there." He bent and kissed her on the head. "You'd better bring your books. From the flyer, the book signing is at ten."

Jenna's phone chimed and she glanced at the caller ID. "It's Carter." She raised an eyebrow and put her phone on speaker. "Morning."

"Hi there, Jenna. Just calling to touch base. With the snow and all, we have nothing to do. Any cases you want to share?" Special Agent Ty Carter out of Snakeskin Gulley, an ex-navy Seal, super-detective, and bomb expert, sounded bored.

Glancing out the window at the threatening snow clouds, Jenna bit back a laugh. "Sorry, we have nothing either. It's all quiet here, thank goodness. How is Jo?"

They'd met behavioral analyst and Special Agent Jo Wells when she and Carter became their local go-to FBI office. She liked Jo and her little girl, Jaime, and they'd all become friends. She figured working on murder cases created a close bond between people. She had a close-knit team: Deputies Jake Rowley and Zac Rio and the medical examiner, Shane Wolfe. He and his daughters were like family. In fact, the entire team were all close friends and worked together like a well-oiled machine.

"She's fine. How are you since the break-in?" Carter cleared his throat. "Having any flashbacks?"

Sighing, Jenna smiled at his concern. Over Halloween, Jenna

had been alone when an intruder trashed her ranch house. "No, I'm good, but I was a bit jumpy living here alone. I'm fine now Dave is staying with me."

"*That's good to know.*" Carter cleared his throat. "*Ah... Jo sends her love and is begging you to call us if you, and I quote, 'Get anything juicy.'*" Carter chuckled. "*We're running out of things to do. Jo's writing a book and I'm whittling.*"

"Really? Is she writing about criminal behavior?" Jenna collected her things and headed for the front door.

"*What else?*" Carter laughed. "*Okay, I'd better let you go. Chat soon.*"

"Bye." Jenna disconnected and pulled on her hat and gloves. She looked at Kane. "Ready?"

"Yeah, as soon as I've put Duke's coat on. Come here, boy." Kane bent to secure the coat and stood. "Let's go."

Jenna stepped out into the cold and surveyed the pure-white landscape. It sure was pretty in winter. It was a shame the deep snowfalls and ice became treacherous. The tall mountain peaks and frosted pines held a deadly deception. The sudden drop in temperature could cause massive tree limbs to shatter, blocking roads and causing damage to houses. The sidewalk or blacktop could freeze in seconds and just making it to the curb to put out your trash could be deadly. As she climbed into the Beast her phone chimed again. She stared at the caller ID. "Hi Jake, what's up?"

"*Probably nothing.*" Deputy Jake Rowley sounded exhausted. "*I just had a call from the ski resort. Apparently one of the room service people found a guest missing and thinks she saw a shoe floating in the fishing hole near one of the cabins. I can't get much from the manager. He said he went and had a look, but the fishing hole is frozen over and covered with snow. They're looking for the guest. That's all the details I have.*"

Jenna leaned back in the seat and thought for a beat. "We'll go up and take a look. Are you okay running the office with Rio until we get back?"

"Sure." Rowley yawned. "Sorry, I had a long night. I took Sandy to the hospital but it ended up to be a false alarm. I dropped her at her parents' house. It's closer to the hospital and her mom will keep an eye on her today."

Rowley's wife was expecting twins at the end of the month, but they'd all laid bets that the babies would arrive early. Jenna nodded to herself. "Well, if you need a couple of hours shut-eye, leave Rio in charge and head down to the cells. It's nice and warm in there. I'd rather have you alert than exhausted from lack of sleep. I'll wake you when we get back, if need be."

"Thank you. That's a very tempting offer." Rowley gave a raspy cough. "I'll have some coffee and I'll be okay for a time. Are you dropping by the office first?"

Jenna checked the time. "No, we'll head straight to the ski resort. Catch you later." She disconnected and rolled her eyes at Kane. "Let's hope this isn't anything to worry about."

"It's a ski resort. The guest is probably in someone else's room." Kane shrugged. "Or she's fallen into a snowdrift and is a Popsicle. Worse case, she's been murdered." He wiggled his eyebrows at her. "The cold weather doesn't seem to slow down killers around here."

"That would complicate things." Jenna blew out a steamy sigh. "I just wanted one hour to have some fun, one itsy-bitsy little hour. Trust me, one more murder in the dead of winter and I'm moving to Hawaii."

TWO

The dark clouds surrounding Black Rock Falls had dropped so low in the last hour they appeared to have cut the mountain range in half. They carried the gray ominous hue that meant more heavy snowfalls and blizzards would soon be making life difficult. Snowflakes built up on the wipers as Kane negotiated the driveway. He pushed on his sunglasses to view the blinding-white vista spreading in all directions. The road ahead was deceptively dangerous and, although he'd equipped his truck with snow tires and had the snowplow attachment fitted, the drive to town would be slow. Due to the sudden drop in temperature, the carpet of white hid a deadly layer of black ice on the blacktop, and unless the salt spreaders had followed the snowplow earlier, the road up the mountain would take some negotiating. The Beast could handle just about any conditions, but if he made one wrong move, it would slide around on the treacherous black ice the same as every other vehicle.

"It's fate, isn't it?" Jenna turned in her seat to look at him. "You know, us wanting to go to the ski resort and we get a call about something suspicious out there."

Dave scanned the blacktop ahead, noting the damp patches. They couldn't be water, not in temperatures this low. "Maybe.

Hang on, I'm going off-road." He eased the Beast over the dirty gray mound left by the snowplow and onto the snow-covered grassy verge alongside the highway. "The truck can handle the drifts, but I don't like the look of the ice. It might be a bumpy ride, but as long as we don't run into an open gate or fence, we should be fine."

"Then why don't you take the pastoral trails?" Jenna gripped the seat. "They go through the woods from the end of my ranch and come back around to the highway about half a mile closer to town. There's a chance the snow won't be deep there. The trees will have given the trail shelter. It's worth the chance."

Unsure, Kane glanced at her. "I've only been along that trail once in all the time I've been here, when we were searching for a killer. We've no idea what condition it's in. No one has used it for years."

"We should try. I know the Beast can handle an overgrown track and it's wide." Jenna chuckled. "Let's live on the edge, Dave. It will be exciting."

He shrugged at her enthusiastic expression. "Okay. I guess we do have a snowplow with us if we get into trouble."

"See the gate about twenty yards on the right?" Jenna pointed ahead. "Let me out and I'll open it."

Dave puffed out a sigh. "It's not posted, is it? I don't want the owner taking potshots at us for trespassing."

"Don't worry." Jenna chuckled. "I won't shoot you." She grinned at him. "I purchased this parcel of land when the Old Mitcham Ranch was split up. Nobody wanted it because they believed it was cursed. As it borders my ranch, I bought it. It's over one hundred acres of natural woodlands. How can something so beautiful be cursed?"

For someone so superstitious, Jenna's enthusiasm surprised Kane. He raised an eyebrow and pulled up in front of the gate. "We haven't been that lucky, Jenna. Just how long have you owned this land?"

"Oh, I got it just before you arrived." Jenna frowned. "It actually cost me one dollar. It had to be sold, not given. I went to the auction just to see who my new neighbor was going to be. I didn't intend on buying anything."

Trying hard not to grin, Kane shook his head slowly. "Not cursed, huh?" He met her gaze. "I thought bad luck had followed me here and now I discover it was just sitting here waiting for me to arrive."

"Oh, and you call me superstitious?" Jenna slipped out of the truck and crunched through the snow to the gate.

He waited for Jenna to open the old steel gate and drove through. When she climbed back inside, bringing the scent of winter with her, he took off slowly along the track, winding through a dense wooded area. Mostly tall pines lined the way and the denser the forest became the less snow-crusted the trail. "Why haven't you mentioned owning this land before now?"

"I don't know." Jenna shrugged. "It never came up. It's not like I need to secure it. There's nothing here to steal." She looked at him. "I bet you have things you haven't told me about either."

Kane barked a laugh. "Too many to count. Some I'll tell you about; some I can't. But you know that, right?" He drove around a fallen log and moved slowly through the darkening woods. The trail seemed to close in around them, and he switched on the headlights.

"Oooooh, do tell." Jenna waved a hand. "This place is creepy good. Tell me a secret."

"Okay." Kane kept the Beast moving. "Let me see... something you don't know about me... um... I'm obsessed with new socks. I buy heaps of them. When they get those little bobbly bits on them, I throw them in the trash."

"That's not a secret." Jenna peered ahead. "Give me something really juicy."

"Oh Lord." Kane grinned at her. "I don't have anything that interesting in my arsenal. Ah, I speak six languages."

"That's not juicy." Jenna frowned. "You know almost everything about me. This isn't fair. You know my real name and I know for a fact you'll never tell me yours."

"My real name is David Kane and I have a birth certificate to prove it." He grinned at her glare. "Okay, okay, something personal. About my family then? My grandpa made his own wine. I think that's where my appreciation of a great wine comes from. His apparently was really good."

"You didn't get to taste any?" Jenna frowned. "That's a shame."

Kane pushed away memories of his past life. "No, I was too young to drink when he died. There may have been some left in the house. I don't know. After my sister died, I had the place razed to the ground."

"You burned down your grandparents' place?" She gaped at him. "Why?"

Unable to continue, Kane shrugged. "I've said too much already. You know, it's dangerous to talk about our pasts. Please, let it go, Jenna."

"Sure." Jenna leaned back in her chair and folded her arms over her chest with a sigh. "One thing and I won't ask another question: You told Carter your dad was a two-star general, was that true or a lie?"

Dammit. "That guy gets under my skin sometimes, but yeah, that was the truth. I let slip a clue to my past that could get everyone I care about killed. You, Wolfe and his family, Rowley... everyone. It doesn't take a genius to trace the families of two-stars and see who has a missing son, does it?" He stopped driving and looked at her. "I have a bounty on my head and, trust me, there are people out there who would pay a fortune to take me down."

"I already gathered that, Dave. It seems to be par for the course when it comes to snipers of your caliber. Don't worry, I understand the need for secrecy, and Carter is a patriot. He might be curious, but I'm sure you can trust him. Wolfe does and he's never been wrong yet." She squeezed his arm. "When we get through the woods, take a sharp left and there'll be another gate for me to open."

Relieved, Kane resumed the bumpy trip through the woods. The light blinded them as they came out of the darkness. He looked both ways along the highway and whistled. "I figure we should come home this way. It was slow the first time, but apart from the fallen log, it was safer than taking the highway."

"I'll call the mayor later and ask him to salt the road to the ranch. We might need to get to town in a hurry in an emergency." She slid from the truck to open the gate.

Kane moved through the gate and waited for her to climb back in. He examined the blacktop. The salt spreader had layered the highway, and the snow was melting on contact. "It looks like we're good to go. If it's as good as this all the way to the ski resort, we'll be there in no time."

"I just hope driving through the cursed woods back there hasn't changed our luck." Jenna frowned. "All we need is a murder to start the week."

THREE

The drive to the ski resort was uneventful, although as they climbed higher up the mountain, the majestic vista was a sight to behold. The deadly yet beautiful snowscape changed the familiar views into a different world, making landmarks hard to detect. Even from this great height, Jenna could see just how many roads the recent heavy snowfalls had blocked. Rows of houses had vanished into the snow and the only clue they existed came from the woodsmoke streaming out of the chimneys. In the distance she made out snowplows, blowing small streams of exhaust into the air as they cut their way through the endless white, leaving a blackened path behind them. Reluctantly, Jenna dragged her attention back to the road. As promised, snowplows had cleared the highway all the way to the top of the mountain. The blacktop glistened with the recent application of salt, and as they turned into the resort entrance, they passed a snowplow heading back down the mountain. Jenna turned to Kane. "Will Duke be okay? It's freezing out there and the chill factor with the added wind will be way too cold for him. He'll get frostbite."

"He's wearing his coat. If he gets too cold, he'll let me know." Kane tugged down double woolen caps over his ears and pulled up his hood. "I don't like it this cold either. The headaches from the metal plate in my head are still causing me problems."

It hadn't been easy for Kane. He'd ended up with a metal plate in his head courtesy of a car bombing that killed his wife. Jenna glanced at him. The last thing he appreciated was her worrying about him, so she just nodded, tucked her hair into her hood, and opened the door. "Okay let's do this." She jumped down, slipped her backpack over one shoulder, and bending her head against the blinding snow, slipped and slid her way from the parking lot to the main entrance. She couldn't resist turning round to Kane and inhaling the crisp clean pine-scented air. "It smells so good up here. We must get a few days skiing in after the convention. Maybe we can see if they have rooms available."

"Hush, don't tempt fate." Kane's sunglasses reflected her image. "Before we make plans, let's see what's going on here first."

As Jenna headed through the double doors and made her way to the front desk, she couldn't help noticing the attention she and Kane were getting from the guests. It wasn't the usual worried glances. People poked each other in the ribs and pointed as if they'd just witnessed an alien encounter. She leaned on the desk and a young woman dressed in a warm uniform grinned at her. "Our guests will be so glad to see you. They've asked about you and Aunt Betty's Café since they arrived for the convention."

Beside her, Kane chuckled and Jenna rolled her eyes at him before returning her attention to the woman. "I hope you didn't drag us up here just to parade us in front of your guests?"

"Oh no, of course not, but the author of the Black Rock Falls series gave a reading last night and it was very popular. I was on duty until late and the place was still buzzing with excitement." The receptionist glanced at Kane, and when he raised both eyebrows at her, she blushed and turned to Jenna. "We called because Agnes, one of the room service staff, delivered breakfast to Miss Storm out at one of our chalets. On her way back past the pond beside the cabin, she claims to have seen a shoe in the water. Our manager, Joe Brightway, went to take a look but couldn't see anything. Then we received a call from the convention organizers. They've been calling Miss Storm since early, to finalize her list of author interviews this morning, but she hasn't picked up or returned their messages. Mr. Brightway went to check on her and found her room empty. She is nowhere on the premises as far as we can tell." She blinked at Jenna. "Mr. Brightway said I was to send you right in when you arrived. His office is just over there." She pointed across the foyer.

Jenna followed the line of her finger and then turned back to her. "Is Agnes still here? We'd like to speak to her."

"Yes, she lives in the staff quarters. Do you need to speak with her now? I'll send her right along." The receptionist went to pick up the phone.

"Just a minute. We'll talk to her later. You mentioned being on duty last night. Did you see anyone with Miss Storm before she left for her chalet at midnight?" Kane took out his notebook and pen.

"Oh, yes, I did. She was chatting in front of the fire with the author of the Black Rock Falls series." The woman waved someone toward the desk. "Here she is now."

Jenna recognized the author at once from the image on the back of the book covers and offered her hand. "Sheriff Jenna Alton. Thank you for putting our town on the map."

"It's surreal meeting you, Sheriff, and this must be Deputy Kane?" The blonde woman smiled broadly. "You're just as I imagined. This is my niece, Rachal Whitley." She indicated to a young woman beside her. "I'm guessing you'll want to know when I last saw Dakota? We all came together, same flight. I was attending a book signing out of Wild Woods, Oregon. Last night we had dinner together and I went to my room around ten. She was making notes and drinking hot chocolate in front of the fire when I last saw her." She frowned. "I hope nothing bad has happened to her. As a literary agent, she has her enemies."

"Explain." Kane removed his gloves and leaned on the counter.

"Well, she is an excellent agent and subsequently receives a ton of submissions for representation, but she can't sign everyone and people get disappointed by rejection." The author opened her hands and sighed. "Such is life."

"Oh, Auntie, you never say a bad word about anyone do you?" Rachal rolled her eyes. "The problem with Dakota is that she's a nasty person. None of her PAs have lasted more than a month or so, and how many husbands has she had—five, or is it six? There would be so many people out there apart from authors she's upset and who hate her. Honestly, she had her entire house decorated by a New York designer and then blogged he'd ruined her home." She shook her head. "Okay, so she claims she's ultra-busy when she declines an author's pitch, and rather than contacting the authors with a personal note, her secretary sends out a form rejection letter." She sighed. "Everyone knows what she's like. For heaven's sake, she insists people call her Miss Storm. It's no wonder she gets awful feedback."

"Is this normal practice for agents?" Kane looked interested. "The form rejection letter?"

"Most agents send out more cordial rejection letters. I've spoken to Dakota about this, but she's not one to be tactful." Rachal sighed. "It's not just about writing a story. Many authors consider their work as 'their baby' and take rejection very personally. Their submission might represent years of hard work, and one single word of encouragement would go a long way."

Amazed, Jenna nodded. "Yes, but there must be a ton of writers who'd never have a hope of being published."

"I would never say never. Writing is a compulsion, and it takes time to learn how to present a manuscript in a way that makes it attractive to an agent or publisher. Dakota never offers any help and makes it worse by adding their names to a list on her rejections page. Can you imagine how embarrassing that would be after getting one of her caustic form rejection letters?" Rachal smiled at Jenna. "Although, a formal rejection might have been nicer in my experience. You see, the only other agent I ever approached replied with one word: *meh.* Whatever that means."

"That's water under the bridge." The Black Rock Falls series author laughed. "Rachal's type of thrillers wasn't to her particular taste, but she has Dakota now." She chuckled. "As a bestselling author, she can laugh now, but rejection and criticism are part of the job."

"I'm sure the agent who rejected Rachal regrets missing out on their percentage of her income." Jenna smiled. "You obviously need a tough skin to be an author and yet you seem so normal."

"We're all *normal*." The author smiled warmly. "For me, sharing my stories and meeting my readers is the charm."

"I've read all your books." Jenna patted her backpack. "I was planning on heading down to the book signing this morning before Dakota went missing."

"Don't worry. You go and find Dakota and I'll be happy to autograph your books." The author smiled. "It would be my pleasure."

Jenna pulled out the books and piled them on the counter. "Thank you. That's so kind of you."

"Is Miss Storm your agent too?" Kane was making notes.

"Mine? No. We're just friends. I don't have an agent." The author smiled ruefully.

Pulling herself back to the missing woman's case, Jenna straightened. "It was great meeting you. We'd better go speak to the manager about locating Miss Storm." She indicated to the manager's office door. "If you leave my books here at reception, I'll collect them when we're done here. Thanks again. Keep those books coming." Reluctantly, she walked across the foyer and knocked on the door.

The door opened wide. A tall thin man with graying wavy hair and what might be called "fashionable stubble," or he'd neglected to shave the untidy growth on his face, stood to one side and waved them into the room. Jenna unzipped her jacket, the heat from the log fire defrosting her cheeks. "Mr. Brightway, I'm Sheriff Alton and this is Deputy Kane. Could you run us through the incident this morning?"

Brightway repeated what the receptionist had said verbatim. Jenna took in his concerned expression. "And you've searched the resort for Miss Storm?"

"As well as we can possibly search a place this big. I've checked the CCTV footage and she left the hotel at twelve-twenty and headed for the chalets. There'd been a few guests before her but the majority left for their chalets around ten. She's not on the footage during the night and hasn't returned here this morning. My people did a sweep of the area and we've made countless announcements, but no one has seen her since last night."

Jenna glanced at Kane and caught his concerned expression. "So, the CCTVs cover only the entrance to the resort? Why aren't they over the entire complex?"

"Snow. It builds up, frost covers the lenses. It gets very cold up here. The camera here is in the lobby. It's inside and covers the entrance and right out to the parking lot." Mr. Brightway shrugged. "It's the best we can do."

"How many fire exits do you have?" Kane looked up from his notes. "I assume there's a staff entrance as well?"

"Eight fire exits and all have alarms, so I'd know if anyone used them, and the staff entrance is the back door to the kitchen." Mr. Brightway pushed a hand through his hair, obviously irritated. "The door from the lodge to the kitchens requires a passkey. It is clearly marked as a staff entrance with a sign above the door. I doubt the guests would take much notice of it. Anyone accessing the staff entrance from outside would need to know the code for the keypad. The passageway the staff uses runs beside the kitchen and opens into a mudroom, where the staff can change their shoes and leave their coats."

Jenna made a few notes and looked up at him. "Did anyone check out this morning, and has anyone else gone missing overnight?"

"No, and no one has checked out. All but two of our guests, both are authors, have booked for the full two weeks of the convention." Brightway was checking his computer.

"Did you notice any vehicles leaving the parking lot since Miss Storm left for her chalet?" Kane walked around Brightway's office, scanning the room.

"Not that I'm aware but I can view the CCTV footage and see if anyone drove out overnight. It might take some time." Mr. Brightway cleared his throat and picked up his phone. "Please check the CCTV footage from midnight through to this morning and make a note of any vehicles leaving the parking lot." He replaced the receiver and looked at her. "I'll let you know at once if we find anything."

Jenna straightened and folded her notebook, pushing it with her pen into a pocket. "Okay, thanks. Now if you could show us Miss Storm's chalet?" She pulled on her gloves. "Did you touch anything inside?"

"No. I knocked, and when she didn't reply after knocking a few times, I opened the door and called out." Mr. Brightway scratched his head and stared into space. "Let me see. I wiped my feet and went inside to check the bathroom and then left. I was wearing gloves but only touched the door handle. The bathroom door was open. The bed hadn't been slept in. I instructed room service to avoid the area until you'd been by." He reached for his coat hanging on a peg by the door. "Follow me. It's not far."

As they walked out into the freezing air, snowflakes whirled around Jenna and the smell of winter seeped into her nose, she could almost taste it. Her mind was working overtime. "Did you notice any footprints around the chalet?"

"Not that I recall." Mr. Brightway frowned as he led the way along the pathway. "Not that I was looking. I'm not a trained observer, more like a trained non-observer. It's often best I don't notice the guests. Hotel staff are more like ghosts. We drift around trying not to be obtrusive. We prefer not to know what the guests do to amuse themselves overnight."

Jenna recalled her last visit to the resort, when she'd had to negotiate the path in the dark looking for Kane. It had been scary, the dark forest all around. The strange noises had startled her and she'd been armed. Now many pathways like a spider's legs spread out in all directions. At least the path had been recently cleared. "How often do you clear the path?"

"It depends on the snowfall. Sometimes two or three times a day. Early in the morning, so the staff can access the chalets to deliver breakfast, or for the guests who want to make an early start on the slopes. The path was cleared last night at five and again this morning at six." He led the way down a pathway. "To the right we have two new chalets in the final stages of building. Workmen are there most days. To the left is Miss Storm's chalet, number forty-eight."

Jenna looked up at the signpost. The chalets' numbers were prominent, with an arrow pointing the way. "So, it would be unusual to get lost. I see the lights are along each pathway. Are they on all night?"

"Yes, it's a safety precaution, and as you see, we've made every effort to make the guests' movements around the complex as uncomplicated as possible." Mr. Brightway led the way along the trail.

As they rounded a bend, a pretty chalet came into view. Very private with a trickle-fed pool and a small creek running close by. "Is that the pool where Agnes said she noticed a shoe?"

"Yeah." Mr. Brightway crunched through the ice-covered snow and pointed. "She said it was there, but as you can see, it's frozen over and I couldn't make out anything."

"Didn't you think to break the ice?" Kane frowned at him. "Even after you discovered Miss Storm was missing?"

"Ah... no... I didn't think to." Mr. Brightway looked abashed.

Bending to clear a coating of snow from the edge of the pond, Jenna used her Maglite to see through the ice. The beam moved over a flash of blue. She pointed. "See that? Find something to break the ice."

"Sure." Kane walked off the pathway and into the forest with Duke on his heels.

The sound of wood cracking broke the quiet and Kane pushed

back through the trees, peeling the branches from a pine bough. Jenna eyed the stick with doubt. "Do you think that will work?"

"Yeah, it will when I'm finished." Kane pulled out his hunting knife and sharpened one end of a heavy branch. He moved toward the pool holding the stick like a javelin. "Stand back."

An uneasy feeling fell over Jenna as Kane lifted the branch and smashed it through the ice. In seconds a pair of ski pants, with one leg pushed up to reveal frozen stark-white flesh clad in a bright blue snow boot, floated just under the surface. "I guess we've found Dakota Storm."

"I'll call Wolfe." Kane pulled out his phone.

Jenna frowned. "I'd use the satellite sleeve. If the call cuts out halfway through, Wolfe will figure we're in trouble."

She turned to look at Mr. Brightway. His face had drained of color and she led him some distance away. "Do you have a spare key to the chalet? I'll need to look inside." She touched his arm to get his attention. "Mr. Brightway... this could be a crime scene. I'll need the key."

"I have a master key and can open the door for you, but I'll need it to gain access around the resort." Brightway frowned. "I'll get someone to bring you one of the room service passkeys, but you must return it when you're through. We have a limited supply for the staff."

"A passkey will be fine, but this could be a crime scene and I need you to keep everyone away from this cabin." Jenna walked with him to the door, and when he opened it, she pinned it to a hook on the wall. "Thank you." She led him down the path. "Go back to the ski lodge and be ready to direct the medical examiner, Dr. Shane Wolfe, here when he arrives. Give him the passkey. Don't speak to anyone, especially the media about this. Any leaks at this stage of our investigation will cause a problem. Right now, we don't know if this is an unfortunate accident or a murder." She stared at him. "Do you understand?"

"Yes, I do." Mr. Brightway turned and hurried back down the path without a backward glance.

Jenna turned back to Kane who was staring at the ground. "What is it?"

"I figure the ice under the snow formed after she fell or was pushed into the water. The flow from the falls keeps this water moving, but the sudden cold snap has frozen it solid. That happened early this morning, which means if this is a homicide, there's a chance there'll be evidence trapped in the ice layer." He crouched down and gently brushed away the recent snow, revealing a patch of ice. "That looks like blood spatter. We'll need to mark this area." He pulled off his backpack and took out crime scene tape and yellow markers.

Jenna took in the distance from the chalet to where Kane was standing. "Maybe someone followed her from the ski resort? It's noisy here at night with the forest creaking, branches cracking and falling. It would have concealed the sound of someone walking behind her."

"Maybe, but the manager said nobody left the resort after her last night." Kane wrapped tape around a tree and paced to the next one.

Jenna placed a flag near the spot Kane had uncovered. "Who says they came from the resort? They could have left there and been in any one of, what, fifty or so chalets littered around the place?"

"True." Kane tied off the tape and went to her side. "Why do you figure she took such an isolated cabin? I mean, this one is perfect for a honeymoon, but a woman alone who maybe has enemies at the conference would be taking a risk. You'd think she'd stay in the hotel where it's safe."

Heading back to the chalet door, Jenna turned to him. "I wouldn't stay out here alone at night, that's for sure. It looks great during the day, but walking back here alone at night isn't my idea of fun." She pulled booties over her shoes and followed him inside. After scanning the room, and finding nothing, she waited for Kane to walk from the bathroom. "Anything?"

"No sign of a struggle. I don't think she made it inside." He opened closet doors. "Her cosmetics are in the bathroom and her clothes are here. Laptop on the bed." He bent to peer under the bed. "Not even a dust bunny."

Taking her time, Jenna swept the room. Nothing was out of place. A dirty coffee cup sat on the bedside table, but the breakfast inside the delivery box was untouched. "So we can assume she left after drinking coffee last night." She examined the garbage in the bin under the dresser. "The fixings wrappers for coffee are here, so she made it herself." She turned around. "Can you see her purse?"

"Nope." Kane stared around the room thoughtfully. "The author you spoke to mentioned Miss Storm was making notes, so she'd have a purse large enough to carry a notebook." He moved to the door, where Duke was sitting watching them intently. "Let's see if Duke can sniff out anything." He picked up the laptop and held it under Duke's nose. "Seek."

Aware of the limited ability dogs had of tracking in the snow, Jenna wasn't surprised when Duke sniffed around and walked into the chalet and barked. "Well, he's right. I doubt he can track her in the snow, but I guess it was worth a try."

"I'll take him into the forest alongside the path. It's not so thick in there. Someone might have tossed her purse into the bushes." Kane headed into the trees with Duke close behind. "Seek, Duke. Find the lady's purse for me."

Jenna rubbed her arms and started after him and then stopped. Someone had to remain on scene and guard the body. Her thick jacket should be keeping the cold at bay, but the wind howling through the forest pushed the cold into every gap in her clothing. Her feet had turned into blocks of ice and she couldn't feel her fingers. She walked back inside the chalet out of the wind and stared at the few items that made up Dakota Storm's life. "I sure hope you slipped and fell into that water."

FOUR

Medical examiner for Black Rock Falls, Louan and Blackwater Dr. Shane Wolfe arrived at the ski resort. His team included his assistant Colt Webber, a badge-holding deputy, and his daughter Emily. Emily, a talented ME in the making, was anxiously waiting to commence studies in medicine at Black Rock Falls Medical College after successfully completing a degree in forensic pathology. Emily worked closely with him, starting off as an intern, and Wolfe had soon discovered she had a natural instinct for the work. Not content to join the team as a forensic pathologist alone, Emily's goal was to complete all the necessary qualifications and become a state-registered medical examiner. He'd welcome the day when she could take over for a time. It would be nice to be able to go fishing once in a while.

Wolfe climbed out of the van and blinked into the swirling snow at the impressive frontage of the main ski resort building. Walls of glass offered guests panoramic views of the valley below. The inclement weather was obviously keeping most of the visitors inside. The place was deserted. He hadn't gotten as far as the main entrance when a man bundled up in a green hoodie came toward him. Waiting for the man to speak, he glanced around at his team.

"Grab the gurney, body bag, and the forensics kits out of the van. It looks like we're heading straight out to the scene." He looked at the man. "Mr. Brightway? I'm the ME. What have you got for me?"

"I'm to direct you to the accident." Mr. Brightway handed him a key. "Sheriff Alton said you'd require a passkey for Miss Storm's room. The chalet is that way, number forty-eight. Can you be as unobtrusive as possible, maybe hide your van somewhere else? We have important guests this week. I'd rather they didn't see your van parked out front—or the body. I won't allow you to parade it out here in full view of everyone. You'll have to find a way to disguise it. This is a very prestigious event. The last thing I need is bad press. They'll never come back again."

Annoyed at the man's total lack of regard for the demise of one of his guests, Wolfe took the key and lowered his sunglasses to look at the man. "Bad news travels fast and I figure most of them know by now. I'm not moving the van and will be bringing the body out the easiest way. Or would you rather I left Miss Storm to decay in your pond until the melt?"

"No! How would I be able to have guests in number forty-eight with a body in the pond? Get the job done and leave before any of the guests wander outside." Mr. Brightway gave a dismissive wave of his hands and stepped closer, gesturing wildly as if trying to push him down the pathway. "The path is that way."

"Uh-huh." Wolfe straightened and pushed his sunglasses back up his nose. Behind him he heard Emily make a strange snorting noise. He took a step closer to Brightway. "I suggest you keep your guests inside until I've retrieved the body. If I believe a crime has been committed here, I'll lock down this establishment, and your guests will have to remain in their rooms until further notice." He looked away and then back at the man. "Until I examine the scene and make a determination, no one will be allowed in or out, including you."

"You can't do that." Mr. Brightway's mouth twisted into a determined grimace. "I won't allow it. We have bus tours of crime scenes organized. I can't call them off, the guests have already paid for them."

Wolfe shrugged. "You don't get a choice. When it comes to a crime scene, I make the decisions." He puffed out a cloud of steam. "Is the sheriff on scene?"

"She is." Mr. Brightway turned to leave.

"Just a minute." Wolfe shook his head in disbelief. "The sheriff asked you to direct me to the body, I believe?"

"Yes, she did." Mr. Brightway's head nodded like it was attached to a spring.

Wolfe glanced around as Webber and Emily moved to his side and then slowly back to Brightway. "Good, then take me to cabin forty-eight. I don't have the time to search the entire complex to hunt down a body."

The man gave him a look of contempt and stomped off along a trail, moving at light speed. Wolfe ushered Webber in front of him with the gurney and dropped into step beside Emily. "Some people, huh?"

"What an arrogant little man." She grinned at him. "You sure have mellowed over the years since Mom died."

Wolfe looked at her. "Not really... Inside I'm the same. Bad-mannered people still annoy me. I've gained more control as I've gotten older. Which is just as well, when I run into people like Brightway. That man hasn't got one ounce of sympathy in him." He sighed.

"Yeah, I remember when Mom was pregnant with Anna and that man came running out of a store and knocked her over." Emily grinned. "You grabbed him and hung him over the fence. And then there was that boy at high school who kept on bothering me. You sent him packing with a death-ray glare."

Wolfe frowned at her. "In hindsight, I shouldn't have touched the man who knocked over your mom, but I have to admit I do tend to be a little overprotective when it comes to you and your sisters. That, I'm afraid, comes with being your dad." He gave her a hug as they walked.

"I wouldn't have it any other way, Dad." Emily smiled up at him. "It's kind of nice knowing you'll be there for us if we ever get into trouble." She chuckled. "Although, the parent teacher nights were freaky. I love seeing people's expressions when you walk into a room. You look kinda scary sometimes, you know?"

Wolfe smiled. "Your mom called it 'intense.' She'd say, 'Take that intense look off your face, you'll scare the neighbors.'" He sighed. "At the time I was working through a difficult situation, so my mind was on the job, not at a cookout." He looked ahead and spotted Kane coming out of the trees with Jenna close behind. "I think that's the cabin up ahead."

When the manager pushed past them and practically ran back up the path, Wolfe stared after him and then turned his attention to the area inside the crime scene tape. He waited for Jenna to make her way to his side. "Did you break the ice?"

"I did." Kane kicked the toes of his snow-caked boots against a tree stump. "The report we had was when Agnes delivered room service to the chalet, she spotted a shoe in the pond. By the time the manager contacted us, it was frozen over. I broke it using a branch."

Wolfe nodded. "Any sign of a struggle in the room?"

"Nothing." Jenna waved a hand toward the door. "Breakfast is delivered through a hatch, into a sealed compartment accessed only by the guest. It wasn't touched. The bed hasn't been slept in. We found nothing unusual inside at all." She walked toward the pond. "She was last seen making notes in the foyer by the fire. It's a meeting place, everyone congregates there, but she was the last person seen leaving on the CCTV footage. We haven't found her purse and it must be substantial to carry a notebook." She waved behind her. "We've been searching the surrounding area looking for any signs of disturbance."

"I tried to get Duke to track her, but he couldn't pick up a scent. We found nothing." Kane shrugged. "If someone else was here last night, whoever cleared the snow this morning has obliterated any evidence." He led the way to a cleared patch of ice. "We did find blood spatter, sealed in the ice."

Wolfe followed and bent and examined the evidence. "We'll need to clear the snow from this entire area and expose the ice." He pointed to a metal box set beside the pathway with a padlock hanging from the door. "That looks like a maintenance shed. Take a look inside. It should have something we can use."

"It's padlocked." Emily looked at him. "We'd need bolt cutters to get in there without a key. Do you want me to go and get the manager?"

As Wolfe turned around, he heard the metal door creak open. He smiled to himself. There wasn't a door Kane couldn't open. "Anything in there?"

"Yeah." Kane pulled out a snow pusher and went to work.

Wolfe moved closer to the pond and bent to look at the body. The water had already iced over but it broke easily enough. He peered at the legs and turned to Webber. "I'll glove up and pull her out by the feet. Be ready to support her head when it leaves the water. The snow will protect the body, but I don't want any post-mortem injuries."

"Gotcha." Webber snapped on gloves. "It's going to be damn cold handling her." He moved into position.

Rolling up his sleeves, Wolfe dipped his hands into the bitterly cold water, gripped the body by the ankles, and tugged. Amazingly, she slid from the icy depths in one move and with Webber's help he settled her on the snow. The fully clothed body was frozen solid. The face stark white, lips blue, and hair sticking out like a bundle of wet twigs. The hands had been pushed into the pockets of her coat in an almost casual pose. He heard Jenna's sharp intake of breath beside him and glanced at her startled expression. "Now you don't see that every day."

"Let's hope we never see anything like that again." Jenna shook her head. "So much for falling into the pool and drowning."

Wolfe dried his arms on a wad of cotton Emily had handed

him and pulled down his sleeves. "Ah well, we'll see what else happened to her when she thaws out."

He never made a snap judgement on cause of death, but it was obvious they were looking at a homicide. The strap of the missing purse was drawn so tight around the victim's neck that the skin had bulged on each side and, in a bloody mess of destruction, a gold pen protruded from one eye.

FIVE

As Wolfe did a preliminary examination of the body, Jenna kneeled on an aluminum blanket beside Kane and examined the ice layer under the snow using her Maglite. The wind howled around them, chilling her to the bone. The cold seemed to slice through her jeans and right through her thermals. As they shuffled slowly from the pathway to the pond, she noticed something glinting in the ice. "By your left hand. I see something shining. What's that?"

"It's an earring." Kane pulled out his phone and took a few images. "Nothing around it at all. No footprints, scuff marks, zip." He waved to get Wolfe's attention. "Is the victim wearing earrings?"

"Nope." Wolfe zipped up the body bag. "Pull it out and bag it. Maybe it belongs to her attacker." He lifted one end of the bag and with Webber slid it onto the gurney. "You can head back to the van, Colt. I'll be right along." He turned back to Kane. "At least we have some evidence to go on for a change. The blood spatter is a bonus and I was able to collect a good sample."

Jenna looked up at him. Her teeth chattering. "We're done here and I need to get back to the hotel."

"You'll have a ton of work ahead of you." Wolfe removed his

gloves and balled them up. "I don't have to rush to get the body back to the morgue. It will take days to thaw. We can assist with the investigation for an hour or so." He held out his hand to Jenna and pulled her to her feet. "I figure the manager is going to be uncooperative. He started complaining the moment I arrived."

Jenna rolled her eyes. "Did he now?" She brushed snow from her jeans and straightened. "I guess this book convention is a big deal for the resort. This would be the last thing they'd want to happen."

"Maybe not." Kane bagged the earring, wrote on it, and tossed it to Wolfe before removing his surgical gloves. "What would be better at a crime-book convention than a murder?"

Speechless, Jenna pulled on her gloves and tried to stamp warmth back into her feet as she gaped at him. "Oh, come on, Dave, that's crazy talk. Do you think someone would actually commit murder as a publicity stunt?"

"It depends how desperate they are to sell books, I guess." Kane folded the aluminum blanket. "Considering what we've discovered so far, what conclusions have you come up with?"

Turning back to the path. Jenna ran the evidence through her mind. "Well, I'm sure, Dakota Storm was someone admired by those she brokered deals for, but I guess that she upset the majority of authors she declined."

"All true, but it would be the same for many agents." Kane shrugged. "I'm guessing as most agents represent less than one percent of the authors who pitch to them, many would feel some degree of animosity toward the person who rejected them. It's human nature."

Staring into space, Jenna considered the case. "Enough to murder someone?"

"We've seen psychopaths triggered by a lot less than being rejected by an agent." Kane wiped his sunglasses and pushed them back on. "I could think of a ton of reasons to kill someone, jealousy being one. Authors seeing others getting agents and making money would be a bitter pill to take, especially if a writer believes their stories are superior. If it's a psychopath, that alone would be something to consider because it slips right into their behavior pattern. They believe they're better than everyone else and going down in history as the Book Convention Killer would be the type of notoriety they'd crave."

As usual, Kane was already building a profile. "I agree, and we can rule out it being sexually motivated as her clothes seem to be intact. It will be interesting to watch the autopsy. I couldn't see any defense wounds, but then someone tampered with the body after killing her. No one being strangled would keep their hands in their pockets."

"I'd naturally consider looking for a male suspect first, but I couldn't help noticing the majority of people in the lobby were women, many over sixty." Kane pulled his woolen cap more snugly over his ears. "So, we could be looking at a female killer. She'd need to be of only average fitness to push the body into the pond. So I figure we can rule out anyone over seventy." He turned to her. "Everything I see here is personal. The strangulation was committed in a frontal assault, face to face is just about as personal as it gets and the pen in the eye is symbolism. Someone who works in the publishing business committed this murder. Not a reader but one of the three main players: author, agent, or publisher."

"Reviewers can be caustic as well." Emily chewed on her bottom lip. "Although I can't imagine how that involves agents."

Jenna blew out a puff of steam. "So, it could be anyone and we have two hundred people at the convention."

"And a bus load from town arriving at eleven." Wolfe fell into step beside them.

"Yeah, that's right." Emily peered over her scarf at Jenna. "Julie's been talking about the convention for ages. She has a ticket for the book signing and will be riding on the bus organized by the library with a bunch of her friends."

Jenna rubbed her temples. "More people? How are we going to keep track of everyone?"

"We know no one checked out last night or this morning, and if we discover no vehicles left the parking lot, we'll have to assume the killer is on site." Kane pushed his hands deep inside his coat pockets. "Remember we're dealing with a group of people who either write, read, or publish crime novels. Unless it's one of the staff, which is highly unlikely, whoever did this would be aware of police procedure, forensics, and the like."

"And hiding in plain sight." Emily shivered. "They could be watching us right now."

"Yeah, and Julie will be in the thick of it. You know your sister, she can't keep out of trouble." Wolfe frowned. "Maybe I should take her home with me."

"She won't appreciate you ordering her home in front of her friends." Emily glared at him. "Honestly, Dad, did you hear what Dave said before? He thinks it was personal. Julie doesn't know any of the authors, agents, or publishers. She's a reader. There's no reason to believe she'd be targeted."

"In fact, she'd be the best person to pick up scuttlebutt." Kane flicked a glance at Wolfe. "The entire population of the ski lodge is a suspect, and right now we'll need all the help we can get."

"Well then I'll need to arrange things so we can assist you." Wolfe peered at Kane over his sunglasses. "I had planned to remain here for a time, but I'll stay with Em to assist you. Colt is quite capable of taking the body to the morgue and setting it up to thaw without cross-contamination. We've done it enough times." He heaved out a long cloud of steam. "You have a captive audience in there and, with all but two of them booked to stay for two weeks, you shouldn't have a problem keeping them locked down. Like you said, all are interested in crime, most of them enjoy solving mysteries in books, and they may be more help than you believe."

The list of procedures Jenna needed to complete for a homicide slid into her mind. "The resort will have a register of the guests. If Brightway refuses to give it to us, I'll send Rio to ask the judge for a warrant. We'll need to lock it down completely with no one leaving the mountain, except for the people arriving on the bus for the day trip. I figure we allow the convention to go ahead and get the people back on the bus and away from the area this afternoon. They'll be one group we can rule out as possible suspects." She looked at Kane. "It's too cold to leave someone here to guard the scene and I doubt we'll need to search it again but in case we do, we'll need to block this pathway. It only leads to chalet number forty-eight, and once we tell Mr. Brightway it's off limits, no one will have a reason to come this way."

"Okay. Give me a second." Kane turned around and headed back to the chalet with Duke tearing after him, his long ears flying in the wind.

Jenna stamped her feet and rubbed her arms against the bitter cold and waited for him to return. A few minutes later he came back dragging a large red and white sign with the words DANGER, FALLING ROCKS and set it across the pathway. She smiled at him. "Oh, that will work."

"I noticed it in the maintenance shed." Kane wrapped the wire attached to the sign around two pine trees. "No one will risk wandering up there now."

Jenna met his gaze. "Unless the killer returns to the scene."

"With us at the ski lodge, I doubt they'd risk it." Kane led the way down the path. "We'll need some help to interview everyone. You'll have to call Rio in to stay overnight, someone needs to be on scene. We can't expect Rowley to leave Sandy when she's so close to her due date."

"They're staying in town with her folks, so it shouldn't be an issue working here during the day. It's what, half an hour to the hospital if anything happens." Jenna followed Wolfe and Emily along the pathway. "We really need to stay here too but it's impossible. We'll need to tend the horses and Pumpkin."

"That's not a problem." Kane turned to look at her walking backward. "We could drop the horses at the stables in town and ask Maggie if she'd care for Pumpkin for a couple of days. She loves her and the horses never seem to mind being away for a few days. With all the people we have to interview, being on scene would make life easier." He bent to pat Duke. "Duke can stay here with us. The resort never minds him being here."

Snowflakes brushed Jenna's cheeks like butterfly wings and she brushed them away. "That would make sense." She glanced at her watch. "But we don't have the time to arrange everything and go home to collect the horses. We just can't leave. Someone might try and slip away."

"I'll go alone. You have Wolfe and Emily to get the investigation rolling. If we don't need a court order to see the register, then Rio will be here in no time. It will take me two hours max."

Jenna considered his idea and nodded. "Okay, but the moment people hear about the murder they'll be leaving in droves. I guess locking them in the building is out of the question?"

"We can't lock the resort doors as people need to move back and forth to their chalets." Kane looked at her. "But we can lock it down. There are two roads in and out of the resort, and with a blizzard forecast, no one will try and escape on foot. Many came here on buses, in rental cars, or their own vehicles. Once the bus has left, we'll ask the guests to remain on site and suspend the cab and bus services until further notice. We'll say there's been an avalanche or something and the road is blocked. They'll comply, and most of them are booked here for two weeks anyway, according to the manager."

Jenna thought for a beat. "What about the staff?"

"Everyone who works here lives in the staff quarters on site. Even married couples. Nice work if you can get it."

Jenna squeezed his arm and then moved away under Emily's eagle stare. Keeping their relationship private was getting harder, especially when close friends were involved. "Okay, make the arrangements for the animals, and I'll get the rooms organized and call the transport companies." She pulled out her phone, attached the satellite sleeve, and glanced down at her wet jeans. "Can you pack me a bag? I'll need a few changes of clothes and more pairs of boots. You'll need to tell Rio to grab some clothes while he's in town too. We'll need him here."

"Sure." Kane leaned into her and rested one arm over her shoulder. "Although I love the tune your teeth are playing, I wouldn't want you to get frostbite."

"Well, aren't you two a picture of domestic bliss?" Emily looked over one shoulder at them and narrowed her gaze. "Is there something you're not telling me?"

Jenna waved her away with a smile. "When there is, you'll be the first to know."

SIX

Alone in a sea of faces, I'm one of many but I'm special. I blend in so well. You see, I've always been above the crowd in everything I do. I'm perfect. I know how to act, to use my charm, and make people believe the image I portray. It's like acting a part and I'm so used to doing it now, it comes naturally. People call me friend, but I have none. I use people for my own endgame and they're so deliciously vulnerable to an ego stroke that I could ask them to slit their own throats and they'd do so.

It's amusing when people believe they have power over me, but it's the opposite. Why can't they understand I always win in the end? You see, it only takes a few seconds to silence them forever. I'm smiling now and attracting the attention of people around me. Their curiosity draws them to me like a magnet and I smile back as if I'm their friend. I'm not. Each of them is a potential clog in the drainpipe of my life, but I acknowledge them because that's what people are expected to do. It's all part of the charade, the deception, because I know inside they're just as empty as me.

It's just as well no one can read my thoughts. Can you imagine if they could? Would they run screaming or nod and say, "I'm just like you"? Most people are like me because I'm not responsible for the six hundred thousand people who go missing each year in the

US. Trust me, there are many of us out there watching and waiting for the opportunity to indulge our passion.

The audience falls silent as another author climbs onto the stage to read the first chapter in a thrilling crime. I watch the audience's eager faces as the author describes a bloody murder. How many here live for that rush? I look at my hands and see warm, sticky blood running over my flesh. I inhale, craving the addictive metallic smell of the crimson delight. I'm trembling and it's not because of the cold. It's becoming more difficult to control the craving when I sit among them—but I must.

Learning to be compliant is crucial to success—no tears came when my mom beat that simple truth into me. *Don't tell or they'll lock you away*, being her mantra. I'd stand in the choir every Sunday dressed in my white smock and sing to the heavens. Each day, I'd pray for someone to take me away from the pain and suffering. Nobody came and then I heard the priest say, "God helps those who help themselves." I waited, allowing my strength to grow and my mind to accept the words given to me in answer to my prayers. But it was against all I'd been taught: *thou shall not kill*. But at the time, I was far too young to determine it was Lucifer tugging at my ear. At first I believed I'd been chosen to stop them from hurting other children—and they *would* hurt them. I soon became a fallen angel, never to return to the holy sanctum. I committed the unforgivable sin and killed my mom. I can still see her startled expression as the life seeped from her. Although, knowing her last image was of me standing over her with a knife has never bothered me. At last, I was free. Others followed and I found I enjoyed it—craved it. It was my chosen path. My abusers are all dead now but the hunger remains and I'm forced to choose others. No one can stop me. You see, I know how to cover my tracks and slip through life unnoticed. For I'm no one of interest, just one in the crowd. I'm the person you meet in one second and forget the next.

My heart races at the contemplation of my next kill and sweat trickles between my shoulder blades but I must push the delicious thoughts from my mind and concentrate on the words spilling from the author's mouth. I need to clap at the appropriate time, nod, and make nice comments. It's cozy inside this room and the beads of sweat on my brow are like warm blood spatter and trigger a cascade of memories. The thrill ride of the previous night repeats in color so bright it distorts the truth. I can still hear the sound of her voice. Her pleas have become an amusing earwig, running round and round inside my head. I can see the surprised expression on her face and feel her hot breath on my cheek as I squeeze the life from her. It exhilarated me, but more so seeing her shocked expression when I allowed her to rise back to consciousness to discover I hadn't finished with her yet. You see, I couldn't allow her to miss the climax, the grand finale. I wanted her to look at me as I plunged the gold pen she valued so highly deep into her startled eye.

My only regret is that she died too fast.

SEVEN

The last thing Jenna expected was cooperation from Mr. Brightway after hearing about Wolfe's encounter with him. However, when she explained a killer might be on the premises and the absolute need to know the names of everyone on site, for them to ensure no one else was missing, he printed up lists of both the guests and staff. To her surprise, Brightway offered to check on the staff and split the list with his secretary.

The conference was in full swing. Four halls, usually used for weddings and other functions, were in use. One held the group listening to author readings, one was divided into booths for authors to pitch ideas to agents and publishers, the third was for a book signing, where authors sat behind tables and their fans lined up to have their books autographed. The fourth held panels of various experts from all fields of the publishing industry holding question-and-answer sessions throughout the day. The atmosphere was alive, energetic, and happy. It seemed a shame to spoil it with bad news.

Luckily, the guests had been divided into groups as well, and only ticket holders were allowed to attend the various forums on offer. Jenna obtained lists of the people and where they should be at any particular time. While waiting for Rio to arrive, Jenna

arranged for the road and transport blockade. She decided that
Rowley would stay in town to handle the office. Although the
wireless network was a little sketchy, they could use the landline
and the satellite sleeves for their phones if they needed
assistance from Special Agent Ty Carter and behavioral science
expert Special Agent Jo Wells at the FBI field office in Snakeskin
Gully.

As she organized her team, Mr. Brightway interrupted her
with a cough. She looked up from her notes. "Do you have something for me?"

"I do." Brightway straightened the front of his burgundy
jacket. "My secretary has viewed the CCTV footage and no one
left the parking lot overnight or this morning. The builders
working on the chalets came by this morning but stopped working
because of the blizzard forecast and have returned to town. They
left last night before six and arrived this morning at eight."

That sure made life easier, and Jenna sighed. "That's good. I'd
like you to make an announcement over the PA system. Say a guest
has handed in an earring and it is available at the front desk." She
gave him a hard stare. "If someone comes forward, make an excuse
to keep them there. Ask for a description of the earring. If it
matches the one I gave you, tell them it's in the safe and ask them
to wait while you get it and then call me." She leaned on the
counter. "Remember this person could've murdered Dakota Storm,
so play it cool."

"Okay, I'll repeat the message throughout the day." Mr. Brightway's mouth hardened into a straight line. It was obvious he didn't
like taking orders. "Is there anything else?"

Jenna nodded. "Yes, I'll need to check on the whereabouts of
your staff last night. I want a list of anyone on duty between the
hours of midnight and two this morning. I want to speak to the
person who cleared the footpath to Miss Storm's chalet and Agnes.
Do you have a suitable room we can use for interviews?"

"Not really. Apart from the rooms you've taken for your staff,
we only have the executive suite. It has two sitting rooms."

Brightway raised his eyebrows. "There are a couple of chalets free."

"We'll need to be inside the lodge. The suite would work." Jenna made a note to call the mayor to handle any fallout. "Can we make it suitable? Perhaps have a couple of desks set up, and chairs?" She gave him a long look. "My department won't be paying for the suite as no one will be sleeping there. There won't be any damage. We'll reimburse you for cleaning, if necessary. I'll speak to Mayor Petersham."

"And your rooms?" Mr. Brightway's lips quivered at the corners. "I expect to be reimbursed for those."

Jenna nodded. "I'm sure we can come to a reasonable arrangement. I'm not here on vacation, Mr. Brightway. I'm trying to catch a killer." She met his gaze. "Make that announcement and get onto the whereabouts of your staff. I'll need to know who to remove from my list of suspects."

"Who have you got on your list so far?" Mr. Brightway fiddled with a pile of flyers.

Jenna shrugged. "Everyone here." She turned, glad to see Rio heading toward her with Wolfe and Emily.

"What's the plan?" Wolfe fell into step beside her.

She headed to a quiet corner and turned to face them. "It's going to be an arduous job. We'll have to restrict the people to the convention rooms. Get them to come up one at a time, copy their ID with your phone, and ask them where they were last night and if anyone can verify their whereabouts between midnight and two." She glanced at her notes. "Apart from the majority of featured authors, agents, and publishers I've listed, who have come here alone, most of the other people attending the conference have traveled in groups. Many are sharing rooms. Everyone, apart from two of the authors, have booked their rooms for the full two weeks."

"That seems like a long time for a conference." Emily frowned. "Most are over weekends or four days."

Jenna nodded. "Yes, or over holiday weekends. This is a little different. It combines a conference and a writer's retreat where they can enjoy the peace and serenity of Black Rock Falls." Jenna rolled her eyes. "I'm reading from the flyer. In their downtime they can enjoy all that Glacial Heights Ski Resort can offer and so on. So, a two-week vacation with a conference thrown in and a chance to meet people of like mind and celebrity authors."

"And a murder to liven things up for crime-hungry patrons." Wolfe scanned the busy foyer. "It seems too much of a coincidence to be true." He sighed. "So, we'll need to know who are staying in the same rooms and can alibi each other, who traveled together, and how they arrived here. Gotcha."

"We'll need to mark the ones we've spoken to, somehow. There's a ton of people here." Emily tapped her bottom lip. "I have it! We have a box of toe tags in the van. They'll love them. It will be all part of the crime conference for them. They'll wear them with pride. Can we use them, Dad?"

"Sure, we have a ton of boxes at the morgue." Wolfe frowned. "What about people arriving on the bus? Do you want me to do the same? As in take images of their ID and tell them they must be checked in and out of the resort? They'll need to be checked back on the bus before they leave this afternoon. The killer could sneak in with them otherwise. I'll make sure you have the image file on your phone before I leave."

Jenna sighed with relief. Trust Wolfe to make life easier. "Yeah, thanks and then maybe take the book-signing room?" She glanced at her notes. "There's a desk at the front where the people check in. You can talk to people as they arrive. Every room runs the same timed sessions, so the guests will be moving around soon. The next session starts at midday, so with the bus due in at eleven, you'll have time."

"Copy that." Wolfe scanned the lobby. "We've already gained a lot of interest. I'll go and meet the bus. Emily come with me and I'll grab those toe tags for you." He headed toward the main door.

"Are the attendance desks set up in all the conference rooms?" Rio pushed his hands into his front pockets. "They'd have lists of people with all-access passes. I noticed everyone here attending the conference are wearing lanyards. We should ask them to attach the toe tags to them, so they're easily visible." He rubbed his chin. "Are all the guests with the conference this weekend, or are there other people we need to hunt down?"

"Yes to the tables, and no other guests." Jenna handed him a list of the guests and a map of the complex. "Start here. It's the author book readings. Wait until the current reading is completed and then you'll have time to check everyone who comes through the door before the next session. Lock the doors if possible once you're done to prevent people wandering around. Any problems, call me." She tapped the papers into a neat pile and ran through her mental to-do list. "Wait outside the door for now. I'll have Emily bring the tags to you. Send her to the panel room. She'll be able to catch people as they arrive too. I'll take the pitch room." She nodded. "Okay, let's do this."

EIGHT

Look at them moving around like ants chasing sugar, all wanting the same thing: fame and fortune. But in truth, no one can ensure success. I've heard the empty promises and seen the despair on the faces of the denied and yet the all-powerful refuse to acknowledge me, a surefire winner. I'm watching now as the local sheriff and her cohorts move through the guests. Have they found Dakota's frozen corpse or is she still missing? It's so hard to tell by their actions. Cops always seem to be faceless, devoid of expression, as if they have no faces at all.

I'm smiling because the one who took my place, Jedidiah Longfellow, calls me friend. He is so arrogant in his success he can't see me. I'm one of the lowly he graces with his presence. My "friend" turns to me and I bend my head to listen, feigning interest. His breath, a stinking mix of coffee and cigarettes, wafts over me in a cloud of nasty. I'm smiling at him as my fingernails dig deep into the flesh of my palms. The sting a reminder not to casually reach forward and dig out his eyes—but I want to.

"I overheard the cops talking to the receptionist this morning. My literary agent, Dakota Storm, is missing." Jed looks at me and a slow smile spreads across his face. "I wondered when the games would begin. She's not missing at all. This is a mystery, set up for us to solve." He chuckles. "The next thing, they'll lock us in the resort and more people will go missing."

"You really think they will?" A girl with pink hair and green fingernails leans forward inserting herself in our conversation. "Oh, I love a mystery game. I wonder who will vanish next?"

Before I can reply, an announcement comes over the loudspeakers about an earring someone has found. I join in the fictitious game. "Oh, there's the first clue." I pull out my iPod and make a note.

A second announcement echoes through the hallways, and it's as if everything is falling into place for me, as if they anticipated my plans and created a perfect environment—a captive audience just for me. I chuckle with absolute glee as I join the line for the next session and turn to Jed. "You're correct that they're restricting us to the complex. It's like living in a cozy-mystery story. I wonder what they'll have for a prize?"

"Yeah, it looks like we have the time between sessions to do some investigating." Jed grips my arm. "I know where Miss Storm's chalet is. She told me just after she arrived, in case I needed to speak to her. She was complaining it was close to a construction site. Coincidentally, the crew working there left at the first blizzard warning. I overheard the manager complaining about the delay to finishing the cabin." He lowered his voice. "She's given me a very subtle clue. We'll sneak out later and take a look around. Just us, I'm not giving anyone else any tips. The prize for winning will be substantial and I always win."

I nod and smile, picturing the amount of readily available weapons on a construction site. I'll need to sneak away and set the scene but I already have a way to ensure we're not seen leaving the lodge. I'm far too smart to be caught. The need to kill surges through me like an uncontrollable rage but I hide it before I meet his gaze. I look away and cover the delay with a laugh. "You're right, that is a perfect place to commit murder."

NINE

The blizzard hit the mountain just as Kane made the last turn into Glacial Heights Ski Resort. He'd had to stop to haul open the road-closure barriers wide enough to fit the Beast through and then replace them. It was obvious Jenna had covered all the bases by the time he'd returned from the stables in town. Rowley was at the bottom of the mountain supervising the men setting up the road-blocks. He'd been informed the roadblocks would be opened at six to allow the snowplow to cut a path for the bus at the resort to return to town and then the barriers would be replaced until further notice. The mayor had offered to clear the service road to the resort twice daily if necessary, and Rowley had volunteered to supervise.

As he drove into the parking lot, his satellite phone buzzed to life. He pulled into a space and took the call. "Dave Kane."

"*Hi, Dave. It's Colt. I've been trying to reach Wolfe, but he's not picking up. Maybe he isn't using his satellite sleeve on his phone.*"

Kane raised both eyebrows and bit back a sigh. "I've just arrived back at the resort. Is there a message you want me to give him?"

"*Yeah. As I was unpacking the body, the hair has thawed out and I noticed blood in the water. I examined the back of her head* and there's a contusion. I picked out bark fragments from the wound. Wolfe will be able to tell if this injury killed her, but there must be a murder weapon up there. A log or similar? I noticed outside each cabin there's a box of wood for the fire. You might be lucky and find it."

"Okay, I'm on it." Kane slipped from the truck and opened the back door to unclip Duke. "He won't be back in town until after six. He'll have to wait until the snowplow's been through and the barriers lifted. We've shut down the resort until we find the killer. Gotta go. I'll get him to call you." He disconnected and lifted Duke down into deep snow. "Sorry, boy, but I need to carry in the supplies."

He went to the back of the truck and pulled out a large box and, moving slowly, made his way inside the double doors of the resort. He went to the counter and spoke to the receptionist. "Mr. Brightway gave me a passkey for the cabins. Will it work on the suite you've reserved for interviews?"

"No. The lodge has a different system. I'll get one for you." She tapped on her computer and a card slid out of a machine. "Here you go." She smiled sweetly at him. "Just let me know when you want me to send up the staff. The sheriff mentioned you'd start interviewing them the moment you arrived."

Kane nodded. "Do you know where she is right now?"

"I'm afraid I don't." She frowned. "They all split up and went to different rooms, so one of the four, or she may be already upstairs. I just came on shift."

Placing the keycard between his teeth, he headed for the elevator. The carton contained all the notebooks, statement books, and pens they'd use during an investigation and a pile of snacks to keep them going. He'd grabbed boxes of energy bars and cookies, and dropped by Aunt Betty's Café for a good supply of individual fruit pies. The resort had enough supplies to feed everyone for over a month, but he preferred to have things he liked on hand. He'd taken the twenty-pound sack of dog food he kept in his truck up to his room before leaving, so Duke was set. As the elevator doors opened, he grinned around the card in his mouth at the sight of Jenna.

"Oh good, you're back." Jenna plucked the key from his mouth. "Everyone's upstairs. I came down to wait for you. I called you before but got a busy signal." She bent to rub Duke's ears and then pressed the button on the elevator.

Kane rested the box on the handrail. "Yeah, it was Colt, he found a contusion on the back of Dakota Storm's head. We need to look for a murder weapon. He thinks a log maybe. The wound has wood chips in it."

"Oh, out in the snow during a blizzard—wonderful." Jenna sighed. "We'd have found it if it were close to the chalet. We searched every inch of that place." She paused a beat. "We'll need to talk to the person who cleared the footpath this morning. If he found a log on the footpath, he might have tossed it somewhere." She led the way out of the elevator and then stopped and turned to him. "Did you remember to pack me a bag?"

Kane smiled at her. "Yeah, our bags are in the truck. I figured the food was more important right now. I'll go back and get them as soon as I've dropped this off in the interview room." He looked her over. "You look dry."

"I used the hair dryer in my room to dry my jeans. It was Emily's idea. Leave the bags for now, we can grab them later." Jenna smiled back. "We've made some headway since you left. The manager gave us a spare printer to use, which will make life easier as we've gathered information on everyone here. I'm using hard-copy sheets to keep track of everyone as they move throughout the conference. Rio is looking over the guest lists and sorting them into groups. Having a close to a photographic memory is quite an advantage."

Kane walked into the suite, and warm air from a log fire warmed his cheeks. At once Duke walked over and dropped down in front of it with a long doggy sigh. He whistled softly and Duke looked up at him with a "what now?" expression. "In here, I'll dry you off and remove your coat and then you can sleep in front of the fire."

Duke rose slowly and with great reluctance and sad eyes dragged himself into the other room behind him.

"Come here, boy." Jenna called Duke to the fire in the next room. "I'm all ready for you. See, food and water and a log fire. Doggy heaven, right?" She bent, removed his coat, and rubbed him all over with a towel. "There you go." She stood and grinned at Kane. "I'm his best friend now."

Kane chuckled. "Thanks. He started getting worried when I put Pumpkin into a cage and took her to Maggie, he kept looking at me with those sideways glances he gives me if he figures he's going to the V-E-T or due to take a B-A-T-H."

"You have to spell in front of your dog?" Rio looked up from his notes. "This is a story you have to tell me one of these days. I'm intrigued."

"He's smarter than you think." Jenna hung the dog's coat near the fire to dry. "Those two things send him hiding under the bed is all. It's a real long story."

The manager had reorganized one of the rooms to hold interviews, the other as a headquarters for the team. Tables had been pushed together to make a central workspace, and two fridges had been set against one wall beside a counter with a microwave. Kane placed the heavy box on the counter and smiled at Jenna. I picked up one of the coffee makers from your office and coffee. I figured we could get the fixings here."

"Yeah, there's cream and milk in the fridge and a coffee machine with those pod things in the other room as well." Jenna looked over at Wolfe, Emily, and Rio scanning the lists of guests they'd gathered earlier. "Everyone is famished. I've ordered a ton of sandwiches for now, and they should be here soon. We'll eat in one of the restaurants later. Rio is staying over for a few days to work on the case. His brother and sister will be fine with the housekeeper."

"Yeah, his brother called me. He packed a bag for him and I

collected it on my way back here." Kane unpacked the box. "The snowplow will be doing a run so the bus can get back to town, and Webber is planning on following it up the mountain, so Wolfe will be able to leave with him around six. All the roadblocks are up. Rowley is supervising."

"You've been busy." Jenna went to the house phone. "If you'll bring Wolfe up to date, I'll call the manager and have him arrange for the person who cleared the path to come up so we can talk to him. I'll have Agnes come by as well."

After bringing the others up to date, Kane peered at the list of people staying at the resort. Rio had organized it in record time, and they all gathered around as he explained his theory.

"I correlated all the data we gathered from the guests and sent it to Bobby Kalo, mainly so I had a clear overall picture of who was where and when." Rio glanced up. "I've sent a copy of the final groups to your iPads. It makes it easier to remove potential suspects in one block at a time, leaving us with a few potential suspects rather than hundreds. We'll need more personal data from the, let's say, *main players* to make sure we include any potential suspects from one of the other groups. I'm going to assign each person a group letter as they arrive into the next session after lunch. It will be written on their toe tag as well." He sighed. "At this point, the majority of guests believe they are involved in a mystery game and are more than willing to go along with anything we suggest. I've no idea where the rumor came from but it's spreading like wildfire. The fact we locked the place down and they believe Miss Storm is missing is apparently part of the mystery they're all trying to solve."

Understanding but finding everything surreal, Kane nodded. "So, like, Mr. Smith was in the lobby with the candlestick, you mean?"

"Yeah." Jenna turned at a knock at the door. "That will be room service. After we've eaten, I'll be leaving you to interview Agnes and the path-cleaning guy, Mr. Sparks. The rest of us will be dividing the guests into their groups at the next session."

Kane stared after her. "I'd like to know more about these groups."

"Sure, Rio will bring you up to speed while we eat." Jenna opened the door to a man pushing a cart.

Inhaling the smell of freshly brewed coffee and food, Kane smiled. His stomach rumbled in appreciation. He looked at Rio. "Okay, feed me the information."

TEN

Zac Rio waited for everyone to collect sandwiches and coffee. It had been a long exhausting morning without a break and everyone was running on adrenalin. He handed out the sheets he'd compiled with the assistance of Bobby Kalo and laid his copies on the table. He stood and indicated to the lists of people. "Okay, I've worked with Kalo to break the guests into groups and graded their possibility of being involved in the murder of Miss Storm. Group A or people with alibies, are guests who arrived together and share rooms. This luckily comprises over ninety-five percent of the guests. It seems that author organizations around the country arranged for members to come to the convention. When I compiled the list, using the data gathered as the guests entered each hall, we were able to eliminate everyone who had a person to confirm their whereabouts at the time of Miss Storm's death."

"So, everyone with a rock-solid alibi is in Group A?" Kane looked at him over the rim of his cup. "How many slipped through the gap?"

Lifting his attention to Kane, Rio cleared his throat. "Would you believe only six I'd consider probable. These people aren't affiliated with organizations and have their own rooms at the lodge or are out in one of the chalets. They are Group D, for potentially *dangerous.* As the elevators have CCTV coverage on each floor, like the main entrance, we'll need to view the footage and see if anyone left the lodge during the time Miss Storm died, which we're assuming is between the time she left the lodge and when Agnes noticed her shoe on the pond, so from midnight until six."

"From preliminary findings"—Wolfe leaned forward—"I figure she was killed close to the time she returned to her chalet. She didn't enter her room, so for now assume she died between twelve and two. She must have been in the water for some hours to be frozen."

Rio nodded. "Once we've viewed the footage, we'll be able to add or subtract people from Group D."

"There's a loophole in Group D." Jenna peered at a map of the complex. "Anyone who can't account for their movements and has a room out of the direct line of the CCTV cameras could have used the fire stairs. There's a set of steps at each end of the building. They'd be easily accessed from either end of the hallways. One exits in the lobby, the other to the delivery bay outside. So anyone inside the building would more likely use the lobby exit and entrance if they didn't want to take the elevator." She pointed to her map. "See, the CCTV cameras are clearly marked, and my copy came from the information folder given to everyone attending the conference. Perfect for anyone trying to elude detection. Also, those out in cabins could have easily murdered her without anyone seeing them. You'll need to mark them on the list as staying in the lodge or in a chalet." She looked at Rio. "Send all the names on the D list to Bobby Kalo to do a background check for us. The blizzard will slow down everything we try to do online." She nodded approvingly. "What about the staff?"

Rio nodded. "All the staff who work at the resort are accounted for, including the teams of builders constructing the new chalets. From what I understand, they left in a hurry when they heard the blizzard forecast and were all gone by six last night, so we can take them off the list of suspects as well." He pointed back to List A. "We also have a team of media who are staying in a suite together and can account for their whereabouts. The media are listed under the heading 'Media' to keep them separate from the publishing industry or the readers."

"That all sounds good." Kane chewed on a sandwich. "And as we're all trapped here with the killer, who might strike again, who should be considered as possible victims? We'll have to take every possibility into consideration."

Rio smiled. He could see it all clearly, as if each group were lit up in different colored bright lights, but explaining it would be difficult. He sighed. "Okay, so going on the information about Dakota Storm from the author Jenna spoke to when she arrived, and if the pen found at the murder scene is symbolic, we can assume jealousy or revenge as a possible motive. Using this data, I've compiled a list of possible victims: List C. But there's too many for us to watch twenty-four/seven."

"So, you figure all the agents and publishers are possible victims?" Jenna stared at a list. "Okay too many to watch, but you have agents and authors on the suspects' list. How are you differentiating between them?"

Rio leaned back in his chair. "I asked Bobby Kalo if he could access the pitching schedules from the last two years' crime writers' conferences. He used the list of guests staying here and cross-checked them against the authors who pitched to Dakota Storm." He poked one finger at a list. "Those she rejected and have no alibi are on the list of possible suspects."

"But there's published authors on here as well." Jenna frowned. "Why would they be pitching at a conference?"

Rio's enjoyment of the arts had put him in contact with playwrights, authors, and many people in the industry, so he had insider information. "It's all about the golden ring."

"The what?" Jenna scanned the list and looked at him skeptically.

Rio opened his hands wide. "There are millions of authors published and unpublished but few reach the 'golden ring,' the career they've dream of, like being a *New York Times* bestseller, for instance, or having their books turned into screenplays." He smiled. "This is a place for unrepresented authors to avoid the slush pile and go straight to the top of the list. Deals are made and dreams realized at conferences. Reaching the golden ring is what every author wants in life."

"Slush pile?" Jenna raised both eyebrows. "Okay, I'm gathering that's where the unsolicited manuscripts go that don't make the cut?"

"Exactly." Rio tapped a list. "So, on this list is a group of rejected authors and I've added the names of two agents and an editor who lost clients to Dakota Storm and weren't too happy about it. I figure it has to be one of the people on List D and this method is our best chance of finding the killer."

"Okay." Kane reached for another sandwich. "This was a brutal murder and no one has taken for the hills. Everyone is still here, so either our killer is hiding in plain sight or we have a wounded vigilante out to get revenge on more than one person."

Rio nodded. "Yeah. So, are we all on the same page? The A-list people are in the clear, the B list are possible victims, the C list contains the bus people, and finally the D list are our suspects, without alibis and with probable motive."

"So, from this you've narrowed it down to a possible six suspects?" Jenna scanned the page. "That's impressive. So, we have:

August Bradford, an author out of Eagle Ridge Glen, Colorado
September March, an author, out of Spirit Lake Montana
Bexley Grayson, an author out of Lyons Bay, California
Murphy Finnian, a literary agent out of Black Canyon, North Dakota
Parker Rain, a literary agent out of Twisted Forest, Montana
Ike Turnage, an acquiring editor out of Devils Bend, Colorado.

Rio nodded. "They're the most probable, yeah. I've emailed you all their details and driver's licenses. Kalo is running background checks on them now. He'll send the info along as soon as possible."

"Great work." Jenna smiled at him. "You and Kalo have saved us hours of grunt work."

Suddenly feeling part of the team, Rio smiled. "Collecting the data and having Kalo to run things for us made all the difference."

"Okay, people." Jenna swept her gaze over the room. "Let's get to work. Kane, you can start by interviewing the staff members. Call the desk and have them send them up." She looked at Wolfe. "Can you and Emily go and find August Bradford?" She turned to Rio. "You can take September March. I'll find Bexley Grayson."

"Just a minute." Kane looked dubious. "Anyone we interview must be here voluntarily. We can't Mirandize anyone and hold them. For one, we don't have anywhere to keep them, and two, we'll be denying them legal representation. We've one lawyer in town and if he's not snowed in, I figure he'll be flat out getting up the mountain in this weather. If he did get here, would he be able to represent a ton of suspects? There's no chance in hell of anyone from Louan or Blackwater making it through in this blizzard."

"Then we make sure they know it's voluntary at the get-go. I could suggest they talk to a lawyer over the phone, but the law does state they must have a lawyer present during questioning if requested. If this weather keeps up and we find a solid suspect, I'll call the DA and get advice, but I figure we'd have to get the killer off the mountain—somehow." Jenna's mouth was set in concentration. "Your profiling skills will tell you the killer will come forward to have his say. He wouldn't risk standing out by avoiding us in a crowd of cooperative people." She sighed. "We'll be as nice as pie. With luck, the guests will think it's part of a conference mystery game."

"Yeah, that idea is floating around already." Kane smiled. "It might just work."

"Okay, go find the possible suspects." Jenna waved them away.

"Wait up, Jenna. We'll be chasing our tails." Wolfe pushed his hands into the back pockets of his jeans. "I figure the best way to locate these people is to call them to the reception over the loudspeaker. We can meet them there, explain why we need to speak to them, and escort them up here."

Rio smiled. "Maybe we should wait here for them or we'll scare them away."

"I'm sure we can make ourselves inconspicuous, if we spread out." Jenna pushed hair behind her ears and lifted her chin. "We'll bring them all up here at the same time. The tables are set far enough apart in the interview room next door to allow for privacy. Okay, get at it. Kane, will you call the lobby and ask them to call out the names? We'll head downstairs."

"Copy that." Kane picked up the phone.

ELEVEN

Jedidiah Longfellow's life couldn't be any better. He'd secured Dakota Storm as his agent and she'd gotten him a great deal for his novel. His book *Nailed It* had flown to the top of the charts world-wide and paid out his very generous advance within a week of publication. He'd become an overnight success and although he'd missed the opportunity of being one of the featured authors at this convention, he'd been booked for others later in the year. He enjoyed being in the audience and absorbing the atmosphere. Listening to the speakers had sparked his imagination and he'd made copious notes on a new thriller he planned to write the moment he walked back into his office. For now, he'd enjoy the conference and all it had to offer. Being involved in a real mystery, even if it were just a game, was as good as it gets. He tucked his coat under one arm and turned to his friend. "We'll have to sneak out. If anyone sees us going out the front door, they'll know we have a clue. I'm not staying in a chalet and no one would venture out in a blizzard for fun." He sighed and gestured to a fire exit. "They all have alarms. We can't use them. Any ideas?"

"Of course." His friend gave him a mischievous smile. "Follow me but keep at a distance. Now you're famous, we wouldn't want to draw attention."

Jed moved through the crowd, keeping his friend in sight as they approached a set of double doors with a sign above it that read STAFF ONLY. His friend flashed a keycard over a scanner and walked inside. Jed hurried along, catching the door before it shut and caught up with his friend. "How did you manage to obtain a card to open the door?"

"I accidently on purpose tripped over the housekeeping attendant and snagged it from her. It was clipped to her belt. Hurry, we haven't got much time. We'll be missed if we're late to the next session. The sheriff is checking everyone on the way in. It's like a real murder mystery." His friend slipped into a thick coat, pulled up the hood and headed down a long passageway. "We have to pass by a door to the kitchen. Keep your hoodie pulled down low, sunglasses on, so nobody recognizes us. Although most of the kitchen staff will be too busy cleaning up after lunch to notice."

"Sure." Jed shrugged into his coat and covered his head with the hood. He pushed on sunglasses and pulled on his gloves. "I'm ready, let's do this." Head down, he followed his friend out into the brilliant-white turbulent snow. He spotted the keypad on the outside door. "How are we going to get back inside?"

"They write the code on a chalkboard by the door." His friend chuckled. "It doesn't take a genius to know what it's for. Worse case, we trek back to the front door. It's all good, don't worry. It'll be fun."

Jedidiah looked at the blinding-white snowscape. "Do you know where to go?"

"Yeah, Miss Storm was in chalet number forty-eight, so the ones under construction will be numbered from forty-nine." A low chuckle came from his friend's throat. "I bet we find another clue on the construction site. I figure it will be a photograph or something to guide us to the next one."

As the blizzard howled around them, they took a pathway thick with snow and hustled along, but the going was slow and underfoot the pathway slippery. The icy wind buffeted them, chilling Jed to the bone. As the construction site came into view, he heaved a sigh of relief. "Thank goodness." He pointed to a gap in the trees. "Look, there's a temporary access road. I bet that's how she slipped away."

"It looks deserted. There're no vehicles here. I figure the workers left in a hurry." His friend tried the door, and finding it locked, headed around back to a utility shed and peered inside. "Well, just as I figured. Lookee here. There's a board with keys for the new cabins. I guess they leave them here because so many different contractors come by." His companion took down the key for chalet forty-nine. "We'll look in here first."

Jed trudged through the snow. The cold had reached his bones. He should have worn his thermals, but inside the ski resort it was as warm as toast. He moved inside the chalet and looked around. "See anything?"

His companion was peering at the framework for a closet and turned back with a smile. "Hey, look at this. What does this remind you of?" Hoisting a nail gun in the air, his friend walked toward him.

Alarmed, Jed took a few steps away, but his back ended up against the bathroom door. "Put that down. It's dangerous."

"Not unless the compressor is turned on." His friend grinned widely and walked to the machine and pressed the switch. The compressor hummed into action. "Oops, now I'm armed and dangerous." The jerk aimed the nail gun at the wall and pressed the button. A nail flew out in a *thunk* and buried deep into the drywall. "Oh, that's got quite a kick."

Raising his voice above the machinery noise, Jed held up his hands. "Turn it off. We'll get into all kinds of trouble if they find out you've damaged the wall!"

"They don't know we're here, Jed." His friend moved closer. "I said, 'What does this remind you of?'"

Alarmed by the strange look on his companion's face, Jed lifted his hands in the air and dropped them back to his sides. "Okay, it's the murder weapon I used in *Nailed It*. So what?"

"You didn't research it very well, did you?" His friend

shrugged. "You completely forgot to mention the compressor or how loud it is. It was a great choice of a weapon though. I've been thinking about a better use for it for some time."

Not liking the way his friend looked at him, a chill ran down Jed's spine. It was as if his friend's personality had changed in a split second. "Well, you can't just copy my killer's MO. Find something original and you might get someone to publish you."

"I figure, nobody owns a method of murdering someone. Let's face it, just how many ways are there to kill someone? But I digress. Let's get back to you. Did you consider how much pain your victim went through, when his killer shot nails into him? Did you feel his pain as you wrote the story, because to me, your depiction of the victim was weak. He was an easy kill. He refused to fight back even with words." His friend rolled his eyes. "You know, I do believe you modeled the victim in your novel on yourself." His companion snorted with laughter. "Here I am, brandishing a weapon at you and you should be afraid of me, but you're just standing there waiting for something to happen."

An uneasy feeling crept over Jed and he shook his head. "What do you want me to do? I'm not frightened of you. You're hardly a threat to me, are you?" He looked around and noticed a hammer on one of the benches, grabbed it, and waved it. "There does that make you happy?"

"Deliriously." His friend aimed the nail gun at the wall beside Jed and squeezed the trigger. The noise was frightening, almost like a real pistol. "But if you're going to pick up a hammer, at least use it. Make it interesting. Thrill me, Jed. Can you at least try?"

Jumping away, as another bolt from the nail gun came way too close, Jed felt his gut tighten at the amused expression on his friend's face. "Stop acting like a jerk or I'm going back to the lodge."

"Oh, I'm not acting." His friend's expression had changed from amused to deranged. "I just wanted to know how it felt to kill someone with a nail gun. You didn't give your killer a voice in your story, so no one will ever know what it was like, but you will."

As nails shot from the gun, horrified, Jed turned to run, but it was as if his legs refused to move. The hammer fell from his grasp and clattered to the floor. He had to get away, call for help, something. Gasping for air, he held his bleeding chest. "You're crazy. You'll kill someone with that thing."

"Isn't that the idea?" His friend's lips twisted into a strange grin. "You wrote this scene and now I'm allowing you to experience how the victim felt. You should thank me." The compressor hummed and hissed as the nail gun fired.

Writhing in a world of pain as metal pierced his flesh, Jed staggered and held on to a doorframe. This couldn't be happening. Surely his friend didn't intend to kill him. He stared into dark menacing eyes, uncomprehending. "Why are you doing this?"

"Because you're not as good as you think you are, Jed." His friend raised both eyebrows. "You have to experience pain to write about it. Shame it's too late for you now. We both know how this story is going to end, don't we?"

Dizzy, white spots danced in front of Jed's vision, his fingers slipped on the doorframe and the sawdust-covered floor came up fast. The nails dug deep into his neck, and he cried out in agony. A metallic taste coated his tongue and each labored gasp sprayed the wooden floor with crimson droplets. As he dragged his heavy aching body toward the door, his hands slipped in the warm blood pooling around him. Footsteps, slow and deliberate came close behind him and he turned to look into the black eyes of a killer. In one last effort to stop this madness, he lifted his head, but his voice was less than a whisper. "Help me, somebody, help me!"

"What a fool you are." The tip of the nail gun pressed against the base of Jed's skull. "Not a soul knows we're here."

TWELVE

Watching the guests milling around, Jenna glanced down at her iPad at the images from a list of driver's licenses belonging to their suspects and tried to pick them out in the crowd. It was noisy as the conference guests moved from one session to another, everyone chatting and exchanging notes. Excitement hovered in the air and every person she looked at smiled at her as if they were on a secret mission and she'd become part of their team. The requests for people to come to reception repeated and when a cold blast came from the front door and two men walked inside shaking snow from their coats, she recognized them as Murphy Finnian, a literary agent, and Ike Turnage, an acquiring editor. She walked toward them. "I'd like to talk to both of you. Are you busy right now?"

"No, our next session starts at three." Finnian removed his heavy coat. "Is there a problem?"

"This will be about Miss Storm." Turnage pulled off his gloves and stuffed them into the pockets of his ski jacket. He looked at Jenna. "Lead the way."

"It's all over the conference that the organizers are running a murder mystery competition." Finnian raised an eyebrow as they rode up in the elevator. "It's news to us if they have."

Jenna rested one hand on the butt of her Glock and met his gaze. "I have no idea. I'm not involved in the conference."

"So why do you want to speak to us?" Turnage unzipped his jacket and took his time removing it.

"I want to know people's whereabouts last night, so we'll be interviewing guests all day." Jenna led the way into the suite and sent Finnian to a desk where Kane sat and sent Turnage to the space she'd chosen for herself. She turned as Kane stood and beckoned her and she followed him across the room out of earshot. "These two just came in together. So, find out what they were doing out in a blizzard."

"Copy." Kane glanced over at the two men and then moved his attention back to her. "I've spoken with Agnes. She repeated what we already knew. She spotted something in the pond. It was icing over. She didn't notice anything out of place at all. No footprints. Zip. I've spoken to Sparks, the guy who keeps the pathways clear. He said the only thing he noticed was one of the logs had fallen out of the bin beside the door to Dakota Storm's chalet. He put it back on the pile." He smiled. "I'd bet that's the wood the killer used to incapacitate Dakota Storm. We'll have to go back and check it out. Sparks mentioned he clears the paths regularly, so we'll be good to go when you're finished here."

Jenna nodded. "Okay. We'll head out as soon as we've spoken to these two. I'm not planning on waiting and searching in the dark."

"I'll grab our bags from the truck on the way back." Kane indicated with his chin toward the two men waiting patiently. "I hadn't realized what a cutthroat business publishing was. I had the idea it was kinda peaceful. You know, people living in their own worlds writing stories."

"Oh, that part is." Jenna smiled at him. "All the authors say that part is pure magic, but after the writing comes the hard work of getting the story to market. I'm just glad they share their stories. I sure do love a good book."

"Me too." Kane headed back to his desk.

Jenna sat down and opened her notebook. She looked at Turnage. "As you know, we asked everyone a few questions as they entered the halls earlier. We're just following up on those people who are staying alone or had no witnesses to prove their whereabouts."

"Okay." Turnage gave her a confident smile, his overuse of cologne almost stifling, but better than the smell of damp clothes and sweat that seemed to hang around everyone. "I'm not in the habit of sharing accommodation when I'm away at these confer-ences. It can lead to misconceptions. Plus, I'd probably end up nursing someone who'd had too much to drink and was spending the entire night hanging over the toilet." He leaned back in his chair. "Trust me, I'd rather be alone. As I told that officer," he indi-cated to Wolfe, speaking to a woman at his desk, "I left the lodge after dinner and went to my chalet. I made some calls on the land-line, drank a few glasses of wine, and went to bed around ten. I didn't venture out until after breakfast."

"Okay." Jenna made notes to check the time of the calls made from Turnage's room. "So, what made you venture out into a bliz-zard just before?"

"Oh, I made a huge purchase of books and had them signed by some of my favorite authors. I have a busy afternoon with inter-views and I didn't want to carry them around all day." Turnage's mouth turned up at the corners. "I took a chance and gave the authors my card. Any one of them would be a huge acquisition for my publisher. I admit to schmoozing as many authors as possible over lunch, and after, I took the books back to my cabin. I'm out in number thirty-eight. They did say they were clearing the pathways at lunchtime in case anyone wanted to return to their chalets and the man on his machine had just finished when I dashed back to my room."

Jenna observed him. His overconfidence gave her concern. She'd seen too many killers, who'd convinced themselves they'd gotten away with a crime act in a similar manner. After making a note to check the CCTV footage to determine when he left the lodge, she lifted her gaze back to him. "And you met Mr. Finnian where exactly? I noticed you came in together just before."

"He was coming from the parking lot and stopped to speak to me." Turnage let out a long sigh. "He found an author with the next best thing and wanted to discuss it with me. That's what agent's do, Sheriff. They find suitable authors and send their work to me. We don't want a one-book wonder. We want an author who can produce a string of bestsellers. It's all about sales."

"Interesting." Jenna made a few more notes. "Thank you for your time. I think that will be all for now."

"I can go?" Turnage gave her a rueful smile. "No handcuffs?" He stood and chuckled. "Now wouldn't that have been a story to tell around the water cooler back at the office?"

Jenna closed her notebook and got to her feet. "Maybe next time."

She walked him back to the elevator and waited for it to arrive before turning back in time to see Kane waving Finnian toward the door. As Finnian walked past her, she cleared her throat. "Mr. Finnian, where did you meet Mr. Turnage before you both came back to the lodge just before?"

"I ran into him on the pathway, as I was coming out of the parking lot." Finnian's eyebrows knitted together in a frown. "I had to go back to my SUV to look for a flash drive I'd mislaid."

Jenna smiled at him. "Okay, thanks for your time." She headed back into the suite and walked to Kane. "Find out anything interesting apart from them meeting outside just before?"

"No, not really." Kane scratched his cheek. "Finnian is a little on edge. He is the nervous type. He said, he goes to his room in the lodge after dinner at all the conferences or else he is constantly pursued by annoying authors looking for an agent. He said he spent his time reading the submissions he'd requested earlier in the day. He mentioned that the internet is great here, only the wireless phone service is intermittent. The landlines are working just fine."

Jenna smiled. "Good to know." She sighed. "It looks like

everyone has things in hand for now. Grab your coat and we'll go and look at the woodpile outside Dakota's chalet."

They headed for the elevator, and as the doors slid open, a man stepped out and looked at them. Jenna vaguely recognized him as one of their suspects. "Can I help you?"

"Yeah, thanks." The man straightened and his gaze flitted to Kane and back to her. "My name was called out and I went to the receptionist. She said to hang around and someone would be down soon. I waited for a bit, then decided to come on up." He gave her a slow almost intimate smile. "Did I win a door prize or something?"

"Ah no." Jenna narrowed her gaze. "What name was it?"

"Bexley Grayson."

Jenna checked her list. "Thank you. If you'd like to take a seat, someone will be with you in a moment." She noticed Rio had nobody waiting and he'd be free after interviewing the woman at his desk and pointed to him. "You won't have to wait too long. Deputy Rio will be finished soon."

As Grayson walked away, Kane moved to her side. She caught his stony expression. "What's up?"

"Nothing, but everyone who walked in here has wet boots... or damp boots." Kane indicated to Grayson. "Him too."

"Yours are damp too. So are mine." She pressed the elevator button. "It's a fact of life up here. Not everyone has a ton of dry boots with them."

"It's a must-have in the snow." Kane shrugged. "Most people would have more than one pair of outside boots and inside shoes or whatever with them. Wet boots mean frostbite." He followed her into the elevator. "The two guys coming in from outside have an excuse but not the others. It seems strange is all. I told the team to include it in the questioning. It might be relevant."

When the doors closed, Jenna leaned into him. "Good to know, but everyone is here to enjoy the snow. Their boots could be damp from before we locked them down. One thing's for sure, I'm changing my boots the moment I get back and setting them in front of the fire." She squeezed his arm. "You should too."

"I sure will. I've packed everything we'll need for at least a week, and they do laundry here if necessary." Kane smiled down at her and one hand snaked around her waist. "Our ski gear is in the truck, so we won't get wet after today. I packed indoor and outdoor boots, our spare sheriff's department coats, and four pairs of gloves each. If I've forgotten anything, I'll buy it at the store in the foyer." He chuckled. "Don't look so worried. I do have some idea of what you need for a trip. I even packed your toiletries."

Jenna burst out laughing. "Well, that's good to know. I was visualizing sleeping in one of your T-shirts."

"It wouldn't be the first time." Kane dropped his arm as the doors slipped open. "Darn it, the press is supposed to be following the convention, not us. What are they doing in the foyer? They've gathered quite a crowd of onlookers. That's all we need."

As the reporters moved forward, microphones in hand, men with cameras followed close behind. Jenna composed her expression and met them head on. She recognized Deni Crawford, a reporter from Blackwater News who could sensationalize a snail race, and avoided her prodding microphone.

"Sheriff Alton, why have you locked down the resort?" Crawford moved closer. "Does it have anything to do with Dakota Storm going missing?"

Jenna waved a hand toward the tall glass windows being pelted with swirling snow. "The slopes have been closed and all nonessential travel postponed until the blizzard passes. The weather forecast suggests this may take some time. I can assure you Mayor Petersham is working hard trying to keep essential roads clear. As everyone here has come for the convention, I suggest you all stop worrying about the weather and enjoy your stay. I'd strongly suggest, if you do plan to venture outside, then go as a group or in twos. It will be safer. The phones are unreliable at the moment, and if you're alone and take a fall, you won't last long out there."

"I noticed the medical examiner's van here earlier." Crawford waved the microphone in front of Jenna's nose. "Why was he here?"

Jenna smiled at her. "Dr. Shane Wolfe is in the building, yes. He is here with his daughters enjoying the convention. It is a crime convention after all." She looked at the gathered crowd. "The van will be back again this afternoon to collect him, or maybe his medical examiner's truck. He doesn't spend all his waking hours on the job."

"And is Dakota Storm missing or is the rumor just part of an official mystery game?" Crawford narrowed her eyes. "Was the ME's van parked outside as a red herring? Are you involved in the game, Sheriff?"

"I've no comment on anything to do with the running of the convention." Jenna stared at Crawford. "The people of Black Rock Falls don't pay me to play games. Now if you'll excuse me. I'm going to collect my bags from the truck. Just like everyone else, we're here for the duration of the blizzard." She pushed her way past the reporters and headed out the door.

"Deputy Kane." Crawford ran after them with her entourage close behind. "Is the earring a member of the staff found on a pathway one of the clues in the game? No one has claimed it yet."

"No comment." Kane waved her away.

Jenna walked beside him through the first set of doors. "How the hell are we going to complete an investigation with her watching our every move? If we tell the guests there's a killer running loose at the resort, they'll all panic and try to leave."

"Then we'll have to be careful." Kane pushed open the outside door. "And hope like hell this is an isolated incident."

THIRTEEN

Rumor is everywhere. It nibbles its way through the crowd like a swarm of locusts. People all around me are wide-eyed and exchanging gossip as if their lives depend on it. Maybe that's closer to the truth than they think. I smile to myself as someone close by is discussing why the cops asked them about their wet boots. What a deliciously misleading clue, because as I cast my gaze around the room, almost three-quarters of the people have watermarks on their boots. For me, since the sheriff locked down the resort, I have a captive audience, and when excitement turns to fear, it will be like catching fish in a barrel. There'll be no place to hide, no place to run from me. I'll leave no clues, and no law enforcement officer will suspect me, for I am a master of deception.

I know this ski lodge. I spent a wonderous vacation here last winter enjoying the slopes and planning my revenge. I used my time to map every CCTV camera, every safe exit and entry throughout the complex. I can move from place to place, floor to floor like a shadow.

Obtaining a supply of passkeys had just become easier. I couldn't risk using the same one more than twice, or the management might be able to track me. But as luck would have it, when I returned through the staff entrance earlier, cleaned off my boots, and shook the snow from my coat, I noticed a PASSKEY CARDS sign above a small metal box just inside the door. It wasn't locked and I grabbed a few and stuffed them inside my pocket. The one I took from the room service attendant I'll be sure to toss in a hallway somewhere.

I catch sight of someone I know. We started out together many years ago both studying literature and creative writing. I often helped her write pitches and it was one of my greatest that scored her the agent she'd craved. But when it came time to pass it forward, she turned her back on me as if I wasn't worth her time. I knew her as Doris Slaughter out of Chicago, but now her bio has her name as Kitty Pandora out of Superstition Oregon. Here she sits, as readers come by, books in hand, to collect her promotional handouts and ask for an autograph. I join the line but I haven't purchased a book. I figure my eyes would catch fire and burn at the sight of the words she'd written but I have read the reviews. At last, it's my turn and I smile at her. "Doris, how good to see you again."

"It's Kitty Pandora now." She preened and puffed up her hair. "My second book is due out next fall."

I lean closer and drop my voice to just above a whisper. "How about we celebrate with a few drinks later? You always said we'd celebrate with champagne when you made it."

"Champagne? Have you hit the big time?" Kitty's eyebrows rose in surprise.

I laugh and shrugged. "Oh, I can't tell just yet."

"I can't have a drink with you tonight. I'm having dinner with my agent." Kitty's mouth curled down. "It's all business, you know. You'll soon find out there's no time for fun."

I keep smiling. She was always a greedy woman and I'd play to that weakness. "I so understand. This is a busy time for me too. At least allow me to send a bottle of champagne to your room. For old time's sake?"

"That would be nice." Kitty actually smiled. "I'll drink it in my bubble bath. I have one every night to sooth the aches and pains.

These conferences will be the death of me." She wrote something on a bookmark and handed it to me. "Here you go."

I glance at the number, 3/24, and her messy signature, scrawled on the bookmark promoting her latest book, *Frizzled*. "I'll be sure to order it now. What's a good time for you?"

"Ten. I'll have my bath waiting." Kitty waved me away. "You'll have to go now. I have people waiting."

I chuckle. My day just got a whole lot better. "Ten it is."

FOURTEEN

Snowflakes melted on Kane's cheeks, sending trickles of ice water down his neck. As he walked beside Jenna, he could hear Mr. Sparks on his converted Bobcat snowplow, clearing the pathways. He took Jenna's hand and they hurried along the recently cleared trail. "I spoke to Emily earlier. She's keen to stay here for a couple of days. Apparently, there's an ex-FBI agent who wrote a book about profiling and he's running a Q & A tomorrow. She wants to attend and can get a ticket without a problem. Julie wants to spend more time here too. The only problem is getting a room. You have a suite with two bedrooms and I have a room with two single beds. If I bunk with you, I can give my room to the girls." He gave her a long look and smiled at her bemused expression. "If you're worried, I'll make sure anyone coming and going will see we're using both rooms."

"I'd like that." Jenna squeezed his hand. "I'm getting used to having you around. I was wondering why you took the other room in the first place."

Kane chuckled. "Well, you wanted to keep our relationship private, so asking for one room would have placed the cat among the pigeons. Now, people will see women going in and out of my room. That will put an end to any romance rumors about us." He met her horrified gaze with a wide grin. "Oh, for goodness sake, Jenna, don't look at me like that. I won't be staying in the room, will I? But media reporters, especially Deni Crawford, wouldn't know who they are, will they? With luck she'll leave us alone for a time."

"You have a very strange sense of humor, and I know when it comes to Wolfe and his girls, he has none whatsoever. God help you if Emily is mentioned in the newspaper as your date." Jenna was scanning the way ahead. "This snow is so heavy I can't see a thing. Anyone could be out there watching us."

"I doubt it." Kane peered into the dark forest. "It's so cold. Stand still for long and you'll become part of the landscape."

They reached the barrier Kane had constructed across the pathway outside Dakota's chalet and he moved it and walked around it and headed for the woodpile. He pulled out a brush he'd taken from his forensics kit and gently brushed away the snow from the pile of wood. "I'd assume Sparks would have placed the wood where it couldn't roll back down, so maybe against the wall. I'll look there first."

Starting at one end of the pile closest to the wall, he examined each log. He'd gotten to the last one in the top row and spotted a splash of red. "Got it."

"Here." Jenna waved an evidence bag at him. "Drop it in here."

Kane looked at the log through the plastic bag. "We're lucky it's frozen. All the evidence has been preserved." He glanced at his watch. "Webber will be on his way back by now to collect Wolfe. This is a great find."

"Good, let's go. I'm freezing." Jenna led the way back down the pathway. "I thought I'd be used to the cold by now, but this year it's beyond cold."

The engine sound of the Bobcat rumbled close by and Sparks came riding toward them waving frantically. Kane moaned. "What now?"

"Is something wrong, Mr. Sparks?" Jenna walked toward him, a worried expression on her face.

"There's a body at the construction site." Sparks was breathing heavily, sending great plumes of steam all around him. "The door to one of the new chalets is wide open, with snow getting inside. I went to close it, seeing as the contractors left before the blizzard hit, and saw a man lying in a pool of blood." His brow wrinkled. "This isn't one of those staged murder scenes with a dummy and a murder mystery for the guests to solve, is it?"

"We'll take a look. Show us where to go." As the Bobcat turned around and chugged away, Jenna looked at Kane. "This can't be good."

The way to the construction site had been cleared and a good amount of sand and salt had been laid, but Kane gripped Jenna's hand when she slipped on a patch of ice. "Hang on to me." He pulled her hand through his arm. "We'll move faster together. Our snow boots are in the Beast. We should've thought to wear them this morning."

"I wasn't expecting to be hiking in the snowfields when I left home." Jenna held on tight. "These boots are usually fine in the snow in town but not good enough for alpine conditions." She pointed ahead. "There's the construction site and, look, there's an access road out back for the tradesmen. I wonder where that leads to?"

Kane scanned the area all around the chalet but snow had obliterated any footprints or signs of anyone being in the area and the plow had cleared the pathway. He'd seen the plan of the resort many times. It was on the noticeboard in their front office. "That maintenance road runs parallel to the ski slopes and up here behind the cabins. If you remember the last time we were here, someone had used the back road beside the slopes to commit a crime."

"Vividly." Jenna's mouth turned down as she moved to the chalet door and visibly shuddered. "Oh, I'll never get used to seeing murder victims."

Kane squeezed her arm. "I'll check for vitals and then come right out. We'll need to preserve the scene and I haven't brought my forensics kit."

"Go right ahead." Jenna peered inside the door. "I'll wait here."

Without hesitation, Kane skirted the room, examining the floor for any evidence, but there was little of significance. He approached the body, keeping well away from the pool of frozen blood, and checked for a pulse in the man's neck. He looked up at Jenna and shook his head before retracing his steps. "Frozen solid."

"Dammit, this means anyone could've used the back road to get to Dakota Storm's chalet as well, without anyone seeing them and escaped down the mountain before we arrived." Jenna peered in the door.

"If the same killer murdered this man, I don't think they used the back road." Kane's gaze moved to the open door and the body in a pool of blood. "They closed the road after we arrived and Mr. Sparks would have noticed the door open before now." He walked up to Sparks. "Did you clear this path earlier today?"

"Yeah, I'm clearing them a few times a day. I finished that area before seven and I've been going back and forth all day. The snow is relentless and people have to get back to their rooms." Sparks lowered his sunglasses and peered into the chalet. "Is that body real?"

Kane frowned. "I'm afraid so, but it's not clear how he died. It could've been an accident. Don't mention this to anyone. We don't want people to panic and we'll need time to call the medical examiner and contact the next of kin before we release any details."

"Sure, sure." Sparks looked at Jenna. "Do you need me to stay around, Sheriff?"

"No thanks. We can handle it from here." Jenna glanced back at the road. "Are you in contact with the person clearing the road from here to town? We'll need the back road open urgently, so we don't disturb the guests."

"Yeah, I'll call him on the two-way. He's due to come by this afternoon so the bus can return to town, so he's already on the mountain. I'll get him to come by and clear it now." Sparks's forehead wrinkled into a frown. "If you need the road cleared more often, call the council. The snowplows are working around the clock, so I hear."

"Okay, thanks." Jenna gave him a wave as he turned the Bobcat around and headed back down the trail, spilling salt and sand from a spreader set behind his machine. She turned to Kane. "I'll call Wolfe. While we're waiting, we'll make a start at processing the scene. I have a pocketful of evidence bags we can use. I doubt there'll be fingerprints. No one in their right mind would come here without gloves. We'll just have to do our best. Move slow and check out everything." She made the call.

Kane moved closer to the door and something shiny in the snow caught his eye. He bent and pulled out a gold earring. "This is a match to the one we found outside Dakota Storm's chalet."

"An impossible coincidence." Jenna opened an evidence bag and Kane dropped it inside. She peered at the earring. "I hope this has DNA on it. What's the chance the killer dropped it?"

"More like they left it deliberately. They wouldn't want to be seen wearing one earring after the announcement this morning." Kane peered inside the chalet, the puff of steam from his breath clouded up his sunglasses. He removed them and edged into the room, taking in the entire scene. The man lay on the floor spread-eagled in a pool of frozen blood. Snowflakes dusted the body, covering any signs of injury. But as he moved closer, he caught the glint of something in the fall of hair. Using the pen from his pocket, he lifted the hair to reveal three small pieces of metal protruding from the victim's neck at the base of the skull. With care, he brushed away the snow from the man's bloody coat and jeans. "Oh, Jesus."

The body was peppered with bright silver nails. He turned, searching the immediate area for a weapon and his gaze settled on the nail gun. "He's been shot with a nail gun."

"He suffered." Jenna's face paled. "He'd have bled out with this many bolts in him."

Kane shook his head. "There's not enough blood to indicate he bled out. The body shots were aimed to cause maximum pain. I figure the three in the temple killed him." He straightened and peered around the room. "And there's the nail gun still attached to the compressor."

"It's been a while since we've found a murder weapon. Wolfe will be ecstatic." Jenna stepped carefully across the small space, scanning the ground. "Look at the floor. It's already covered with footprints from the many contractors who've visited, and no doubt the victim and killer." She pushed her hands into her pockets and looked at him. "Take the photographs. There's blood spatter everywhere—floor, bathroom door—and there's a handprint on the doorframe. All no doubt from the victim, but he's wearing gloves and in this weather the killer would have been wearing them as well. I'll call Webber and direct him to the back road." She pulled out her phone.

Kane took photographs with his phone and examined the entire chalet with care, making sure not to overlook anything. Collecting fragments of evidence was vital to solving a murder, but apart from a few dusty footprints on the wooden floor and damage to the walls from the nail gun, he found little else to document. There was no sign of a struggle. The dead man had no other contusions visible, nothing on his face, and apart from blood on his gloves and marks where he'd tried to crawl away, it was as if the man had been in the room alone.

He bent down, avoiding stepping in the blood, and searched the victim's pockets. The inside pocket of his jacket held a wallet with four hundred in cash and a driver's license. In another pocket he discovered cards promoting a book titled *Nailed It* with a photograph of the author. He stared at the driver's license photograph and compared it to the man's blue frozen face and stood. He waited for Jenna to disconnect and showed her the license. "We have Jedidiah Longfellow out of Wilderness, Wyoming." He handed Jenna the pile of cards. "Now this is weird."

"It looks like the victims in his book were killed by a nail gun." Jenna pushed the phone back in her pocket. "We'll need to find out if he writes true crime. It might be payback from someone involved."

Staring down at the face of the man, Kane rubbed his chin. "Possible motive but I think we'd have heard about a previous nail gun murder. It's not the usual weapon of choice. I figure he wrote fiction. Two murders in chalets next to each other. They must be linked. I wonder what connection he has with Dakota Storm?"

FIFTEEN

During a homicide investigation, Deputy Zac Rio regarded every suspect he interviewed as a possible killer. He didn't have the intricate profiling skills of Kane or Special Agent Jo Wells, the behavioral analyst from Snakeskin Gully who often dropped by to lend a hand on some of the more difficult cases, but he had an instinct about people. Alas the woman seated opposite him, an author who went by the name of September March, had skewed all his senses. Miss March informed him she lived out of Spirit Lake in the foothills of the Black Rock mountain range. He'd never heard of the place. He'd met some strange people in his time in Los Angeles, but September March was weird with a capital *W*. With long charcoal-black hair and dressed in long flowing robes over army boots, September obviously had a penchant for snakes, a silver one with red eyes curled around her neck and hung down the front of her black top to nestle between an ample bosom. The same silver design adorned both wrists and snake earrings dangled from her ears. She had a long face, pointed chin, and green eyes topped with highly arched eyebrows. Rings covered every finger and when she walked bells attached to the bottom of her voluptuous skirts tinkled. He looked up from his notes and met her disinterested gaze. "What kind of books do you write?"

"Everyone here writes crime." September leaned forward and tipped her head to one side as she peered at him. "I write supernatural crime thrillers."

Rio nodded and made a note. "Are you published?"

"Yeah, well, self-published." Her gaze drifted to the other hotel guests in the room. "I'm here to pitch my latest manuscript to agents. I've been trying for some time to secure one. It's really annoying when they reject me, especially when I see the exact same story as mine being represented by them."

Oh, you have a chip on your shoulder. "I'm sure that happens all the time." Rio shrugged. "I'd imagine most agents have a slot for a particular genre and ask for submissions, so the best one in their opinion is offered representation."

"But mine is the best one." September narrowed her green gaze on him. "I've proved it. When I self-publish the books, they do quite well, but it's like being stuck in a rut. I need a bestseller to get an agent, but I need an agent to get a good publisher to give me that bestseller."

Rio decided to change tack and find out a little more about Miss March. "So do you enjoy writing crime?"

"I like murder, the bloodier the better." She chuckled and wet her lips. "I want the reader to be too scared to get up and walk to the bathroom at night. Too scared to drive anywhere alone."

Rio nodded. He'd decided, after looking closer at the strange green eyes with black slits for pupils, she had to be wearing contact lenses, or he was talking to an alien from some distant planet. "Do you live alone?"

She pushed her hair from her face, tucking it neatly behind her ears. "Yes, I live alone and right now I'm hoping, when the conference is over, I won't find my cabin under a ton of snow." She sighed. "I'll manage for the winter if I can get back. I hunt for all my food and my meat locker is full."

Rio cleared his throat. "Before you leave, call for an update on the roads and ask when the access to your property can be cleared by the snowplows. We have many working around the clock. It is what we pay our taxes for, after all."

"Thanks, I will." She gave him a curious stare. "I'm sure y'all didn't haul me up here to ask me about my books. Cut to the chase. I don't want to miss anything."

After checking his iPad, Rio smiled. "Sure. You're out in cabin forty-six. You left here at nine-forty-five last night and returned this morning at nine. You told one of the deputies, you didn't see or speak to anyone during the time you left and when you returned. I'm just following up on that. The CCTV footage shows a few people leaving around the same time."

"Well, I may have followed a few people out the door and along the footpath, but when it splits up and I headed to my chalet, I didn't see a soul. I didn't even see who delivered my breakfast this morning. It was snowing hard when I left, so I pulled up my hood and ran. I changed in the ladies' bathroom and my bag is in one of the lockers. I didn't see anyone."

After adding a few notes, Rio looked up at her bored expression. "How well do you know Dakota Storm?"

"I pitched my book to Miss Storm." She made a show of examining her rings, setting each one in the correct position. "I waited, like nine months for an email rejection from her assistant."

Rio frowned sympathetically, although he'd never experienced professional rejection. In his case, people headhunted him. "And how did that make you feel?"

"Oh, you're good." Summer smiled at him. "You want me to say, 'Like putting her in one of my books and murdering her.' As much as I'd like to, it just wouldn't be enough."

"I see." Rio nodded. "Did you hear anything unusual last night or this morning?"

"Nope." September checked her phone. "If that's all, I have to go. I have an agent pitch in fifteen minutes and I don't want to miss it."

"Sure." Rio stood and offered his hand. "Thank you for your cooperation. Good luck with your pitch."

Her handshake was more than firm. Her hands were rough and he could make out the outline of a muscular forearm. He sat down and made a note. *September March, strong tall mountain woman, more than capable of committing murder. Hunts her own food. Motive: Has a beef with agents. Rejected by Storm.*

After moving his brief notes to the file, he glanced up at the next suspect. Having a long-term memory had its advantages, as well as its downfalls, but he recognized the next person as Bexley Grayson, an author out of Lyons Bay, California. Grayson, at forty-two, sported blond highlights in his hair. He was a stocky muscular man. His fake tan had a distinct orange tone and his too white smile could have lit up the room. He'd dressed, as had most of the guests, in ski pants topped with a brightly patterned sweater. Rio stood and walked to greet the man. "Mr. Grayson, thank you for dropping by. We're following up on the whereabouts of guests staying alone, in an effort to find Miss Storm."

"You haven't found her yet?" Grayson raised both eyebrows and gave him a look of incredulity. "I assumed the worse after seeing the medical examiner's van arrive."

Rio observed his behavior. He seemed genuinely surprised. "We're short-staffed and Dr. Wolfe offered to lend a hand. His assistant is a badge-holding deputy. It's what we do in Black Rock Falls. We help out where we can."

"Ah, and everyone believes the conference is holding a murder mystery game." Grayson chuckled. "They often do over these long conferences." He gave Rio a long considering look. "I'm wondering, if you are all actors, roleplaying for our benefit to make it seem real." He glanced around the room. "The locals attending the conference mentioned Sheriff Alton and Deputies Kane and Rowley, but they seem to be conspicuous by their absence. Now we're called mysteriously one by one to answer questions, when we've already given the sheriff the information previously." He leaned back in his chair and smiled. "This is all part of the game, isn't it?"

Not to Dakota Storm it isn't. Rio tapped his pen on the desk and shook his head. "I'm not aware of any game." He glanced at his notes. "How well do you know Dakota Storm?"

"I've met her a few times at conferences, pitched my stories to her. She is one of the best dealmakers around." Grayson sighed. "I haven't been lucky yet, but there's ten other agents all interested in acquiring crime thrillers here, so I'm still in with a chance."

Rio twirled the pen in his fingers. "You're not bothered by her method of rejection?"

"Who isn't? She'd make the Wicked Witch of the West look like a nun. The emails can be harsh but face to face, she's blunt... no, darn right offensive." Grayson sighed. "I gave her my best pitch and she said, 'Why are you wasting my time with this trash? Go away, forget writing, and get a day job. You'll never make it in this business.'"

"I see." Rio made notes and then looked at him. "It seems she has a habit of being rude."

"More like a reputation." Grayson chuckled. "She isn't called the Viper for nothing, but I figure that's too nice. Maybe the Destroyer of Lives would come close."

Rio leaned back in his chair, allowing questions to form in his head. "Uh-huh, so, now you've had time to think, do you recall seeing anyone last night at all who could verify your whereabouts between midnight and, say, six this morning?" His satellite phone buzzed and he held up one finger. "Just a second. I need to take this." He stood and walked some distance away. "Rio here."

"It's Jenna, we've found a body, a male we believe could be Jedidiah Longfellow out at the construction site. It's a homicide. So you'll need to ask the suspects where they were this morning as well."

Rio nodded. "Sure. I'm on it. Do you need any help?"

"No, you'll have to hold the fort there. Wolfe and his team will be heading our way as inconspicuously as possible. I'm leaving Emily there with you. Webber is bringing the van via a back service road. I'll bring you up to speed when we get back." Jenna disconnected.

Rio returned to his seat. "Anyone see you last night?"

"Not that I'm aware. I went straight to bed. I'm sure you'd see me on the CCTV cameras. They're everywhere." Grayson stared into space. "This morning, I ate breakfast in my room and then came downstairs to join in the conference. There were people milling around, but I don't recall anyone in particular."

"Okay." Rio looked up from his notes. "And this morning, what have you been doing?"

"Ah... I went to the book signing and then to a reading." Grayson shrugged. "I spoke to many people. I can't remember all their names. Let me think. A young woman, blonde hair, oh, what was her name? Ah yes, Julie." He glanced across the room to where Emily was talking to someone across a desk. "She looked a lot like her. We were in a line to get an autograph from the Black Rock Falls series author and chatted. There was someone else there too I've met on social media. He's a bestselling author. Jedidiah Longfellow. Nice guy."

Rio's radar went on alert. "What time was this?"

"In the session before the lunch break." Grayson sighed. "At least fifty people would have seen me at the book signing and the reading. The halls were packed." He moved around irritated. "Is that all? I paid good money to enjoy this conference, not to sit around here talking to cops all darn day."

Rio held up a finger. "What time did you speak with Jedidiah Longfellow?"

"Oh, I don't know, eleven maybe." Grayson stood. "He had a few people around him, asking him about his book. He was in the hall when the author was reading her book as well." He narrowed his gaze. "Is he missing too?"

Rio put down his pen and closed his notebook. "Not that I'm aware." He stood and offered his hand. "Thank you for your time."

Grayson seemed reluctant to shake his hand, but when he did his palm was ice-cold against Rio's flesh. It was like shaking hands with a corpse. After the man's touch lingered on his skin for an eternity, Rio used the hand sanitizer on the table, suddenly glad he'd had all his shots. He finished up his files and looked to see who was left to interview. He found the room empty apart from Emily, finishing up with Parker Rain, a literary agent out of Twisted Forest, Montana. When she'd finished entering her notes into the files and closed her laptop, he walked over. "Do you want to get out of here for a time?"

"Sure." Emily stretched like a cat. "I'm stiff from being out so long in the snow this morning. I don't figure I'll ever be warm again."

Rio smiled at her. "We have some time before Jenna gets back. I figure we deserve hot chocolate in front of the fire and maybe a snack. The diner in the foyer has some delicious cakes and pastries in the window."

"That sounds wonderful." She picked up her purse. "Do you have a card to get back in here? I don't want to leave the door unlocked."

Rio waved a keycard. "Yeah, we all have one. How did the interview go? Did you find a suspect?"

"I'm not sure." Emily followed him out the door to the elevator. "I've never met people like this before. They're really obsessed with their books. And they take everything so seriously, like it's life or death. Honestly, from the stories I've heard today, if Dakota Storm had been one of the toxic reviewers they have to deal with, I wouldn't be surprised if an author or agent murdered her just to get even."

SIXTEEN

It was as if a calming breeze came over the murder scene when Wolfe appeared out of the snow. The big hulking figure carrying a forensics kit in one hand wasn't recognizable, with a scarf over his mouth, sunglasses, and a fur-trimmed hoodie hiding his features. If it weren't for the medical examiner logo on the front of his jacket, Jenna would have had one hand on her weapon. She stepped out into the snow to greet him. "Emily not coming?"

"No, she's tied up with the suspect interviews. As you know, my daughters insisted on staying to help out even with a killer on site." Wolfe removed his sunglasses and rolled his eyes. "Julie arranged for Webber to collect their things. My housekeeper packed bags for them." He let out a long sigh. "Okay. What have we got?"

Jenna held out an evidence bag containing the victim's wallet. "Driver's license says Jedidiah Longfellow out of Wilderness, Wyoming. From the promotional cards we found on him, he's an author."

"Oh, this is interesting." Wolfe's eyebrows rose as he peered through the door to the chalet. "Just before I left, Rio spoke to a guy on our suspects' list named Grayson and he mentioned speaking to Jed Longfellow at around eleven this morning." He glanced at his watch. So what time did Sparks find the body?"

Jenna checked her notes. "He called at three-thirty. We were out hunting down the log that was used on the Dakota Storm homicide, and we found it." She pointed to a plastic bag resting beside the front door. "We came here directly and the blood around the victim was frozen. Dave's taken shots of everything. The nail gun appears to be the weapon of choice."

"It's pretty hard to kill someone with a nail gun unless you hit them over the head with it." Wolfe looked skeptical. "On the bright side, the fact we have Grayson as a witness to the last time someone saw Longfellow alive is fortunate, because we can put the time of death between eleven and three-thirty. It's a small window and better than I can calculate with science, especially in subzero temperatures." He placed his kit inside the door and scanned the room. "Find anything of interest?"

"Not much. The matching earring to the one we found outside Dakota Storm's chalet was just outside the door and there's more blood over there." Kane waved a hand toward the blood spatter on the wall. "I'd say the victim backed up against the wall to get away from the killer, but the whole scene looks way too amiable to me."

Jenna nodded. "Yeah, no defense wounds we can see. I figure he knew the killer and could've come here to meet them."

"A lovers' meeting perhaps?" Wolfe glanced at her and approached the body. "Pointing a nail gun and pushing a woman into a pond doesn't take much strength, so I'm not ruling out a woman suspect in these cases. Like Kane said, women of average fitness would be quite capable of sliding Dakota on the ice and into the pond."

Jenna allowed Wolfe's words to percolate through her mind. "Would an average woman know how to use a nail gun? It's a noisy thing most women would avoid, I'd imagine."

"Women work in all trades these days." Kane raised an eyebrow and smiled at her. "You'd use one, wouldn't you?"

"It would be easier than swinging a hammer. I'd imagine you'd turn on the compressor and then fire it." Jenna frowned. "I wouldn't know how to load it, but we can assume it was loaded. This is beside the point. What if this is a love triangle? We need to find out the connection between Dakota Storm and Longfellow. If they had an affair and caused a breakup, maybe the injured party could've done this." She looked at Kane. "Can you actually shoot the nail gun like a pistol?"

"Most of them have a safety mechanism to avoid unintentional discharge, but it can be overridden, and that's an old model." Kane examined the nail gun. "This is a framing nail gun, so it fires three-and-a-half-inch nails, which I believe is code for structural framing. Most nail guns must be pressed onto a surface before they work. On this one, holding both triggers down together allows it to shoot nails, but it becomes less effective over distance. I'd say probably twenty percent effective as a twenty-two-caliber pistol, at best." He turned his attention back to Jenna. "There are easier ways to kill someone if that had been the intention. This indicates this method of murder means something to the killer. Finding a nail gun wouldn't be easy, so the killer must have scouted out the place before they lured the victim here."

"I think it's staring us in the face, Dave." Jenna stared at the evidence bag in her hand. "Longfellow's book is called *Nailed It*. It seems too much of a coincidence not to be part of the killer's plan."

"I guess we'll need to read it for ourselves." Kane rubbed the back of his neck. "Oh boy, if the killer is murdering authors because of fictional crimes they created, it hits the dog barking messages to the Son of Sam out of the ballpark."

Jenna swallowed hard at the implications. "So, a deliberate act and lack of empathy would indicate psychopathic behavior. It would be classed as an organized psychopath, right?"

"Yeah, especially if the killer encouraged the victim to come here in the middle of a blizzard. They do have charm in spades." Kane indicated to the floor. "From the evidence in front of us, it's clear the victim didn't try to fight back. Look, not so much as a scuff mark from a shoe. The place would've been in a shamble if someone I didn't know had come at me with a nail gun." He pointed to a hammer on the floor. "There are weapons everywhere and look down here. The victim was an arm's reach away from the electric cord running to the compressor. He'd only have to pull it out and his killer couldn't shoot again. It seems to me there was a lot of discussion going on before this went down."

The crime scene didn't make any sense. *Who just stands there and allows someone to shoot nails into them?* Jenna watched Wolfe roll the body over and bent to take a closer look. "I'm seeing chest and leg wounds, none on his arms. From what you're saying, Dave, to make the nails penetrate, the killer must have been close, and it's as if this guy just stood there and took it. Anyone being attacked usually has marks on their hands. I'd expect him to be shielding his face at least."

"Maybe he didn't believe his friend would kill him?" Kane stared down at the body. "Disbelief, shock maybe. What do you think, Shane?"

"Yeah, both shock and disbelief can render a person almost paralytic." Wolfe frowned. "His eyes are closed as well. That's unusual. It's as if he'd given up."

Jenna looked at Wolfe. "You've seen violence in all its forms. Why didn't Longfellow defend himself?"

"From my experience, some men wouldn't try to defend themselves against a woman they knew." Wolfe shrugged. "Maybe they'd start out by trying to talk them down and reason with them. I know spousal abuse happens, but thank God it's not the norm."

"That makes sense." Kane narrowed his gaze. "Although, the pain would've been unbearable—those nail guns hit with force and everyone has their limit—and yet he just stood there and took it, rather than disarming his attacker." He shot a look at Jenna. "What kind of idiot does that?"

Jenna shrugged. "A devoted idiot or a very close friend, maybe?"

"It's not easy to kill someone with a nail gun, as Kane explained, it doesn't shoot nails at the same velocity of a bullet."

Wolfe lifted his gaze to Jenna. "Most people could survive random shots, but whoever did this had some knowledge of anatomy. I see nails concentrated around his femoral artery, his carotid artery, and abdominal aorta. This would have caused the major blood loss needed to bring him down. The kill shot, if you like, was well placed, and I'd say when I open him up, I'll discover the shots to the base of the skull severed his brain stem."

Amazed by the lengths people would go to to kill, Jenna straightened. "He must have suffered."

"Yeah, but not for very long." Wolfe used a probe to take the body temperature, removed the victim's glove, and scanned his prints. "The aim of the killer was to inflict pain rather than kill. No head shots, at first, all legs and torso. I'd say from the amount of blood, the time between the body shots and the kill shots would have been a few minutes at most. This was torture and I'd say time restraints rather than choice forced the killer to cut it short. I figure we have a link. This murderer gained gratification, same as in the strangulation of Dakota Storm. Up close and personal."

"This would tell me not only an organized psychopath but a controlled psychopath." Kane's mouth formed a thin line. "There's no frenzied attack, both murders are methodical and well planned. We've one of the most dangerous of psychopaths in our midst. Most follow a pattern and this one is random and impossible to predict."

A cold chill crawled over Jenna. "Then there's the earrings. One left at each crime scene." She chewed on her bottom lip. "It's deliberate. It has to be. Maybe they're a trophy from a previous crime?"

"It must tie the two murders together." Kane stared into space. "It's all part of the big picture inside the killer's mind, like a jigsaw puzzle. We just have to find more pieces. It's as if he's laying out clues for us like in a game. Maybe this is the conference game? Us against an organized psychopath."

"Oh, I hope not." Jenna rubbed her arms, suddenly cold. "I'm sick of being dragged into criminals' delusional minds."

She watched Wolfe and Kane roll the victim into a body bag. Once zipped up, Wolfe moved around, taking samples of blood from every location. "Anything we can do to help?"

"Call Webber and see how close he is. I told him to come directly here as soon as he could get through the back road." He straightened and looked at Jenna. "I'll take the hammer and the nail gun with me as well. We'll have to seal this chalet. I'm not finished with it yet." He huffed out a cloud of steam and shook his head. "I'll do what I can to get formal IDs of the bodies and then you can notify the next of kin." He waved a hand toward the door. "This weather slows down everything."

A phone buzzed and everyone checked their pockets.

"It's me." Wolfe stared at the screen. "Where are you, Colt?" He paused a beat. "Uh-huh, look out for Kane, he'll guide you in." He disconnected and looked at Kane. "He's on the road looking for the entrance. Can you go find him?"

"Sure." Kane put on his sunglasses, pulled up his hood, and vanished into the snow.

Jenna sighed. "You head off with Colt, we'll grab the girls' bags and take them back to the lodge."

"Keep a close eye on them for me." Wolfe looked suddenly anxious. "Trust me, when it comes to killers, those two are like magnets."

SEVENTEEN

Darkness presses against the windows, trapping us inside. There's no moon and only the continuous fall of snow—and the hoot of an owl to break the monotony. Heat from the many woodfires, warms my exposed flesh as I move around, enjoying the scents and flavors of the conference. The smell of books is everywhere, and tables stacked high with the latest volumes adorn the hallways manned by sellers. Authors' images are displayed like in a hall of fame, each with their current bestseller and the times of their readings and book signings. The atmosphere is electric, exciting. People here are like me on the outside—they may write, edit, publish, or read the fine art of murder—but I live it.

I walk through the hall, deciding which author I should grace with my presence. You see, not all are bestselling authors and lucky enough to attract a line of people waiting for an autograph. There are others who arrived with suitcases filled with copies of their books hoping to sell one, or maybe two, and are desperate for me to stop by their table. I've been watching them and a few have appealed to me, but some, I must admit, make no effort to attract readers. I know being an author can make one impoverished. The long wait between book advances, or no sales, can grind a person down, but my urge to kill rises at the sight of one woman, hiding behind a pile of books, stuffing her face with cream donuts. The cream hangs on her chin in a grotesque dripple. She gives all of us trying to succeed a bad name. I wish I could slip her out the back door and strangle her, but I must concentrate on being the social butterfly. I want to be noticed for the time when the sheriff mentions my name to witnesses and asks, "Did you see this person?"

An alibi is a nonnegotiable asset for someone like me, so I move through the crowd, nodding here, smiling there until I see someone I recognize. Ah yes, Julie. The sweet-as-honey blonde creature is used to getting what she wants. I slid by when she spoke to the medical examiner to eavesdrop. From the demands she made and the exasperated expression on the poor man's face, he must be her father. His refusal to allow her to stay had been valid, considering I'm here as a constant unknown threat, but as soon as she batted those long eyelashes, he melted like snowflakes on a log fire. She hasn't meant more to me than an excuse for an alibi but something about her has changed since the last time I saw her. My attention fixes on the way she's touching her hair. As she curls a lock around a red-tipped finger the image of my mother's face catapults across my vision. I am back in time, a vulnerable child, with no one to hear me. I hated my mother's bleached-blonde hair and long red fingernails. She took my dignity and spent it like a commodity, only thinking of herself, her next drink, or new pair of shoes. Countless men came to our house. So many insisted I call them Daddy or Uncle. I'll never forget the sea of faces, or the first one I killed. The warm blood on my flesh, the smell as they breathed their last, and the horrified expression on their face was a relief. At last, I'd gained my voice.

The room comes back into focus, chatter fills my ears, and the warm smell of bodies and woodsmoke bring me back to my senses. It's just as well. I have things to do, but my attention keeps slipping back to Julie. She's become an insatiable magnet and my fingers tingle at the thought of closing them around her slender neck. It would be so satisfying to look into her big gray eyes and see my face reflected in her confusion as I squeeze the life from her. I smile to myself. You see, once I'm done with my list, I'll have time to play. A literary conference is supposed to be fun, right?

EIGHTEEN

After returning with their bags, Jenna took a hot shower and changed out of her damp clothes. She added them to Kane's pile and arranged to have them picked up by the hotel laundry service. She headed back into the cozy sitting room that joined the two bedrooms together and waited for Kane to finish feeding Duke. He'd walked him, rubbed him down, and settled him in front of the fire on his blanket before heading for the shower. She loved seeing this gentle side of Kane. He cared for their animals so well, making doubly sure each one of them was always loved and happy. Even Pumpkin, who really wasn't a social cat, would curl around his neck when they watched TV. A pang of regret grabbed her. He'd make a great father, but would he risk marrying again?

"Everything okay?" Kane had caught her staring at him. "You have that faraway look again. Have you any conclusions on the case?"

Jenna's cheeks heated. "I'd like to hear what everyone discovered today before I make any conclusions." Deciding to be honest with him, she sighed. "Then there's the autopsies, but I wasn't thinking about the case. I love seeing this side of you. You know, the way you care for the animals. I was thinking you'd make a great dad is all."

"The thought has crossed my mind, Jenna." Kane straightened and walked to her. "In fact, I think about the future a lot these days."

The phone rang and Jenna let out an exasperated sigh and went to pick up the receiver. "Sheriff Alton."

"It's Emily. Do you want me and Zac to hang around so you can bring us up to speed?" Emily sucked in a breath. *"The reason being, we booked a table for dinner at seven for all of us and it's six now."*

Jenna pushed the hair from her face and thought for a beat. "Are you dressed for dinner? We are, or do you need time to go change? And where is Julie? We're supposed to be keeping an eye on the pair of you."

"Oh really?" Emily sounded annoyed. *"Dad still thinks we're kids. He trusts me in the lab but not in a ski lodge. It doesn't make any sense."*

Blowing out a breath, Jenna rolled her eyes at Kane. "It's not that your dad doesn't trust you, Em. It's because we have someone on the premises killing people. Shane doesn't want to get a call to find out one of you has been murdered. I can see his point. I'm armed and you're not. It wouldn't be the first time one of you has been targeted. He's just being cautious."

"Okay, sure. I see your point, but as neither of us is involved in the publishing business, like both of the victims, I hardly think we have to worry." Emily sighed. *"So, do you want us to wait for you in the suite or meet you in the lobby and go to dinner together?"*

"We're on our way to the suite. See you in five." Jenna replaced the receiver. "We'll need to go and speak to the team. They've booked a table for dinner at seven." She pushed the room keycard in her pocket and headed for the door.

In the suite, Jenna pulled up the files. She and Kane gave them details of their suspects' interviews and then listened to Rio's account of the interviews from Bexley Grayson and September March. "So, conclusions?"

"Grayson is an unknown quantity. He's a façade. He's trying to fit in with a younger crowd—fake tan, so much Botox—he has no expression, too white teeth. He reminds me of a fast-talking car salesman depicted in the movies. He named people who saw him around during the murders, Julie being one of them. I think he's a creep." Rio opened his hands. "September March is a nut job. Away with the pixies and, yeah, she'd slit your throat without a second thought."

Concerned, Jenna highlighted both suspects on her list. "What about your suspect, Em?"

"Parker Rain, seems pretty levelheaded. I asked her if she knows Dakota Storm or Longfellow. She said that she and Dakota were both trying to sign an author, Joel Stanley, who'd written two books, *Frozen in Time* and *Body in a Frozen Lake*. Dakota apparently had an editor all steamed up about the story and could literally offer the guy a deal from the get-go. As Parker was offered the manuscript first, she feels cheated that Dakota signed the author, especially as the first one has sold over a million copies and the second even more." Emily raised both eyebrows. "So as Dakota was found in a frozen pond, it seems like a very strange coincidence. I figure we need to keep Parker Rain on the list too."

"Wolfe's interview with August Bradford didn't get us anywhere either." Kane stared at Wolfe's notes. "Bradford was dropped by Dakota at the end of last year. He's here trying to get a new agent. His comment to Wolfe was that he hopes Dakota rots in hell."

Pushing both hands through her hair, Jenna stared down at the list. "Six suspects. I'll contact Bobby Kalo and ask him to dig deep. I want to know what these people have been doing, whatever state they live in, and he's the best person for the job." She composed an email and sent it away with all the details she had on each suspect and then turned off her iPad. "Until Wolfe confirms the victims' IDs and conducts the autopsies, we're in limbo. As soon as we've contacted the next of kin, Rio can write up a media report that says virtually nothing. I don't want to panic people but I'll need to keep them as safe as possible."

"When you're moving around the resort, listen and keep your

eyes open." Kane looked at Emily and Rio. "One of the suspects will slip up, boast or do something. We'll need to be ready for them. I just hope whoever did this is stopping at two, but if this is a vendetta, they might strike again at any time and we need to be ready."

"Okay, I'll talk to Julie." Emily's blonde eyebrows met in a frown. "She'll be in the midst of them, now that she's staying and she's gotten tickets to everything. The passes the convention organizers gave Dad to allow us to move around during the investigation also get us into everywhere free of charge." She looked at Jenna. "They didn't want us parading around wearing our coroner's jackets."

"I see." Jenna stood. "They want us to keep a low profile, no doubt." She glanced at her watch. "Let's head down to eat now. Is Julie meeting us there?"

"Yeah." Emily walked beside her to the elevator. "It feels weird being trapped inside a hotel with a killer on the loose." She looked over her shoulder at Kane. "I'm sure glad our room is next to yours, Dave." She shuddered. "If someone creeps into my room, you'll come running, right?"

"Sure." Kane smiled at her.

Concern suddenly dropped over Jenna for the girls' welfare. She held the elevator door as they all stepped inside, but she gave Emily an encouraging smile. "We both will. Don't worry."

NINETEEN

Kitty Pandora checked the time, it was close to ten and it had been a long day. She'd undressed and put on her robe before heading into the bathroom to run the tub. The idea that someone below her social status had offered to send up a bottle of champagne amused her. For heaven's sake, the old acquaintance acted as if she owed them something. She ran her fingers through the bubbling suds and smiled. Kitty's room was very luxurious. Her husband was a very wealthy man, and she deserved to be the best author his money could buy. Oh, she came up with the ideas, usually based on her own extravagant lifestyle and, she had to admit, gleaned from every book or TV show she'd enjoyed. Every word of her manuscript had been polished and primed by the best editors her husband could employ. She'd pitched them to a host of literary agents and had always been rejected until, at a time of vulnerability, she'd reached out for help to a fellow author who had the ability to write an engaging pitch letter. The offer of help had come as an act of compassion and done the trick. After all, as a person of standing, she deserved to be published. Now, she just had to make a best-sellers list. She'd encouraged all the workers in her husband's employ to buy her books and vote for every coveted readers' award available until she'd gained one. When she'd volunteered to do an authors' workshop free of charge at the convention, how could they have possibly refused? People would flock to see her. After all, being the best had its own attraction.

The room filled with fragrant steam and piles of foam bubbled to the lip of the tub. Kitty sighed as she turned off the tap. She dried her hands, took out the hairdryer, and checked to see if it was working before placing it beside the basin. She searched her makeup bag for products she'd need to style her hair. After removing her watch, she shrugged. The offer of champagne was obviously a lie, but then she didn't believe her friend had the money to buy champagne. She walked into the sitting room and poured a glass of white wine and headed back to the bathroom. The tub looked inviting and after placing the wine on the edge of the tub, she turned to remove her makeup and peered at her reflection. Condensation covered the mirror and, irritated, she grabbed a towel to wipe it clean. As the mist cleared, she gaped in horror. Someone was standing right behind her.

She opened her mouth to scream and then recognized her friend's strange twisted smile. Annoyed, Kitty glared at the reflection. "How did you get into my room—and where's my bubbly?"

"What an ungrateful excuse for a person you are." Her friend leaned casually against the vanity and lifted a pistol and aimed it at her. "Get into the tub."

Heart thundering in her chest, Kitty stood her ground. Nobody gave her orders and not this lowlife. "I'm not getting naked in front of you."

"Well as sure as hell, I'm not turning my back." Her friend waved the pistol. "You're an author. Use your imagination. Once you're in the suds I won't see a thing."

Terror gripping her, Kitty tried to reason with them. "But the water is getting cold."

"Do I look like I care?" Her friend's lips quivered into a grin. "Better hurry."

Unnerved by the pistol aimed at her, Kitty stepped into the tub, turned her back, disrobed and dropped down, sinking to the shoulders in the rich foam. She pulled the suds around her. "Now what?"

"Duck under and wash your hair." The intruder pressed the muzzle to her head. "Hurry, we need to talk."

Trembling with fear, Kitty complied. "Okay now say what you need to say and leave and I won't tell anyone you broke into my room."

"You're in no position to bargain with me, Kitty." Her acquaintance took a nonchalant pose. "You've used people all your life, haven't you? Bought your way rather than earned it. Most of the unpublished authors here have more talent in their little finger than you will ever have. The talent to write is a gift and not something you can buy. You can go to all the classes you like, employ the best editors, and attend all the seminars, but the magic comes from inside. Your first mistake was writing about yourself. You see, nobody cares because you've never actually achieved anything on your own merit."

Annoyed, Kitty shook her head. "That's not true, my published book is about a wealthy woman crime fighter. I'm not a detective, so how could it be me?" She pulled more suds around her. The water was cooling fast. "I've done a ton of things in my life. All my friends admire me."

"Have you ever heard of the expression *cupboard love*? No?" Her acquaintance grinned broadly. "It means when people visit, pretending they're friends to get handouts. They believe if they crawl up your ass, they'll get something from you, but that's not the case, is it? You see, I know you for what you really are and, in a crisis, you'd step over a dying child to save yourself." Her friend put down the revolver and picked up the hairdryer. "This brings back memories. I've read the back cover of *Frizzled*. That was an idea I brainstormed with you for my own story. It was such a great idea to electrocute someone with a hairdryer. Why did you steal it? That could've been my breakthrough novel."

Panic shivered down Kitty's spine. Vulnerable and naked in the tub, she scrambled for a way out of the situation. This person didn't have her wealth and she could usually buy her way out of anything. "Oh, I don't remember. We talked about lots of things, but I don't recall discussing the climax of my story with you."

"You've used my ideas almost word for word and you sure didn't mention it when you asked me to write the pitch. I wouldn't have helped you if I'd known you'd intended to change up the ending to the same as my story. Clever though. Did you get one of your editor friends to change the pitch so it matched the new ending? I guess so. That would've been out of your ballpark, right?" Her friend turned on the hairdryer and wafted the hot air over her.

Teeth chattering, Kitty shook her head. "I never used all of your pitch. Well, just the elevator pitch because that was ambiguous and very catchy. What was it now? Ah yes, I remember: *No place to run, no place to hide. She knew he'd always be there right behind her.* I must admit you do have skill in writing an elevator pitch and we all know agents love a hook." She wrapped her arms around her. The once-warm water was cooling fast and goose bumps prickled her arms. "You've had your say, now leave. I'm getting cold."

"Oh, I haven't finished with you yet." Her acquaintance waved the hairdryer around. "Aren't you enjoying our little chat?"

Not that she cared what this nobody thought of her but relieved not to have a gun pointed at her, Kitty lifted her gaze. "No, I'm not. You're batshit crazy."

"I think I am too and I kinda like it." Her friend laughed. "Well? Is there anything else you want to say to me? An apology, perhaps?"

This was just another jealous person Kitty could do without. A leech wanting to bathe in her success. They wouldn't dare hurt her. She'd call their bluff. "I've nothing to apologize for. You're acting as if you wrote my book. Get it into your head that I wrote the damn book. Now, I need to get out of the tub, my skin is wrinkling. I'll look a mess in the morning and the press is everywhere."

"Oh, don't worry, I figure you'll make the news headlines." Her friend smiled and moved closer. Dangling the hairdryer a few inches from the water.

Terror gripped Kitty as she stared into the menacing face but she refused to back down. "Get that hairdryer away from me. I've had enough of your stupid games. I'm getting out the water." She gripped the sides of the tub, her feet slipping on the bottom as she tried to rise.

"Sit back down. You do know what will happen if I drop this?" The smile widened as her friend twirled the hairdryer from the cord just a few inches above the water. "You'll be frizzled."

Trembling with fear, Kitty swallowed hard, trying to think. "What do you want? Money? There's a few hundred in my purse."

"A few hundred?" Her friend moved the roaring hairdryer up and down like a teabag. "Nope, that just won't do it."

Blinking away tears of frustration, Kitty stared at the uncaring face. "What then? A job. You need a job and my husband—"

"I'd never work for you." The voice was as cold as the blizzard outside.

The hairdryer swung back and forth like a hypnotizing pendulum of death. Rigid with fear, Kitty dragged her eyes away. "Please, we can work this out. Whatever you want—money, real estate... My husband will give you anything I ask him to."

Her friend seemed to consider her words, the hairdryer stilling and twirling just above the suds. She pushed wet hair from her face with trembling fingers. "Tell me what you want."

"An apology would have been nice." The hairdryer dropped another inch. "Or an acknowledgement in your book."

Sucking in a breath, Kitty lifted her chin. Oh, she'd get even. How dare this person treat her like this? She'd call the cops the moment her friend left.

"You don't believe I'll drop it do you?" The hairdryer brushed the suds sending foam blowing into the air like snowflakes. "I'd like to see you fry in hot oil. In fact, it's been a fantasy of mine for some time, but I guess water will just have to do."

Suddenly very afraid, Kitty watched the air from the hairdryer make holes in the suds. Teeth chattering, she looked up at her friend. "If you insist. I'm—"

"Too late." With a wide grin, her friend let go of the cord.

Horrified, Kitty opened her mouth to scream just as the hairdryer splashed into the water.

TWENTY

After supper Jenna followed Kane, Emily, Julie, and Rio into the elevator. "I'm ready to get back to work. What about you?" She looked at Kane.

"There's nothing else we can do until Wolfe completes the autopsies and we hear back from Bobby Kalo." Kane shrugged. "We'll just have to put up with all this luxury."

Plunged into darkness without a warning, the cab dropped. Brakes shrieked before the elevator bounced to a stop, throwing everyone in all directions. Jenna moved around on hands and knees. "Is everyone okay?"

"Yeah." Kane touched her shoulder. "Give me your hand."

Jenna grabbed hold and was pulled to her feet. "Em? Julie?" She peered into the dark, seeing nothing at all. "Zac?"

"We're okay." Emily's voice came out of the pitch black.

"I'm good." Rio had tumbled into Jenna as they fell. "Are you? Sorry I trod all over you."

"I'm fine." Jenna fumbled for her phone and lit up the space with her flashlight. "What the hell happened?"

"The power's out is all." Kane's voice was calm and steady. "Don't worry, the backup generator will kick in soon, unless there's a fire or it's an electrical fault. They have many backups in the resort. Power problems on a mountain in freezing temperatures are normal."

"Normal?" Jenna stared at him. "I thought the elevator cable had broken."

"It's fine, don't panic." Kane squeezed her hand. "Trust me, okay? We're not in any danger."

The elevator moved, dropped, and then settled again. Julie let out a wail, phones hit the floor, and everyone hung on, anchoring themselves to the handrail. Unease crept over Jenna. She bent to retrieve her phone. "What's happening? That can't be normal."

"The falling is normal. This is a new building and the elevators would be fitted with a braking system that doesn't require power. Once the cab goes over a certain speed, the brakes engage." Kane smiled at her. "The reason we moved again is because it also has a battery backup that takes us down to the closest floor. It only works once and often doesn't open the doors." He looked at the girls. "We'll hang tight for a few minutes. It depends what's happened. As the power didn't come on straight away, there may be a bigger problem. They might have to find the cause before they turn everything back on."

"And just how do they do that? This place is massive." Julie's face looked pale. "I hate enclosed spaces. It comes from being buried alive."

"You were what?" Rio looked at her astonished.

"Long story." Julie shrugged.

"There'll be a circuit board somewhere and they'll check for the fault." Kane smiled at Julie. "Once they locate the fault, they'll turn on everything in sections. But if you're worried, I'll open the doors and we'll take the stairs."

"Please open the doors, Uncle Dave." Julie looked frantic. "I can't breathe in here."

"Sure." Kane turned to Rio. "Give me a hand." He dug his fingers into the seal on the door.

Keeping the girls to the back of the cab, Jenna held her breath as both men, heaved the door open a few inches before it snapped shut again. She pulled off her boot and when they slid it open again, she stuck the heel into the gap. "Hang on, I'll get down under you and help." She dropped to her knees, and with the three of them, they forced the doors back, and Kane used his back on one side and foot on the other to hold the doors open as they all ducked out under his leg.

"That was harder than I thought it would be." Kane frowned. "I couldn't get any leverage. They need to leave a crowbar or something in the elevator in an emergency pane."

"This is Black Rock Falls." Rio chuckled. "If they did that, someone would use it as a weapon to kill somebody for sure."

Jenna moved her phone light around. People were peering out of doors asking what had happened. Phones glowed in the hallway. "It's just a power failure. Go back in your rooms and try to keep warm. It shouldn't be too much longer." She looked at Kane. "Maybe we should call the manager. People are worried."

"What floor are we on?" Kane walked to the door to the stairs and pulled it open. "Second floor. We might as well go back downstairs and see what we can do to help." He looked at the girls. "I think we should stick together. Grab hold of Zac's arms and take it slow. I don't want anyone falling down the stairs."

"I've got them." Zac held out his hands for the girls. "Em, use your phone to guide us."

They made their way down the stairs. Jenna clung to the handrail. The light from the two phones cast unusual shadows, making it hard to see the steps. Used as a fire escape, the staircase had a damp musty smell, as if the cement hadn't dried, and a strange haunting echo seemed to whistle up toward them. Their footfalls sounded like an old man shuffling along in bedroom slippers. She tightened her grip on Kane's warm hand, glad of having him beside her. She sure wouldn't like being alone in this stairwell in the dark.

They finally reached the ground floor and tumbled out into the foyer. It was chaotic, with everyone talking over each other, all huddled around the light from the fireplace. Some had their phone flashlights, but most seemed to believe the blackout was part of a game. Big fat candles had been lit and placed along the front counter. Jenna headed in that direction and waited for the manager, Mr. Brightway, to finish speaking to a guest. She raised her voice. "Is there anything we can do to help?"

"Yes, maybe they'll settle down if you speak to them." Brightway pushed a hand through his hair. "I have the maintenance crew checking for a fault. It must be substantial to prevent the generators from taking over."

"Where are they?" Kane leaned on the counter. "With everything that's been happening, I think one of us should be with them when they check out the fault."

"They're out back of my office. There's the main power box in there." Brightway met his gaze. "Be my guest."

Jenna walked back to Rio. As the only one of them in uniform, he'd be the best person to speak to the crowd. "Try and calm these people down. Get them seated if possible. I'll go with Dave and see what's happening." She looked at Emily and Julie. "Stick to Zac like glue. Any of these people could be a killer. Don't trust anyone. We won't be long."

"Don't worry, we'll be fine." Emily smiled at her.

"Keep out of the crowd until we get the lights back on." Kane narrowed his gaze at the girls. "Are we good?"

"Oh, Uncle Dave, you're getting more like Dad by the day. We're all grown up now." Julie grinned at him. "I can scream real loud and Zac is armed. Do you really think anyone will try to kill us with everyone watching?"

"Humph." Kane walked away shaking his head.

Jenna chased after him and they walked into the manager's office and soon found the men examining the circuit board. It was a huge complicated contraption and men were moving power from one grid to another manually. "Have you found the fault?"

"Yes and no." A man in coveralls was peering at a gadget in his hand. "We have a major problem on the north corridor on the third level. I've isolated that floor and we'll power up the rest of the complex, but it means going door to door to find out which room has the fault. As you are aware, the passkeys require electricity to gain access to the rooms. We have master keys to use in an emergency, so we'll head off there now. The guests won't be able to use the elevators until all the floors are reconnected." He handed Jenna and Kane a passkey. "You'll need these. They open everything. After a power cut, some of the doors to the stairwell lock to prevent the spread of fire and the lights go out. You'll find battery-operated card readers beside the doors inside and out if you get into trouble."

"Copy that." Kane pocketed the key. "So, you can use these to lock the doors as well?"

"Yeah, and if you need to turn on or off the lights." The man smiled. "There's a box inside the stairwell. It's pretty simple to use. One switch is all."

"Okay, we're coming with you." Jenna lifted her chin. "We need to know if this was an accident or a deliberate sabotage."

"Sure." The man smiled at her. "But it's probably water leaking onto something. In a blizzard anything is possible."

"We'll go tell the manager. Maybe he can move the people back into a restaurant or something." Kane shrugged. "This may take a while."

Jenna nodded. "Good idea. I'll go and speak to Mr. Brightway."

After bringing everyone up to date, Jenna and Kane headed up the stairs following the four-man maintenance crew. The flashlights made it easier to negotiate the stairwell, but it seemed even darker than before. Finally, they spilled out onto the third floor. In the pitch black, the crew's flashlights made round arcs on the walls that reminded her of the Hollywood searchlights. They pushed out into the hallway and split up to door-knock. They asked the guests if anything had happened to the appliances in their room and found nothing. Many rooms didn't reply and the crew used the master keys to enter. They had a quick look around and left until they came to room 3/24 and Jenna heard one of the crew swear.

She hurried toward him, Kane close behind, his phone light bobbing in the dark. "What's happened?"

"An accident, it looks like. There's someone floating in the tub with a hairdryer." The man's face was ashen in the flashlight beam as he stepped out into the hallway.

The maintenance man turned to go back inside the room. "I'll pull the plug from the wall and we can get the power back on."

"Wait! Everyone stays here. Don't touch anything." Jenna grabbed his flashlight and pushed inside with Kane on her heels. Her gaze settled on a naked woman floating just under a film of spent bubbles in the bathtub. A blue hairdryer lay across her chest. The woman's eyes were fixed in death and staring, her mouth hung open. Pushing shock to one side, Jenna turned to Kane. "Get a few shots and then we'll disconnect the hairdryer." She pulled out her notebook and wrote down the time they'd discovered the body. "We don't have to worry about the time of death. It would have been when the lights went out. It must have been close to ten-thirty."

"It was ten-twenty-five." Kane accessed the camera on his phone. "I checked the time on my phone."

As Kane went to work, Jenna pulled on surgical gloves and went back to the sitting room. The smell of perfume hung heavy in the air and a bottle of white wine sat open on top of a bar fridge. She walked into the bedroom. Discarded clothes littered the bed and an overflowing suitcase suggested the woman hadn't bothered to unpack. A phone sat on top of a laptop beside the open suitcase. She could see Kane through the door moving around the bathroom. The room had two doors. She'd taken the other to the sitting room. After moving the flashlight around the bedroom, her gaze settled on a purse on the nightstand. Inside, she found a few hundred in crisp bills, credit cards, the woman's ID, and some promotional bookmarks belonging to Kitty Pandora out of Superstition, Oregon. She stared at them, shaking her head and looked up as Kane walked from the bathroom. "Take a look at this. Is this a coincidence or what?" She walked to a box of books on the luggage rack and, juggling the flashlight, read the back cover. "This book is about a woman who was murdered by electrocution."

"*Frizzled*, huh? It's not a coincidence." Kane aimed his phone light on the cover. "This is a homicide. I found hairbrushes and product on the vanity. There's no way she decided to dry her hair in the tub. No one is that stupid, and it's all set up for her to style it in front of the mirror."

Jenna replaced the book and looked at Kane. "This is creepier than you think. During the background check I did into Dakota Storm, her last big deal was for a book titled *Body in a Lake: Frozen in Time*." She paused a beat. "Jedidiah Longfellow's book is titled: *Nailed It* and now her book is titled *Frizzled*. More than a coincidence, don't you agree?"

"What!" Kane's eyebrows shot almost to his hairline. "I was joking when I suggested that before. This has to be a first."

A shiver ran down Jenna's spine. "Yeah, and we're trapped in a resort with the killer. Now we must figure out what connects these people, and who will be next on his list."

TWENTY-ONE

Pulling up his collar, Deputy Jake Rowley left the warmth of the barn and made his way through the blinding snow to his ranch house. It had been a long hard freezing-cold day managing the sheriff's office alone. He could've asked old Deputy Walters to come by but dragging the elderly man out in a blizzard wasn't his style. He'd eaten at Aunt Betty's Café after picking up his very pregnant wife from her mother's. They'd been staying there overnight, mainly because it was closer to the hospital, but Sandy had become restless and hadn't been sleeping, so they'd decided to stay at home. The driving back and forth to tend the horses had been an extra chore, but in his world, Sandy came first and he'd walk through fire if it kept her happy.

He kicked the snow from his boots and shook his coat before entering the mudroom. After hanging up his clothes, he showered and crept into the bedroom. Sandy's soft breathing met him as he padded silently across the floor. The warm room carried the scent of her shampoo and he slipped in beside her not making a sound. Sleep called to him and he fell into the blissful warmth. The next moment, something jammed into his ribs. Awake in an instant, his hand went to the Glock on his bedside table.

"Jake, are you awake?" Sandy poked him again. "I think the babies are coming." She turned on the light.

Blinking away the red spots in his eyes, Rowley put down his weapon with a sigh. They'd had three false alarms in the past two weeks. "Then we do what the doctor said and time the contractions. It might be another false alarm." He checked his phone for the time. It was a little after midnight.

"I have, they started twenty minutes ago. They came regular at ten minutes apart and now they're five." Sandy sat on the side of the bed and then with some effort pushed herself up. She pressed one hand against the wall. "Shoot, my water's broken."

Rowley had completed a course for delivering a baby some years ago, but his mind suddenly went blank. "I... err. You need to get dressed. I'll go get the truck. Thank God, it has the snowplow attachment on the front."

"Don't you dare leave me." Sandy was puffing and blowing through a contraction. "Don't wake up my folks. I don't want Mom fussing over me. I don't think we should risk driving. Call the paramedics. That contraction was really strong. I don't want to deliver my babies in the truck."

As Rowley was the 911 emergency operator for Black Rock Falls, he dialed the hospital direct and spoke to the ER nurse, explaining the situation. "How long before the paramedics can get here?"

"Right now, we can't get through the end of Stanton Road to get to you. The road is blocked. The snowplow broke down and has left this end of town isolated at least until morning. You won't be able to get through from your side of town. The drifts there are five feet high. Doc Brown is isolated as well. You could try Dr. Wolfe. He's on your side of the blockage."

Rolling his eyes, Rowley glanced at Sandy. "Okay, thanks." He disconnected. With his mind racing, he realized they were in trouble. As Doc Brown was also on the hospital side of Stanton Road, he had no other option than to call Wolfe. How was he going to break the news to her? He smiled at her in an effort to reassure her. "Best you take a shower."

"A shower? Have you lost your mind?" Sandy gripped the wall.

He had to get her out of earshot. "The warm water will help and you're soaked through. I'll check you have everything in your bag, mop up the puddle, and then come and help you dress." He helped Sandy into the bathroom, said a silent prayer, and called Wolfe. The phone rang three times max before Wolfe answered. Surprisingly he was wide awake. "Sorry to wake you, Shane. Sandy's in labor, pains are five minutes apart, her water has broken, and the road to the hospital is blocked. I don't know what to do."

"How is the road from your ranch to town?" Wolfe sounded as if being woken in the middle of the night was usual.

Rowley rubbed a hole in the frozen condensation on the windowpane and peered outside. "No worse than when we drove in. My snowplow attachment cut through it okay, and once I hit town, Main will be clear. Why? I can't get through to the hospital the road is impassable."

"Yeah, but you can make it to the morgue, right?" Wolfe sounded serious. *"I can get there too. I'll meet you there. Drive around back and I'll open the door. It will be easier for Sandy than taking the front steps. I'll head out now and get things ready."*

Shocked, Rowley swallowed hard. "You planning on delivering my babies in the morgue? No way. That will traumatize Sandy for life."

"I'll need medical equipment and I keep drugs on site for my med kit. I'm still an MD after all. Unless you plan to deliver them yourself?" Wolfe sounded amused. *"I won't take Sandy into the morgue. It's way too cold. I'll wheel a gurney into the visitors' waiting room. It's nice and warm in there."*

Unconvinced but without options, Rowley rubbed the back of his neck, wondering how to explain all this to his wife. "She won't be happy."

"I'm sure she'll understand when you explain. She has no

choice. I'll need your help too. Emily is at the resort with Jenna. Are you up to delivering babies?" Wolfe chuckled. *"I wouldn't take too long making up your mind. Babies have a will of their own sometimes."*

A wail came from the bathroom. Rowley cringed. "Okay, we're on our way."

TWENTY-TWO

It's amusing listening to the hushed whispers as people try to discover what's happening. I know what caused the blackout. My escape down the stairs was a nightmare but nobody saw me emerge into the foyer. As candles appear all around the room, casting a soft glow on anxious faces, I mingle with the crowd and listen to the eloquent voice of Deputy Zac Rio. What a charming man he is and how clever to sidestep the many questions by both the guests and the horde of media, all trying to speak at once. It's like being at the Spanish Inquisition, and the young man is handling it with such smooth efficiency. Now that he's finished, we all sit, crammed into a restaurant waiting for the manager to allow us to go to our rooms. Of course, those who had taken cabins had left once the power had been restored to them, but the rest of us, mere mortals, wait for the elevators to come back online.

Today I took the opportunity to listen to a few publishers' presentations. It has been a delight hearing how they work with their authors. It was refreshing to see. I've never received such kindness, and if I had, maybe things would be different. My mind wanders as I cast my gaze around—and there she is again. The red nails draw my attention at once. The way she plays with her hair makes my anger rise and my hands shake.

The rage at seeing her again is already too strong and over-clouds my mission. I need to have my hands around her neck to cool my anger, but for now, I'll just imagine squeezing the life from her. I've done it so many times. It's like eating a special treat. The first touch sends quivers all through me, and as I tighten my grip, they claw at my hands, but I'm always prepared to protect myself. The terror in their eyes feeds me as I press deep with my thumbs. Did you know, they rarely close their eyes? They offer me the delight of watching as tiny blood vessels burst like red stars on a white sky. All too soon comes the vacant stare as life leaves them.

I'm soaked in sweat and force myself to listen as the deputy speaks again, his baritone voice easily heard over the low buzz of conversation. He's asking for a show of hands per floor. Ah, now I know Julie's room is on the fifth floor. Hmm, the top floor holds the better rooms. She must be a spoiled rich kid. The deputy is ordering people to the fifth floor, ten to each cab. I see the blonde sisters head for the elevator and I hurry along to join them. I find myself smiling. Soon I'll know their room number and I have a passkey. My heart picks up a beat as I squeeze into the elevator with them so close. I can smell Julie's freshly washed hair. I wish I could kill both of them right now in front of everyone. The shock on their faces would be incredible. Would anyone try and stop me? How many would try? I nod and smile as my fingers close around the passkey in my pocket. *Not now, my pretty—but your turn will come.*

TWENTY-THREE

Once the lights came on, Jenna walked around the room, photographing everything. "No signs of a struggle. If this was murder, then she knew her attacker."

"I can't see any defensive wounds, no blood in the water." Kane frowned. "Nothing to point to an intruder at all."

Jenna shrugged. "I'll call Wolfe. I hope he'll be able to come back. The service road was cleared at six, but I doubt his van will make it up here. Has he fitted a snowplow attachment to his truck?" She pulled out her phone.

"Yeah, we've all fitted them now." Kane leaned against the wall. "It's a must-have in winter these days."

One of the maintenance crew popped his head around the door and waved at Jenna.

"The elevators are working."

Jenna waved back. "Thanks. You can go. We'll catch up with you later." She called Wolfe using the satellite sleeve. She put her phone on speaker and explained the situation.

"I'm a little busy at the moment." Wolfe cleared his throat. *"Dave has a forensics kit with him. Collect samples of the bathwater. Bag the victim's hands and hand it over to Emily. She'll do a preliminary examination in situ. Then lay clean bedsheets on the*

*floor and lift out the body. Wrap it well. If Kane doesn't have a body
bag in his kit, see if you can find some plastic, wrap it up, and take it
outside. Store it in one of the sheds until I can get there."*

Frowning and a little confused, Jenna cleared her throat.
Wolfe never made excuses. "Is something wrong?"

*"Wrong? No but the road to the hospital is under a five-foot
snowdrift. A snowplow is stuck under there somewhere and there's
no one available to pull it out until daylight—and Sandy is in labor.
Jake is driving her to the morgue so I can deliver the twins. They
should be here soon."*

Horrified, Jenna stared at Kane and caught his shocked expression. "The morgue? You have to be joking?"

*"Nope, it's going to be fine. I'm all set up in the visitors' room.
I'm not taking her in with the corpses. I'm not that insensitive,
Jenna."* Wolfe let out a long sigh. *"It's me and here or Jake at
home on his own, and as he often pukes at the first sight of blood,
I'm a little skeptical of him being able to deliver twins. Leaving
Sandy to cope on her own is nonnegotiable. I'm confident Emily
can handle the body, and with you, Kane, and Rio to process the
scene, you won't need me until the morning. There's no way I'm
driving up the mountain tonight. The snow is thick on the ground
everywhere. The snowplow on Main is running twenty-four
hours. If it's an emergency, maybe you can get one to clear the
back road in the morning?"* Footsteps on tile came through the
earpiece. *"I have to go. I can hear Jake's truck pulling in."* He
disconnected.

Trying to take in the enormity of the situation, Jenna stared at
the screen of her phone and slowly looked at Kane's astonished
expression. "Well, gather the troops, but there's no way I'm hauling
a corpse out into a shed. The back road was cleared at six and you
have a snowplow attachment on the truck. How do you feel about
a trek down the mountain tonight, with a dead body in the Beast?"

"Not overly enthusiastic." Kane rubbed his chin considering.
"Emily will want to come with us and we can't leave Julie here on
her own and there's no way Shane will want her exposed to a

murder victim. I'm damned if I do and damned if I don't take her with us."

Jenna pushed both hands through her hair and paced up and down. "Julie would be safe in her room. Rio is right next door. He can stay awake until we return."

"Maybe, but I figure you'll want to stay until the babies are born and that could take hours." Kane frowned. "Then we'll have to hope we can get back up the mountain. We can't possibly expect Rio to catch a killer on his own."

Mind spinning with all the complications, Jenna shook her head. "We know the time of death. I'll ask the manager to make the CCTV footage of this floor available for us at once. We'll be able to see who murdered her."

"Then get Rio to go look at it now." Kane headed for the door. "I'll go, grab the forensics kit, and speak to the girls. I'll need to make sure Julie will be safe while we're away."

Jenna eyed him with suspicion. "Hang on. What exactly do you mean by that?" She stopped pacing and glared at him. "Don't you dare arm her. Not on my watch."

"Not a handgun, no, but I will leave her my stun gun." Kane had his combat face on again. "I taught her how to use it and you know darn well Shane has had them both on the practice range for years. They don't own guns, but they sure as hell know how to use one safely. With an unpredictable murderer running around the lodge, I'm making a responsible decision to keep her safe." The nerve in his cheek twitched. "She's eighteen, Jenna, and I wouldn't consider it if I didn't believe her to be responsible."

Jenna took out her phone and found Rio's number. "Okay, but it's on your head." She watched him head toward the elevator. "Rio, where are you?"

"In the lobby. I took the girls back to their room and came back down to keep order. People are pretty riled up. The manager put on free hot chocolate for everyone, and things are settling down." The noise around Rio was making it hard to hear him. *"What caused the blackout?"*

Jenna explained and asked Rio to check the CCTV footage. "Let me know what you find. Once we're finished here, we'll take the body down the mountain. Emily will be with us, so I'll need you to stay in close contact with Julie. She won't appreciate it if she thinks we're watching over her, so be subtle, right?"

"Sure thing. My brother and sister are the same." Rio chuckled. *"They're probably running riot while I'm not home. The house-keeper is more like a grandma to them. They respect her, so they should be fine. It's not like they can go out right now and get into trouble."*

Jenna smiled. "Okay, get at it. With luck, you may crack the case tonight." She disconnected and, tucking away her phone, peeled the sheets from the bed and took them into the bathroom. Her gaze moved over the poor woman in the tub. "Who did this to you?"

She headed back to the bedroom and collected the laptop and phone. Setting the laptop on the table in the sitting room, she opened it and smiled. It wasn't password protected. She easily accessed Kitty Pandora's social network and scanned the pages and comments. Nothing nasty there or of interest. Next, she opened the phone and it came straight on. Jenna couldn't believe her luck and ran through all the recent messages, photographs, and calls. Most of the images were of the convention, selfies with various people. The information could be gold, and with everyone trapped in the hotel, she wouldn't have to look far to question them. She heard footsteps and a rattle in the hallway, and Kane and Emily came into the room pushing a gurney. "Where did you find that?"

"There's a first-aid room and a paramedic on staff. We borrowed it to move the body down to the Beast." Kane tossed Jenna evidence bags. "I'll handle the body with Em. Did you find anything of interest?"

Jenna nodded. "Yeah, I'll bag everything and we can go over it later." She looked at Emily. "Are you good to go?"

"Yeah, I've worked alongside Dad so many times, I know the

drill." Emily followed Kane into the bathroom and then paused. "Any news about the babies?"

"Not yet." Jenna shook her head. "I sure hope everything is going okay."

"With Jake helping out, I doubt it." Emily's mouth twitched in amusement. "You know he'll puke. He's a great deputy but he's not so good at crime scenes. I hope he knows what to expect."

"Don't worry." Kane turned to look at her. "Your dad will ask him to be the support team for Sandy. They've been to classes and he'll know what to do. He'll be there for Sandy, if it kills him."

Amazed how nonchalant Kane and Emily acted with a dead woman floating in the bathtub a few feet away from them, she turned back to the sitting room to collect and bag the laptop, phone, and purse. She glanced back at the bathroom and listened to the mumble of conversation. Homicide was never pretty and everyone in law enforcement coped with the mental trauma in their own way. The professionalism Kane always had at a crime scene and Emily's matter-of-fact attitude had calmed her nerves until the sudden realization that, with three murders, they had another serial killer in Black Rock Falls. Here, right in the ski resort. The killer could be staying in the next room. Ice-cold fingers of dread marched up her spine as the need to look over her shoulder gripped her. *They're not finished, are they? They're never satisfied. Who will be next?*

TWENTY-FOUR

Rowley's face ached from keeping it fixed in a happy expression. He'd attended all the classes with Sandy, but now that the time had come, his confidence had flown. Inadequacy hung over his shoulders like a huge weight. He could encourage and do everything he'd been shown, but ultimately it was all up to Sandy. It seemed as if she'd been in pain for hours, but Wolfe had insisted everything was going along just fine. Hmm. With the love of his life's mood swinging from anger to despair, he'd been very close to tears. Being useless to help her and putting on a brave face sounded just fine until another contraction came. Sandy looked at him, eyes wild, as if she hated him. He held her hand as she squeezed the feeling out of it. Where had that strength come from? The bones in his hands grated together. "I'm sorry, sweetheart."

"Sorry for what, Jake?" Sandy puffed out her words. "Did you think they'd come by stork? My hating you right now is normal. Remember what they said at the classes? It's hormonal. I don't really hate you. I just want it to be over."

He rubbed Sandy's back and relaxed his smile, his eyes moving to Wolfe, who nodded at him. The man was so damn calm it was as if he were watching a cooking show.

"I spoke to Jenna earlier." Wolfe was pottering around,

checking things on trays. "They're heading down the mountain with Emily." He turned to look at Sandy. "Do you want a support team or would you rather be alone with Jake?"

"Jenna and Emily came to classes with me when Jake was busy, so yeah, if they arrive in time, that's fine." She looked at Rowley. "I don't mind if Dave comes in. I think Jake needs his own support team right now." She smiled at Wolfe. "Just don't call my mom just yet. She'd pass out cold if she knew I was in the morgue."

"Yeah, it might take some explaining." Wolfe smiled at her. "You have a way to go yet. I'll go and grab a coffee. Jake, do you want one?"

Rowley blinked. Wolfe was going to leave him alone? He swallowed the rising panic. "Sure, but hurry back."

"Everything is progressing normally, Jake." Wolfe headed for the door. "Try and relax. Sandy is stronger than you think. Giving birth is a natural thing. She's fine and the babies are fine. Stop stressing. All is well."

Rowley shook out his numb fingers, wondering if a few of them had cracked under the pressure of Sandy's grip, and forced a smile. "Oh, I know she's strong. Trust me, I know."

TWENTY-FIVE

Jenna rubbed the snow from Duke's coat, dried his feet, and set him in front of the fire in their suite. Not knowing how long they'd be away, she'd walked him and then made sure he was comfortable and she'd given Rio one of their room keys to check on him if they were delayed. She'd spoken with Julie to make sure she was in her hotel room. With Rio staying in the next room, she'd be safe. Looking all around to make sure she hadn't forgotten to do anything, she hustled to the elevator and headed to the ground floor. Surprisingly, the foyer was empty, a sign on the front counter telling guests to press a buzzer if they needed assistance. She sighed with relief. Kane and Emily would have been able to move the body without being seen. With the guests on the verge of mass panic attacks after the blackout, she didn't need any more fuel on the fire. She'd have to make an announcement as soon as the victims' next of kin had been notified. With the media at the conference, she couldn't risk the loved ones of the victims finding out on the evening news.

Bracing for the arctic blast, Jenna pushed her way through the main doors. At once the bitter cold caught in her throat and pained her chest. The temperature must have dropped again. The smell of ozone filled her nose as small shards of ice cut into her cheeks.

Battered by wind howling like a pack of wolves, she put down her head and trod with care toward the Beast. Kane had parked with the engine running as close to the main door as possible. It took a couple of goes to pull open the passenger door, the wind adding an unseeing force that, once she'd pried the door open, threw it back with such force it dragged it from her fingers. She glanced inside as Kane slid out his door and ran around the hood to secure the door before returning. She looked at his concerned face. "The weather is getting worse. I felt ice on my cheeks before. If we get Graupel snow, it will make the blacktop slippery."

"What on earth is Graupel snow?" Emily leaned forward in her seat. "I thought I'd seen everything here."

"It's kind of like ice pebbles made from snow, a bit like hail." Kane stared out the windshield. "It looks like Styrofoam." He turned the steering wheel and headed through the trees. "The back road was cleared at six. It will be our best bet. The Beast has bullet-proof glass. I can assure you it won't shatter. Worst-case scenario, we hit ice and slide off the road and down the mountain, but the snowplow driver told me he salted the road three times in case we had an emergency. Just as well, the back road comes out well past the road blockage on Stanton. If we hit any rough patches, the new snow tires should keep us safe."

Openmouthed, Jenna gaped at him. If it weren't bad enough driving with a corpse in the back of the truck, now there was a chance they wouldn't make it to town. "Oh, well, I feel so much better now. Sliding off a mountain and flying right out there will be fun until we hit the rocks."

"Oh, you of little faith." Kane gripped the wheel. "You trust me, don't you, Em?"

"Implicitly." Emily chuckled. "Although Dad figures I'm missing the fear gene."

"Wonderful." Jenna fixed her seatbelt and hung on as the wipers battled the snow. "Well, mine is firmly in place."

The Beast was a heavy vehicle, but as they negotiated the back road, the wild wind battered snow against the side. Jenna watched

Kane's mask of concentration as he negotiated the winding narrow road through the glow of the headlight beams. It was like driving through a white tunnel. Snow covered everything and draped over fences and trees like dripping white frosting, but apart from a dusting of snow, the road glistened with a thick coating of sand and salt. She held her breath as they rounded each corner, but the snowplow attachment on the Beast took care of any snow that had fallen from trees to settle in great piles across the blacktop.

"I hope Sandy is doing okay." Kane's attention hadn't left the road. "Maybe when we get there, we shouldn't mention we drove down with a murder victim in the truck."

"Do you think she'll tell the twins when they're older?" Emily poured coffee from a Thermos and handed it to Jenna. "You know, that they were born in a morgue during a blizzard and delivered by the medical examiner?"

Pondering the question, Jenna took the coffee and offered it to Kane. "Well, it is a strange story to be sure. What happens if anything goes wrong?" She turned to look at Emily. "I know Wolfe is good but he doesn't have incubators or anything like that does he?" She took another cup of coffee and raised an eyebrow.

"He'll make do." Kane cleared his throat. "You can trust him, Jenna. I've trusted him with my life many times."

Jenna sipped her coffee. "Oh, I know that and I do trust him but babies are a bit different to his usual guests."

"Oh, he has heaps of medical equipment in the storeroom." Emily nibbled on a choc chip cookie. "You probably don't know but in an emergency he's on call for the hospital, being in town, he can get to people faster than the paramedics." She sighed. "This is why I need to get my final degree and work alongside him full time. He works so hard."

Without warning the world spun like a top, the Beast's headlights lighting up the snow-covered forest one second or gaps of blackness the next. Giddy, Jenna gripped her to-go cup. Behind her Emily cried out in terror. The comforting rumble of the engine stopped and an eerie silence descended on them. The lights whipped around again as Kane grappled with the steering wheel, spinning it this way and that to gain control. As the truck slowed, she breathed a sigh of relief but the next second the Beast picked up speed and slid backward down the mountain.

Terrified, Jenna pushed her to-go cup in the console and held on tight as the truck skated closer to the edge. Far below she could make out the lights of Black Rock Falls. Out of control they careered down the mountain trail with death hovering six inches away. Heart in her throat, she stared at Kane. "Do something."

"Nothing I can do until we come out of this patch of ice." Kane was peering over his shoulder into the darkness. "If we don't hit a bend, we'll slide into a tree or something soon enough."

"Or go over the edge." Emily gripped the back of Jenna's seat. "Can't you try and start the engine?"

"I'm not taking my hands off the wheel just now, Em." Kane was spinning the wheel again. "It won't make any difference on the ice. I'll just try and aim for a tree. Hang on tight."

Panic gripped Jenna. "Just how close to the edge are we? Should we jump out?" Her hand went to the door.

"You'll freeze to death in less than five minutes." Kane's breath came out in a puff of steam. "It's going to be okay. We're slowing now."

The truck bumped into a snowdrift with a muffled *thunk*. Jenna's fingers ached from hanging on. She looked all around and shuddered. They'd come to rest inches from the edge of the mountain. "That was too darn close. What happened? Did they forget to salt this part of the road?"

"Nope, a small avalanche is my guess." Kane started the engine, righted the Beast, and moved slowly back onto the salted blacktop. "If you recall, this road runs parallel to the steepest slope. The wind being so strong, snow dislodges and slides down the mountain. The salt can only do so much. That volume of snow coming down would melt some and then freeze fast. Looking at the time, the snowplows will be up here clearing it before we drive back."

He sounded so calm. Jenna gaped at him. "That didn't scare you? We came close to dying, Dave."

"I was too busy to be afraid, Jenna." He smiled. "It's all good. We're at the end of the road now."

They headed along Stanton and into town. The roads were clear right to the medical examiner's building and they drove round back to the morgue entrance.

"We'll deal with the body." Kane turned off the engine. "Go and give Sandy some support. We'll be along shortly."

Jenna hurried along the hallway and through the foyer into the visitors' area. The warm vanilla smell wafted over her as she peeled off her clothes and pulled on the scrubs she'd grabbed from a cupboard outside the examination rooms. She heard a baby crying as she reached the door. Knocking and peering inside, her mouth widened in a huge grin at the sight of Sandy sitting up, holding a baby in each arm. Rowley on the other hand was sitting in a chair with his head between his knees. "Can I come in?"

"Please do." Sandy was beaming. "Come and meet Cooper David Shane Rowley and Vannah Jenna Rowley." She giggled. "And when Jake has recovered from the shock, he'll be asking you and Dave to be godparents."

"Oh wow! They are so beautiful. You named that angel after me? I'm delighted. Thank you so much." Jenna laughed. "Oh, Jake, are you okay?"

"He'll be fine." Wolfe patted Rowley on the back. "He was good until I asked him to cut the umbilical cords." He sighed. "My fault."

"I'm good." Rowley looked up, his eyes glistening with tears. "Look at them. They're so incredible. So—perfect and they're mine. I'm just a little overwhelmed is all."

"That's normal." Wolfe smiled. "I'll go and speak to Kane and Em. I'll be back soon."

Jenna nodded and walked to the gurney, holding out her arms. "Oh, can I hold one of them?"

"Of course. I'm hoping you and Dave will be part of their

lives." Sandy looked at her. "You're the closest person to a sister I've ever had and I know Dave is Jake's best friend." She indicated with her chin to one of the babies. "This is Vannah."

Jenna took the baby from her arms and looked into the deep blue eyes of the tiny face and sighed. "You won't be able to keep us away."

TWENTY-SIX

Julie Wolfe lingered in the tub. The room was better than she'd imagined and the resort supplied everything she needed: soap, shampoo, bubble bath. Being alone didn't worry her. Zac Rio was in the room next door and her sister would be back soon. As the water had cooled, she climbed out with a sigh, dried off, dressed, and headed to her bed. It was already warm from the heated electric blanket and she soon snuggled down to sleep. Although Emily hadn't said much when she left, she had mentioned the electrical problem had been caused by a woman dropping a hairdryer in the tub. She really didn't want to know the details and the idea of her sister, Jenna, and Uncle Dave risking their lives to take the poor woman's body down the mountain in the middle of the night worried her. That was Emily though. She might be years away from being a board-certified medical examiner, but she took the care of any deceased person very seriously. Julie closed her eyes. *No dead bodies for me. I prefer caring for children.*

Unsure of how long she'd been asleep, Julie started awake at the creak of a door. Had Emily returned or was she dreaming? She lay for a few seconds listening and blinked into the darkness at the sound of footsteps brushing the carpet. "Em, is that you?"

Nothing.

Very afraid, her mouth went dry and every hair on her body stood to attention. She peered over the top of the sheets and froze in horror at the outline of a figure standing at the end of her bed. She blinked into the darkness, opening her eyes wide. Was her mind creating an image out of the shadows? Her stomach dropped as the black outline moved. Stunned into silence, she stared, not believing her eyes. No features were visible but she could hear heavy breathing.

Rolling over, her hand landed on the stun gun Uncle Dave had given her. As her palm closed around the handle, she sucked in a deep breath and, brandishing it before her, screamed. The shadowy figure turned to run out the bedroom and stumbled over her boots. Arms waved in the darkness before a soft beam of light from the hallway fell across the floor. They'd left the main door wide open. Terrified and too scared to move, she gaped at the half-closed bedroom door in horror as the sound of heavy footsteps pounded along the hallway toward her.

The intruder was coming back.

She screamed again, and eyes wide with terror, Julie stared at the door as it slowly opened wider. "Get out! I have a weapon and I'll use it."

"Don't shoot. It's me, Zac." Zac Rio's head peeked around the door. "What is it?" He hit the light and keeping his back to the wall, scanned the room, Glock in hand. "What happened, Julie?" He moved inside, his hair ruffled, and he was wearing only sweatpants.

Trembling all over, Julie tried to control the tears spilling down her cheeks. "Someone was in my room. Standing at the end of my bed." She clung to the stun gun. "They ran out when I screamed. Did you see anyone?"

"No, but I'll check the CCTV feed first thing in the morning. Stay where you are. I'll check the bathroom." Rio moved around cautiously and went through the bathroom and did a complete circle out one door and through the sitting room and back. "There's no one here. Will you be okay for a minute?"

"No!" Julie shook her head and her hand gripped the stun gun tighter. "I'm not staying here alone."

"Can you put on a robe and come with me then?" Rio pushed a hand through his hair and dropped the Glock to his side. "I'll grab some pillows and blankets from my room. I'll bunk on the sofa. My room is a single, or you could come stay with me until Em gets back." He walked out and checked the door to the main hallway. "How did he get in here without a key?"

Julie dragged on her robe, stuffed the stun gun in the pocket, pushed her feet into her slippers, and wrapping the robe around her, went to his side. "I don't know." She pointed to the keycard on the table beside the door. "I left my key there. Jenna came by before she left. I shut the door but didn't put the lock on it because Em could be back at any time and she wouldn't be able to get inside." She rubbed her arms. "He must have had a passkey. I heard Jenna talking to Uncle Dave about going with the maintenance crew to check the rooms, and they all have passkeys."

"Okay." Rio rubbed his chin and stared into space for a few seconds. "Before we go, take a quick look around. Is anything missing?"

Taking her time, Julie moved around the room. They had the basics for a few days' stay, but she did notice something. "My scarf is missing but Em could have taken it, we do share things like that."

"You can ask her in the morning." Rio headed for the door. "Coming?"

Julie hustled after him, her legs feeling like Jell-O. In the hallway, people hovered at their doors, peering in their direction. She forced her lips into a smile. Whatever was going on, she knew better than to give away any clues.

"There's nothing happening here, folks." Rio smiled at them. "A spider in the bathroom is all. Go back to bed." He opened his door and Julie followed him inside.

As Rio collected a few things, Julie leaned against the door. "I know you think I'm still a kid. I know everyone does, but I'm eighteen and I'm not stupid. I know there's been two murders and now

I'm pretty sure another one happened tonight. So three makes a serial killer. For everyone to take off in the middle of the night, something is pretty bad. Now this has happened, I want you to be straight with me." She chewed on her bottom lip. "Is Sandy really in labor or was that an excuse to dash off?"

"The twins are coming, so I hear." Rio sighed. "You're right about the murders and nobody thinks you're a kid." He pulled on a black T-shirt. "Jenna didn't want to spoil the convention for you with all the gory details. The woman in the tub, we believe, is a homicide. There are no signs of forced entry, so either she let the person in, which would say she knew them, or they had a passkey." He tossed a pillow to Julie and dragged off the duvet. "But most people engage the lock on the door unless they're expecting room service. No one wants strangers walking into their hotel room." He pushed his feet into his boots, picked up his Glock and key, and waved her toward the door. "Let's go. It's late and I need to get some sleep. All hell is going to break loose in the morning."

Julie followed him back to her room and watched as he settled on the sofa in front of the fire. "Thanks."

"That's what friends are for." Rio snuggled under the duvet with his eyes closed. "Get some sleep."

Still shaking, Julie went into her room and crawled back into her bed, keeping the stun gun within reach. The threat from the figure still hovered in her room like a nightmare she couldn't wake from. She closed her eyes, seeing the shadowed menace watching her. Terror gripped her and her eyes popped open again. Had that shadow moved? Would the stranger come again and kill her next time? Her heart raced so hard, she couldn't sleep. In fact, she didn't think she'd ever sleep again.

TWENTY-SEVEN

My heart pounds as if I'd run a mile and sweat trickles down my brow. The salty rivulets burn my eyes and, annoyed, I brush them away as it reminds me of the tears I once shed. My limbs are slick with perspiration just at being close to her. The long blonde hair cascading over the pillow, the red nails black in the half-light, like blood after lying a week in the sun. She is so like my mom, and when the soft glow from the hotel hallway pierced the darkness of her inner sanctum, I was transported back in time. It was as if I'd shrunk into the young child I once was and had crept into my mom's room.

My mom was so beautiful when she slept, but I've come to know the outer shell of people are deceiving. My mom was not the angelic creature filled with love she portrayed. Inside was pure evil and I was her burden. My punishment was to do her bidding without a word of complaint. At the slightest word of protest, she would scream and lash out, tearing at my cheeks with her nails. I can still feel the sting and how it burned across my face. At school she'd humiliate me by explaining to the teacher how I wouldn't listen to her and had run away to the river through the brambles. She would dab at her eyes, gaining sympathy. How could I ever explain to anyone the torment I'd suffered? I was by all accounts a belligerent child. A liar who made up stories.

The need to see Julie had become overwhelming. My chance came about by sheer luck. On the way to the elevator, I'd seen the sheriff, her deputy, and Julie's sister leave. They'd slipped away with a body on a gurney like thieves in the night. I knew Julie would be alone. I had my passkey and had to see for myself if the beauty hid evil inside. Was she another reincarnation of my tormentor? When I stood at the foot of her bed, watching her breathe, she looked so peaceful, angelic, and then she screamed. Her face became ugly and the glowing hall light reflected in her eyes like a demon. In an instant, my brain shattered—all thoughts of revenge gone. Thrown back in time, I was small and vulnerable again—I had to get away. I'd planned my escape and dashed into the sheriff's room.

Now here I stand, waiting for the calm to come again. The dark room wraps around me like a sanctuary. No one will find me here. My heart slows. I'm in control. To prove it, I press Julie's scarf to my nose and inhale her annoying perfume. Her smell fills my head and my fingers itch again with the urge to kill. All thoughts of murder vanish when a low rumbling growl comes from behind me. I'd forgotten the sheriff's dog. At once, I become a nonthreatening statue, turning just my head to see the beast. In the glow of the fire, a dog rises and draws its fleshy lips back to expose sharp teeth. The growl is low and menacing. If he barks, the deputy will find me. I must try and reason with the animal and lower my voice to a whisper. "Good boy."

Frantic, I search my pockets for the cookies they'd served with supper and toss them to him. To my dismay the beast doesn't move to accept my gift but increases its growling and makes hesitant steps toward me. Desperate to get away from the slobbering menace, I peer through the peephole in the door. Thankfully the hallway is empty. Cracking open the door, I stick my head outside, searching both ways, but all is still. Without delay, I rush for the fire escape. I chance a glance back along the hallway and the ugly image of Julie drifts back into my mind. *Soon.*

TWENTY-EIGHT

The warmth of the visitors' lounge, the happy faces, and the smell that only comes with the joy of birth was a stark contrast to the cold and spartan surrounding of the morgue examination room. Trying to hold on to the good feeling from delivering a pair of healthy twins, Wolfe unzipped the body bag, and stood back as water spilled from the still soaking body. He flicked a gaze to Emily. "Did I mention about wrapping the body in sheets?"

"Yeah, Dad, you did, but as Kane had a body bag in his kit, I made a judgement call and dropped it into the bag." Emily peered at the body. "I did bag the hands but you won't find anything."

Wolfe turned to look at her. "Why?"

"No sign of a struggle." Emily shrugged.

"I sent the images to your files." Kane hovered in the doorway. "No water on the floor. The cord to the hairdryer was attached to the plug above the vanity. If she'd left it on the side and reached out even to dry her hands on the towel before she grabbed it, there'd have been droplets of water on the floor. No one in their right mind picks up an electrical device with wet hands."

Wolfe put the file up on the screen and flicked through the images of the scene. The edge of the vanity, where he assumed the hairdryer might have been, was too far from the tub to have just fallen in and who would be stupid enough to leave a hairdryer running on the side of the sink? He turned and picked up the right and then left hand of the victim to remove the bags and examined each hand closely. He lifted his attention to Kane. "She wasn't holding the hairdryer when she died." He ran his gaze down the body and then rolled it on its side and checked the back. "When the apparent cause of electrocution is suspected, we look for the points of entry and exit of the current."

"Wouldn't the burn mark wash off in the water?" Kane leaned closer.

Wolfe moved his gaze over the victim. She looked peaceful, almost serene. "Good question, but not in this case as the body wasn't submerged for a long time, although even electrocution victims found floating in the ocean still display a burn, a collapsed blister with a brown center fading out to a pale ring. The hands are the most common entry point for electrocution, but I'm not seeing this here."

"So, you don't believe she was electrocuted?" Kane looked incredulous. "The entire complex was without power and we tracked down the cause to her suite."

Wolfe stood to one side to allow Emily to examine the body. He shook his head. "I can't make that judgement until autopsy. It's obvious from what you witnessed that electricity might be the instrument of her death, but she could have suffocated or drowned. Look at it this way. If someone dies from a knife attack, they don't die from a knife, do they? They die from the resulting injury. Electricity is just a tool of death, not a cause."

"Okay." Kane rubbed the back of his neck. "Go on."

Wolfe smiled at him. "In my report, I'll be making the cause of death clear. For example, electrocution resulting in suffocation or whatever." He took in Kane's weary expression. "In some cases, the shock will paralyze the diaphragm, causing the person to suffocate. As she was in the tub at the time, the shock could have incapacitated her and she slid under the water and drowned. To determine the correct cause of death, I'll need to see if there's any water in her lungs. That's why I asked you to collect a sample of the tub water for comparison."

"That makes sense." Kane blinked a few times. "Any progress on the other victims?"

Wolfe nodded. "Yeah, I finished up about ten. I had just gotten to bed when Rowley called. It's been a long day." He zipped up the bag and loaded the body into a refrigerated drawer. "The autopsy can wait for the morning. I'll write up my reports and walk you through all of them over the phone. Are you staying at my place tonight or heading back up the mountain?"

"Driving back." Kane yawned explosively. "I'll grab a couple of cups of coffee and we'll be good to go. With a killer running loose, we don't want to be stuck here in town." He stared at the door. "Are Sandy and the twins okay?"

Wolfe smiled and the tiredness seemed to lift. "Yeah, she came through real well. It was an uncomplicated birth, everything text-book. The babies are strong and healthy. Rowley is a mess, but he'll be good once he stops shaking."

"Can we go and see them now?" Emily washed her hands and arms at the sink. "Do we need scrubs?"

Wolfe chuckled. "No, you go ahead. I'll clean up and make some coffee. I have cookies as well in my office. You go and see Sandy and then come and help me with the coffee."

"Okay." She ran out the door.

"I'll wash my hands too." Kane frowned. "I've not had too much experience with newborns."

Wolfe patted him on the back. "They're tougher than you think. Maybe you'll find out one day." He headed for the door.

TWENTY-NINE

Kane pushed open the door to the visitors' waiting room slowly and peered inside, not wanting to be obtrusive. His gaze went to Jenna, her face flushed and staring at a tiny baby. Her lips were set in a permanent smile as she rocked back and forth as if mesmerized. When she lifted her eyes to him, his heart skipped a beat. There was deep longing in her expression. He smiled and nodded at Rowley, standing at the side of the gurney holding Sandy's hand, his face a picture of rapture. He peered at the babies Jenna and Emily were cuddling. "Congratulations! Wow they have dark curls just like you, Jake. So much hair, and those eyes. They'll have you both wrapped around their little fingers before you know it."

"I welcome it." Rowley grinned. "But that was the most terrifying thing I've ever experienced." He sucked in a breath. "Meet Cooper David Shane and Vannah Jenna. We'd be honored if you'd be their godfather. Jenna has already agreed to be godmother."

"Here." Smiling, Emily held out a bundle to him. "This is Cooper. I'll go and help Dad."

Kane could have held the tiny baby in one hand. The blue eyes looked right at him and little fists waved. A lump in his throat threatened to stop him replying to Rowley. He'd come so close to holding his own son, only to have him and Annie snatched away in an instant of madness. He pushed the thought aside and looked at the tiny Jake Rowley clone. "Hi, Cooper. I'm your godfather. Welcome to the family."

He heard Rowley snort with laughter and looked straight at Jenna. Her eyes were misty with tears. "Let me see Vannah." He walked to her side. "Oh, she has dimples just like Sandy." He looked down at the babies. "So, you decided to arrive during a blizzard, huh, and like true members of the Black Rock Falls Sheriff's Office family, in the middle of a murder investigation." He chuckled and looked at Sandy and Rowley. "We'll babysit anytime. You'll just have to show me how to change a diaper." He walked to Rowley and with reluctance handed over the baby. "Sorry, we can't stay for long. We must get back up the mountain before the road becomes impassable. We've left Julie alone."

"Well Zac is there." Jenna frowned. "He'll take good care of her." She pressed a kiss on the baby's head and with obvious unwillingness handed her over to Sandy. "I could hold them all night. They're so beautiful. Are you staying here overnight?"

"Yeah." Rowley placed his son in one of the baby capsules they'd had in the truck and covered him with a blanket. "I'm sleeping on the sofa and we'll drive back home in the morning unless Wolfe thinks Sandy should spend some time in the hospital."

"I'm not going to the hospital. I'm fine, just tired is all." Sandy looked indignant. "My folks have already offered to stay with us for a few days. Dad will do the chores to take the strain off you, and Mom can help me get the twins settled into a routine."

"Call in Walters in the morning to handle the office for a couple of days." Jenna smiled at Rowley. "Get some rest. No one is going to cause too much mayhem in the middle of a blizzard."

The door opened and Emily came in with coffee and cookies for Rowley and Sandy. She looked at Kane and smiled. "Dad says we need to leave these folks alone to get some rest. He's waiting for you in his office." She hurried out the door.

Kane nodded and turned to the couple. "We'll see you in a few days. If you need anything, just call me." He headed out the door with Jenna close behind.

In the hallway, he took Jenna's hand and pulled her close. "Happy family."

"Yeah, I just love the smell of babies." Jenna leaned into him and sighed. "It's going to be fun watching them grow.'

Biting back the need for a family of his own, Kane dropped her hand and shrugged. "It's a lifetime commitment. Kids need their parents and our job isn't exactly nine-to-five. Could you give up being sheriff to raise a family?"

"I wouldn't give up being sheriff, Dave." She smiled at him. "I'd take my baby to the office with me. I'd change the new back room into a nursery and I'll hire a nanny to watch over her while we're out."

Kane only heard one word. "*Her*? You don't get a choice you know."

"Yeah." Jenna giggled. "Just checking you're awake."

THIRTY

The drive back up the mountain terrified Jenna. She sat as quiet as a mouse as Kane urged the Beast through the fallen snow, although Emily seemed unconcerned and had curled up on the back seat and fallen asleep as soon as they'd left town. Condensation built up on the windows and, even with the heater pushed to full capacity, cold seemed to seep through every crack. Ice piled up on the hood and slowed the wipers. If they stopped, they'd die for sure. Before they'd left, Wolfe had insisted on refilling Kane's gas tank. He had fuel on site for his vehicles and an aviation tank to refuel a helicopter should the need arise in an emergency.

Shivering, Jenna pulled the blanket more firmly over her knees and licked dry lips. Being out in freezing weather caused her lips to crack if she wasn't careful. She glanced at Kane. The trip was taking a long time. The snowplow attachment barely pushing enough snow aside to allow them to pass. She refilled Kane's to-go cup from the Thermos and placed it within reach. "Hot coffee. I'm sure glad we brought the Thermos flasks with us. Do you know where we are?"

"Not exactly but we just passed a sign to beware of fallen rocks, so I figure we're past halfway." Kane reached for the coffee but didn't take his eyes from the road. "Why don't you try and get some sleep? It will take a while yet."

Astonished, Jenna gaped at him. "Sleep? I have enough adrenalin pumping through my veins to run up to the ski lodge without losing my breath." She gripped the seat as the back wheels fishtailed for the hundredth time. "Anyway, you'll need me to keep you awake. You look all in."

"Nah. I'm wide awake." Kane flicked her a glance. "It's been one hell of a night. We'll be lucky to get a couple of hours sleep before we start investigating people's movements again." He sighed. "Oh, that reminds me, Wolfe will send through the autopsy reports in the morning sometime. He said he'll call and walk us through them."

Already making mental notes in her head on what to do the following morning, Jenna nodded. "Did he do a preliminary examination on Kitty Pandora?"

She listened as Kane brought her up to date. "Wolfe must be exhausted—the autopsies and then delivering twins. Don't forget he has a little one at home too and he manages just fine."

"Anna is hardly a baby now." Kane frowned. "And I know for a fact Wolfe is always at home when she finishes school and puts her to bed. He arranges his workload around her and usually works at night when she's asleep. His housekeeper is like a grandma to his daughters. He was lucky to find her."

Jenna smiled at him. "That was Maggie. We have a great receptionist; she can fix just about everyone's problems."

"Maybe we should put her on this case." Kane gripped the wheel and pushed the Beast around a corner. "Right now, nothing is making much sense. I hope Bobby Kalo hunts down something to link them apart from all being involved with publishing, because so far, I've found diddly squat. Having limited resources up here is annoying."

Jenna sighed at the sight of the lights up ahead. "We at least have suspects and nobody is going anywhere. The killer is right under our noses. We just have to catch them."

Suddenly feeling tired, she rubbed at the pain in her temples. Coming down from an adrenalin high was like suffering a hangover minus the alcohol. As they slid into the parking space outside the lodge, Jenna nudged Emily awake. "We made it. It's going to be cold out there."

"I'm good." Emily wrapped a scarf around her head and pulled up her hoodie. "Let's go. I'm so tired I can hardly walk."

Jenna dashed through the doors with the others close behind. It was warm inside and the smell of woodsmoke filled the foyer. She stripped off her gloves and hat and stuffed them in her pockets as she headed for the elevator. She'd pulled down the zipper of her jacket by the time they'd reached their floor and noticed Kane had done the same. The heat inside the elevator seemed stifling and the smell of dampness enclosed her. They headed up the hallway, walked past Zac Rio's single room, and paused at Emily's suite for her to unlock her door.

"Darn, Julie's locked the door." Emily hammered on the door. "Julie, open up, it's me."

"Not so loud. You'll wake everyone." Kane moved to her side.

The door opened and a sleepy-eyed Zac Rio peered at them. The next second, Kane had him by the front of his T-shirt and hauled him out and against the wall. Jenna moved toward him. "Hey, put him down."

"I will as soon as he explains what the hell he was doing in Julie's room." Kane glared at him. "I trusted you."

"You still can." Julie appeared at the door wrapped in a robe. "Put him down, Uncle Dave. He was here protecting me is all."

"You done?" Rio's gaze was as cold as ice as he brushed Kane's hands away. "What do you take me for? Do you figure I'm some kind of pervert? Someone broke into her room. I slept on the sofa in case he had a mind to come back."

"Okay then, I'm sorry. I overreacted." Kane offered his hand. "She's like a daughter to me."

"I feel the same way about my sister." Rio relaxed. "I'm a little overprotective since my parents died too." He shook Kane's hand.

"When you two have finished male bonding, I want some answers." Jenna waved everyone inside. "Get inside, we'll talk there."

After Julie told her story and Rio chimed in with his version, Jenna leaned back in the chair stunned. She gathered her thoughts. "You couldn't tell for sure if it was a man or a woman? Not any clue at all? Any scent for instance?"

"No." Julie's eyes looked so big in her pale face. "It was a shadow at best. It was hard to see. The only glimpse I had was of someone in black, covered from head to foot. They could have been anything from five-seven to five-ten. They were kinda stooped over because they fell over my boots as they ran out the door." She thought for a beat. "I could hear them breathing. It was real spooky."

"How long until you arrived on scene?" Kane looked at Rio.

"A minute, I'd say." Rio shrugged. "I heard a scream and ran out into the hallway. I didn't see anyone and Julie's door was open. She was screaming loud enough to wake the dead. The guests were out in the hallway looking at us when she followed me to my room."

Blinking back weariness, Jenna stared at him. "Why did you go to your room and neglect to search the hallway?"

"I could see both ways when I came out my room. The hallway was empty." Rio sighed. "I came back here to get dressed and grab some blankets is all. Julie came with me—she didn't want to be left alone."

"Whoever did this and murdered Kitty Pandora has a passkey. To move that fast, they didn't leave by the elevator unless they wedged the door to keep it open." Kane scrubbed his hands down his face. "Or they ducked into a room close by. Whatever, it couldn't have been occupied or you'd have heard more screaming."

Jenna nodded. "I don't think anyone on the front counter is a suspect, so who else would know which rooms were empty?"

"No one would give out that information." Rio sighed.

"Then it could've been anyone staying on this floor." Julie

shuddered. "When we came back out of Rio's room, there were people standing at doors staring at us like we were freaks."

Jenna stood. "Okay, we all need to get some sleep. Head back to your room, Zac. Emily, lock the door behind us and always keep it locked when you're in here. We'll talk some more in the morning." She checked her watch. "Well... make that later today. Sleep late and order room service for breakfast. I'm going to bed."

Jenna waited with Kane until they heard the lock click on the girls' door and headed for their room. When Kane slid his card into the lock, they heard Duke growl. She flicked a glance at Kane and pulled her weapon. Flattening her back to the wall, she waited for Kane to push open the door. He went in low, darting to the left, Glock drawn, and she hit the light covering him with a sweep of her weapon. Duke let out a yelp of joy and did his doggy dance. Jenna followed Kane as they swept both bedrooms. The suite was empty.

"Someone has been here." Kane held out a hand to stop her. "Someone's been in our room."

THIRTY-ONE

The rattling of a breakfast cart woke Jenna. She could have slept all day if not for the urgency of the case. The door opened and Kane, fresh from the shower, hair damp like a wet seal, pushed the cart to the bedside. She sat up, pushed the hair from her eyes, and smiled at him. "Oh, how lovely. Breakfast in bed. You do the kindest things. I think I'll keep you."

"Maybe I couldn't wait any longer for you to wake up." Kane gave her a teasing smile. "My stomach is making so much noise it sent Duke under the bed. He thought a storm was coming." He chuckled.

Jenna frowned. "Is Duke okay? He didn't eat any of the cookies the intruder left behind, did he?"

"Nah, I've trained Duke not to take food from anyone he doesn't know. It took some doing, but after talking to Ty Carter, he figured it might save Duke's life someday."

Jenna nodded. "It was just as well. They could've been poisoned." She took the cup of coffee from him. "Thank you. I'm famished." She sipped the coffee and leaned back as he settled a loaded tray of food on her lap. "I'll never understand how you can function on four hours or less sleep."

"It was part of my training." He settled down in a chair beside the bed and rested a tray across his knees. "We went through a little more intense training than you did to make sure we'd endure torture and be able to function under all types of stress."

Jenna peeked under the plate cover and sighed with delight. A stack of buttered pancakes floating in syrup and a pile of crispy bacon. It was Kane's favorite, but she'd forget about the calories over winter and indulge herself. Lost for a few moments in the syrupy delight, she nibbled on a strip of bacon and noticed him staring at her. "What?"

"I like being with you but it scares the hell out of me." He cleared his throat. "I have a confession to make before we head out and tackle this case. I went to DC to visit Annie's grave before the first snow." He looked down at his plate and ate slowly without looking at her. "I went to say goodbye. It was something I needed to do." He lifted his gaze to her. "My life is here now—but that in itself is a problem."

What's up now? Overwhelmed by the intensity of his gaze, Jenna pushed her concern away and smiled at him. "I would have gone with you, if you'd asked me."

"It was something I needed to do alone, and taking you there would have confirmed my identity if anyone had seen us. Your picture has been all over the media lately, and although I've had plastic surgery, we don't know who may be watching and people will do anything for money." Kane leaned back and looked at her. "I needed closure so I could move forward with my life, Jenna."

"I'm glad you told me. That must have been very hard for you." She leaned over and gave him a sticky kiss, almost toppling her tray. She sighed. "I know I can't take Annie's place in your heart—"

"Jenna." Kane cupped her chin. "It's not that—I'm just so darn worried about losing you too." He dropped his hand, looking stricken. "We take down serial killers. Our life isn't by any means normal. You'd have a better chance of survival fighting beside me in Syria than in Black Rock Falls."

A rush of emotion hit Jenna and she bit her bottom lip. "Life is uncertain for everyone, and we all walk the tightrope of fate, Dave.

Worrying about what might happen is so not you. What was your motto when Wolfe was your handler? Ah yes, 'One day at a time,' right?"

"Yeah, but that was different." Kane shook his head. "I only had to worry about myself most times. At the time, I never thought about dying. Since Annie died, I can see the fragility of life. I put you in danger every day I'm here in Black Rock Falls."

It was all too true, and concern flowed over Jenna. He'd risked everything to see his wife's grave. He might have had plastic surgery, but his body shape was distinct and it was common knowledge Wolfe had been in the service. It would only take someone to put two and two together and they'd track Kane down. After all, his fingerprints hadn't changed. She'd known he'd taken a day and headed off somewhere with Wolfe. She'd encouraged him to spend time with the guys, as most times he never left her side, but she had to admit he'd been very subdued for days afterward. Although curious, she'd not asked what was troubling him. She valued her space and private thoughts, and Kane would be the same.

Shaking her head, Jenna examined his face. "Normally I'd say, 'Don't worry. We can face any problems together.' But this is different, isn't it? What's this really about, Dave? You've been distant since you moved into my ranch house. Is this about us? You've been extra quiet since we held Rowley's twins."

"Yes and no." Kane placed his tray on the cart. "My head's not in the game right now."

Jenna leaned back and sighed. "You know, Dave, I'm starting to wonder if I'm wasting my time waiting for you to get your head straight."

"What do you mean by that?" Kane took a long sip of his coffee. "I've never lied to you or made any promises." He shrugged. "That's not my style. You knew I was damaged goods when you took me in."

"Maybe, but every time we get close, you find an excuse to pull back." Jenna pushed the tray aside and flung back the blankets. "We chose this life and understood the risks. I can protect myself against serial killers but I could get sick or die in a car wreck. That's life and we have no control on when our time is up. I've given you three years of intimate friendship and asked for nothing in return, but you know darn well I want a family. From now on, with or without you, I'm going to enjoy every single day. Now get out of my room. I have murders to solve and right now they are my top priority."

"Jenna—" Kane grabbed her arm.

"Don't act like I've hurt your feelings. You don't have any feelings, do you, iceman?" Jenna glared at him. "Drop into the zone or whatever you do because I'm over listening to the same sob story. Now, get out of my room." Fuming, she dragged her arm out of his grasp and headed for the shower.

When she returned a long time later, Kane was missing. She found him in the interview room working on his laptop beside Rio. Both men looked subdued and didn't lift their eyes from their screens when she arrived. "Find out anything useful?"

"Unusual, worrying, but nothing we can use." Kane frowned at the screen but didn't look at her. "I had Mr. Brightway give me access to the CCTV data. Someone disabled the camera on this floor and the one on Kitty Pandora's using a laser pointer. It wiped out transmission for about two hours." He shrugged. "So, we have nothing. I also asked him about passkeys and there's a box of them down at the employees' entrance. The house rules are when the housekeeping staff finish their shift, they drop the passkeys into the box and collect one when they come back on. He said this is because the staff works on shifts and he only has about twenty or so keys, apart from his own master, which he keeps on him at all times." He leaned back in the chair and looked at her. "The interior staff area can only be entered using a passkey. The outside entrance is via the kitchen and anyone entering that way would be noticed. The back door has a keypad and they change the code about every two weeks."

Jenna sat down beside him. "Anything from Kalo?"

"Yeah, he sent a few files. I'm looking at them next." Kane was wearing his combat face and she couldn't read his feelings at all. "Rio is chasing down where all our suspects were last night and who has alibis. Wolfe messaged me. He has the autopsy reports and will be doing a video call in half an hour."

It never ceased to amaze her how her team sprang into action. She stood. "We'll do a breakdown of each case after we speak to Wolfe. I'll go and grab Emily."

She could have called her but wanted a little girl-to-girl chat. When she reached her floor, she ran into Mr. Brightway. The manager was looking a little annoyed. She paused before knocking on Emily's door and waited for him. "Is there a problem?"

"No." Mr. Brightway stood to one side to allow two male members of his staff to walk by. "We managed to squeeze another bed into Deputy Rio's room as requested. Is there anything else you require?"

Confused Jenna stared at him. "Another bed?"

"Yes, Deputy Kane made the request." Mr. Brightway gave her a long look. "Please inform him. We've moved his things as requested."

Swallowing hard, Jenna nodded. "Great, thank you."

So, it was over. Jenna shook her head. Just like that after all they'd been through. She'd stood her ground and he'd walked away without a fight. She banged hard on Emily's door.

"Heavens above. What's happened now?" Emily looked pale and tired. "Another murder?"

Jenna shook her head. "Nope. I had a disagreement with Dave is all."

"Really?" Emily looked amused. "Uncle Dave doesn't argue—not ever. He's more an action man. Did you see him last night with Zac? Oh my, he is so like my dad. Overprotective is an understatement." She stood back to allow Jenna inside. "First fight, huh? Tell me all about it. Julie's not here. Zac took her down to the conference earlier and she's with friends. She doesn't need a babysitter."

Jenna explained but left out everything about Kane's past. "He leads me on, like he wants a relationship, and then backs off and makes excuses. I'm over it. I told him to get out of my room."

"And he followed your orders. No wonder he had a face carved in stone when he came to check on us before. He's in love with you." Emily chuckled. "Everyone knows it and you do too. I figure after so long being single he has a commitment issue. He's probably worried if you get married, he'll become overprotective and you won't be able to work together. He won't find another occupation because he doesn't trust anyone else watching your back. It's catch-22. He's damned if he does, and damned if he doesn't."

Jenna sighed. "Maybe, but I don't want to end up growing old all alone. I want marriage and maybe the chance to have a baby, just one before it's too late. That's not too much to ask and if it's not going to be Dave, then I'll have to start husband-hunting. There are a ton of eligible guys in town." She shrugged. "Grab your things. Your dad is calling soon and he'll want you there."

"Okay, but you're making way too much out of this argument. Don't rush into decisions you'll regret." Emily collected her things. "They say the making up is the best bit, so look forward to that."

Jenna pulled open the door. "All I'm interested in right now is solving this case. Dave Kane is the least of my problems." She headed for the elevator.

THIRTY-TWO

It was the first time Kane had experienced Jenna's anger toward him. It hadn't been a simple disagreement. She was fuming. He'd upset her by telling her the truth and couldn't understand why she'd got so mad at him. She'd made it plain she wanted him out of her life and nothing he could have said would have helped matters. He'd do the only thing he understood in this situation, and that was to retreat and regroup. As she'd made it very clear the case was her priority, he'd work his butt off until they caught the killer. The other stuff would have to wait until she'd cooled down.

He glanced at his watch and using his satellite phone walked into one of the bedrooms of the suite they were using as interview rooms and dialed Special Agent Jo Wells. As she was a behavioral analyst, he'd like her take on the current homicides. She picked up after a couple of rings. "Hi, Jo. It's Dave Kane. How are things in Snakeskin Gully?"

"Cold. I hope you don't need us. We can't use the chopper to get to you. I hear there's been a line of blizzards across your part of the state all week, although I've heard no news of any crime. If it's urgent, we could maybe fly to the closest town and drive if the roads are passable."

Kane shook his head. "No, don't risk traveling in this weather.

We can discuss cases over the phone. Good news first, Jake and Sandy's twins arrived safely. One of each, born last night at the morgue, would you believe? Thank goodness, Shane was there to step in and deliver them. The road to the hospital was blocked."

"Oh, that's wonderful news. Give Sandy and Jake our congratulations. But I'm sure that's not why you called."

"No, it's not. We've had three homicides at the ski lodge. At the moment, we're isolated here at a crime writers' convention. I can get to town by a service road if it's urgent, but it's dangerous. We went close to sliding off the road last night." Kane went on to explain everything in detail. "We're still waiting for Wolfe to confirm ID and notify next of kin before we give it to the press."

"Three different MOs, how interesting." Jo paused as if thinking. *"What's your take on the crime scenes?"*

Having given the subject a lot of thought, he just needed Jo to validate his conclusions. "The killer is an organized psychopath and he's using the ski lodge as his comfort zone. He's been here before, knows the layout, and is aware of all the security features. I believe he has a passkey and was in Julie's room and mine last night. I say 'he,' but I'm not discounting this could be a woman."

"Yes, the evidence suggests the killer knows the victims, although something changed with Julie. A peeping Tom is far removed from attempted murder. It sounds like vengeance kills and, as they are all so different, something specific links the cause of death to the killer or victim."

Thinking over the crime scenes, Kane scratched his cheek. "Hmm, well the last one was electrocuted and her last novel was titled *Frizzled*. The character died by electrocution. The previous one died the same way as in his novel too. So, we have a link with two of the murders."

"There you go. Check out the correlation between the victims' books and mode of death. Are they all authors?"

"No." Kane leaned back against the wall, allowing the crime scenes to filter through his mind. "The first one, in the pond, was an agent but I'll see what I can find. Perhaps, she made another book deal recently and the story was about a peeping Tom? But why target Julie? All the victims have been associated with the publishing industry."

"Check out the agent's webpage. If you find any similar coincidences this could be the same person that entered Julie's room. If so, I believe she is a distraction from the vengeance kills." Jo hummed as if thinking over what next to say. *"I don't want to alarm you, but it seems strange for an organized psychopath, who has obviously planned these homicides, to veer off into another path, unless Julie is a trigger for a previous series of murders."*

Suddenly uncomfortable, Kane rubbed the back of his neck. "In what way?"

"Well, from the cold, calculated murder of his victims, he's killed before and likely often. As you know, a first kill is usually hurried and messy. At first, they lose control, but as they commit more murders, they take their time and enjoy it." Jo paused a beat. *"As vengeance kills, these people have wronged him in some way, so there must be a connection. I'd say he's kept control for a time, maybe years, until someone pushed his buttons and the need to commit murder rose again. The moment he started killing once more it unleashed the beast. When they feel the power over life and death again, it causes a domino effect. The original incident that made him a psychopath in the first place is highlighted in his mind and it doesn't take much to trigger an episode. Perhaps Julie resembles the first girl he killed, for instance, or the person who abused him as a child."*

Concerned for Julie's safety, Kane sucked in a breath. "So, Julie could be next on his list?"

"That depends." Jo sounded serious. *"He didn't strike when he had the chance, so maybe he was testing his reaction to her, or the next kill is more important to him or he just gets off on looking at sleeping teenagers. Whatever, I'd watch her closely, or better still, send her home to Shane. She's obviously not safe at the ski resort."*

Kane cleared his throat. Insisting Julie went home wouldn't be easy and, as the blizzard had hit again with full force, neither would negotiating the back road down the mountain. "Okay, thanks, Jo. I appreciate your help."

"Anytime. Send me the files when you can. I need something interesting to read."

Kane chuckled. "Sure thing." He disconnected and strolled back into the main room just as Jenna and Emily arrived.

"Okay, before Wolfe calls, I'd like an update on everything you have to date." Jenna pulled out a chair and placed her laptop on the table. "Rio?"

"I figure we can remove September March and Ike Turnage from our suspects list. I have March on the CCTV footage leaving the lodge for her cabin at eight last night and she didn't return until this morning. Ike Turnage was in his cabin on the phone talking to the manager during Dakota Storm's murder and he headed for his cabin last night at nine. He called room service at ten to discuss his breakfast order. So both have alibis." Rio leaned back in his chair, twirling a pen in his fingers. "August Bradford, Murphy Finnian, Bexley Grayson, and Parker Rain were all in the lodge last night. All claim to be in their rooms or in the lobby when the power went out, but none of them can offer the name of a witness, which is suspicious."

"Okay, so we concentrate on those four." Jenna made notes on her laptop. "Kane, what have you got for me?"

Kane explained the call to Jo. "I haven't looked over the files from Kalo yet, but with Jo's insight, it will be easier to match up possible links between our suspects and the victims."

"I don't recall asking you to involve the FBI in my case." Jenna lifted her gaze to him. "Do you suddenly feel the need to question your profiling skills, because as sure as hell, I don't need anyone working with me who doubts their ability."

"I've never doubted my ability." Kane stared at her uncompromising expression. "I didn't think asking your permission to call my friends was part of my job description."

"That's the problem, Kane. You don't care what anyone thinks, do you?" Jenna's eyes blazed. "Maybe I'm sick of looking incompetent because you keep running to the FBI for help."

Unaccustomed to dealing with Jenna's anger, Kane ignored her question. "Validating a theory is hardly running to Jo for help. We haven't dealt with an organized serial killer who does a complete three-sixty in his MO. I'm not a behavioral analyst in Jo's class, and with Julie in possible danger, I wanted to ensure we'd be prepared for whatever was coming next."

"Well then, when you get back to Kalo, ask him to find out if any murders of women fitting Julie's description happened during our suspects' lifetimes." Jenna turned back to her laptop. "Rio, if Wolfe has formally identified the victims, contact their local law enforcement office to notify next of kin. Once you have confirmation of all three victims, write me a statement for the media. I'll go and speak to them."

The air in the room seemed to crackle with anger. Kane stood and went to the coffee machine the hotel had supplied. He pushed in a pod and waited for the aromatic brew to drip into the cup. Emily came up beside him and selected a pod. He glanced at her. "It's not safe for Julie here. Do you think we can convince her to go home?"

"Not a chance." Emily slid the fixings across the bench to him. She dropped her voice to a whisper and both her eyebrows rose in question. "First argument, huh?"

Kane added cream and sugar to his cup. "It goes way past that, I'm afraid." He shrugged. "She wants me out of her life."

"No... she wants you to fight for her, Dave." Emily smiled at him. "Not give in and run away the moment she raises her voice. She's a strong woman and needs a strong man." She sighed. "And that's all I'm going to say on the subject. I'm not taking sides, so don't ask me."

Kane sipped his coffee and grinned at her. "Yes, ma'am."

THIRTY-THREE

Wolfe stared at the somber faces on the screen. The isolation must be getting to the team as not one of them, apart from Emily, greeted him. He pulled up files and cleared his throat. "I've identified all three victims. As it happens, all three completed DNA profiles for various things and all showed up on the databases. I've contacted their local law enforcement agencies and all have come back to me that the next of kin have been notified." He waited for a reaction but none came. "Moving right along. The earrings found at Storm's and Longfellow's crime scenes don't belong to Dakota Storm. I found a DNA trace on both the earrings; small amounts of blood and tissue were trapped under the stones. I ran the samples and came up with a cold case from twenty years ago. Many cold-case files, as you know, have been reopened due to the advances in DNA. These earrings belonged to Diane Tate out of Black Ridge, Montana. She died from multiple stab wounds. Before she died, the local cops found two murdered men in the woods, close by the house. They'd been killed at different times. One of them was the local priest. Tate was a single mother. She had a son, Paul, a religious choirboy who was staying over at a friend's house at the time of Tate's murder. He was ten years old and went into foster care. They never found a trace of the killer. These earrings were ripped from Tate's ears during the murder."

"Twenty years ago?" Jenna frowned. *"The ski resort is new. There must be some mistake."*

"Unless our killer is the same person who killed Diane Tate and the men." Kane stared at the screen. *"Do we have a photograph of Diane Tate?"*

Wolfe smiled. "As it happens, I do." He scrolled through the files and sent one through. "Blonde, small boned, and pretty."

"Ah, we have a problem." Kane cleared his throat.

Wolfe listened with incredulity as Kane brought him up to speed with the profiler information and what had happened to Julie. "So, it comes down to the risk of leaving her there and risking another trip down the mountain?"

"From what we experienced last night and the conditions this morning, she has less chance of being murdered." Jenna pushed both hands through her hair. *"She is aware of the situation and isn't a fool. She's with a group of friends right now and we'll be checking on her all day."* She sighed. *"It's up to you. If you want her back home, we'll get her down the mountain. Just say the word."*

Torn between wanting Julie home and the potential risk, Wolfe moved his gaze to Kane. "What do you think?"

"I've given her my stun gun. Her tracker ring won't work up here. We have no reliable wireless signal." Kane stared back at him over cyberspace. *"I'd prefer she were off the mountain, but Jenna is telling it how it is. We came close to sliding over the side. It's dangerous out there right now."*

Wolfe nodded. Kane had made the first tracker ring for Jenna, when he'd arrived in Black Rock Falls, but over the years he'd made significant improvements. With one click, the rings allowed the team to track the wearer on their phones and the one-way communication, sent them vital information, should one of the women be in trouble. "Their rings will work. I've upgraded them to satellite. Like the pair of you since the upgrade on the ranch, your new phones have a red panic button on the main screen. It works with your satellite sleeve or wireless."

"Mine too?" Jenna frowned. *"Is that why you wanted my ring?"*

Wolfe nodded. "Yeah, I thought I'd told you. Anyway, back to the case. Anything else you need to know about the Tate murder?"

"Was she raped?" Kane's attention moved to his laptop.

"No. All the victims died from sharp force trauma. Multiple stab wounds. The woman's main injuries were to the face and neck. The men received similar injuries but had their genitalia removed. It was a gruesome scene from frenzied attacks. I'll send the autopsy reports on all the victims." Wolfe sent the files. "I leave it to you to discover why a killer leaves a trophy behind from one kill to the next. Assuming this is the same person."

"Unless the killer was a kid at the time, none of our suspects would be old enough. The oldest one we have is thirty-two. The son you mentioned had an alibi and it would be hard for a kid to take down three adults." Jenna looked up at him. *"I assume he was considered at the time of the murder of his mother, but what about the others?"*

Wolfe consulted his notes. "I'll send you everything I have, but it doesn't look like they were able to establish the approximate time of death for the men. They didn't look at the boy because his alibi was solid. He was sleeping over with a friend, in the same bedroom. They'd have noticed him missing and he would have been covered in blood if he'd slipped out and then returned. The kid discovered his mother's body after school the next day. From the report, he was acting normal all that day at school but was hysterical when he ran to a neighbor's house to tell them what had happened."

"Where did they live?" Kane raised both eyebrows. *"Nobody heard anything?"*

Wolfe sighed. "Black Ridge, just outside of Blackwater. They lived out a ways, on the edge of the forest."

"Okay thanks. Getting back to our cases. What did you find on Dakota Storm?" Jenna's serious expression was set in stone.

Wolfe surveyed the line of faces. All but Emily had their mouth turned down. The atmosphere was unusual and troubling. "In simple terms, she drowned. The splinters found in the head wound caused by blunt force trauma match the log you found at the scene and the blood is a match. I conclude she was struck from behind but not killed, strangled to the point of unconsciousness. But she was alive when the pen was stuck into her eye. The subsequent injury wasn't fatal but would have rendered her unconscious. She had pond water in her lungs."

"That was overkill." Rio pushed a hand through his dark hair. *"He wanted her to suffer. It didn't last long enough for him. I've heard of killers who strangle just enough to make their victims black out, then bring them around for round two."*

"Yeah, that's up close and personal." Kane sipped his coffee.

"So, this would fit a revenge kill." Jenna made notes. *"We have a theory that this killer has some beef against members of the publishing industry."*

Wolfe nodded. "It seems logical, but there are easier ways to kill. This person toys with his victims, like a cat with a mouse. Have you seen the way a cat tosses a mouse around, lets it go just to chase it down again? They amuse themselves by torturing the mouse. This killer is the same."

"How so?" Jenna stared into the camera.

Wolfe had been waiting to reveal his new investigative tool. "It's a shame you aren't in the office to gain the full extent of this new device. It will make understanding the extent of the injuries much easier." He turned on a machine and adjusted his camera to send the images to Jenna's laptop. "This is a digital anatomy table. By superimposing the images of a victim over a normal body, I can demonstrate the nature of the injuries. This machine also produces a 3D image and, by rotating parts of the body, I can display underlying organs. It will give you a concise and visual explanation of cause of death."

"That is amazing." Kane leaned closer. *"How does it work?"*

Wolfe ran the machine through its paces. "There is a slider

that allows me to manipulate the image, or for indicating or demonstrating injuries, I can just write on the screen with my finger." He sighed. "But you'll be able to get the full benefit when you next come to the morgue. I'd better get on."

He pulled up the images of Jedidiah Longfellow. "From my preliminary examination I would have thought maybe one of the nails had punctured a vital organ, but in fact, on autopsy we see that apart from the paralyzing effect of the one pressed into the base of the skull, this victim could well have survived unless he froze to death—but he didn't. He actually died of heart failure."

"The killer scared him to death?" Jenna looked incredulous.

"The heart wasn't in great shape to begin with." Wolfe displayed the images on the new machine, moving them back and forth to explain as he talked. "The stress of what happened to him caused the heart to fail. Again, from the number of nails I pulled from this victim, it was a different MO, but similar in the fact that the killer was playing with him to cause maximum pain."

"Revenge again." Kane leaned forward peering at the screen of his laptop. *"That's two, but how can you call number three revenge?"*

Wolfe flicked up more images, this time of Kitty Pandora. "No burn marks. She didn't handle the hairdryer in the bathtub. Her prints and only *her* prints are on the hairdryer. No water on the floor. No struggle. What does this say to you?"

"She knew her killer, well to allow them into her bathroom." Rio scribbled on a notepad. *"The killer didn't play with her, he just dropped in the hairdryer and left."*

"Maybe not." Jenna chewed on her bottom lip. *"Think about it. If a friend suddenly arrived in your room, you wouldn't scream. You'd maybe chat a bit. Say things got nasty. Maybe he had a weapon and ordered her into the tub? Then he tormented her by threatening to drop in the hairdryer. He'd want to hear her beg for her life, but he didn't care and dropped it anyway."*

Wolfe smiled at her. "That makes sense because, when Emily took the temperature of the water and the body, they were cool.

You discovered the body within half an hour, and the bathwater should have been at a higher temperature. The room temperature was warm, toasty in fact. Women don't lie in cold baths unless they're forced to. She died of asphyxiation due to a paralyzed diaphragm induced by an electric shock." He checked his notes. "Do you know if anything was left at the scene or taken from the scene?"

"As we don't have anyone to confirm either, we have to assume the negative." Kane shrugged. *"The room hasn't been touched. Why? Did you notice anything unusual?"*

Wolfe nodded. "Yeah, she has an indent, on her finger as if she constantly wore a ring. Third finger left hand above her wedding band. So an engagement ring, perhaps?"

"Okay, I'll do a search of the room, and if we can't find it, I'll contact her husband for confirmation." Jenna sighed. *"Is that everything?"*

Wolfe looked from one to the other. He'd never had such a cold reception. "Yeah, for now. Ah, Emily, can you call me, please? I have some family business to discuss with you."

"Sure thing, Dad." Emily smiled at him.

Wolfe disconnected and waited for Emily to call. When the phone rang, he smiled to himself. Emily wouldn't hold back information from him unless she'd been asked to keep a secret. "Okay what's going on? I get a better reception in the morgue than I did today."

"Well." Emily let out an exasperated sigh. *"Sit down and I'll tell you."*

THIRTY-FOUR

After a stern warning from Uncle Dave about not spending any time alone and keeping the stun gun in her jacket pocket, Julie tried to relax and enjoy the conference. She took a ton of selfies with her friends to remember the weekend and kept a watchful eye out for anyone acting suspicious, but everything seemed normal. There was so much to see and do here, and reading crime was the best thing in her life. She loved trying to unravel the mysteries and follow the clues in the books she read. She preferred to lose herself in the pages of fiction. The true-crime books were too close to home. She'd live enough true crime in her life to read about it. Although the cases her father, Jenna, and Uncle Dave solved were interesting, she didn't really want to know all the gory details.

Julie had at least six friends from school staying at the lodge, and many had intended to ski during their stay, but the events throughout the conference kept them from going stir-crazy. She'd had to bite her tongue a few times during discussions about a mystery game everyone was convinced was playing out over the week to prevent from telling them about the murders. The moment Jenna walked into the hall and took the stage to address everyone, her stomach dropped. She hadn't told any of her friends about the man in her room and hoped Jenna wouldn't say anything.

"Can I have your attention?" Jenna stood and her gaze scanned the crowd. "My deputies are in the other halls, so everyone will be aware of what's happening at the same time. Unfortunately, I'm here to report the deaths of Dakota Storm, an agent out of Wild Woods, Oregon; Jedidiah Longfellow, an author out of Wilderness, Wyoming; and Kitty Pandora, an author out of Superstition, Oregon. Their deaths are unrelated and the causes undetermined at this time."

The crowd burst into a barrage of questions, and Jenna waited in silence for the noise to settle. In an effort to look as horrified as her friends, Julie looked at them and mouthed, "Oh, my gosh."

"Do you know what happened?" Jenny Pritchard elbowed her in the ribs.

Julie shook her head. "Not exactly, but I think something happened when the lights went out. Maybe they were electrocuted or something. My dad doesn't give me any details. It's a privacy issue and, really, I wouldn't want to know. I'd have nightmares."

"During our investigation, I would strongly advise you all to move about the lodge and especially outside in pairs, until we can get to the cause of deaths." Jenna avoided all questions from the media and left the room.

"It's all part of the mystery game, isn't it?" Jenny giggled. "I've lived here all my life and the sheriff rarely leaves town, and not in the dead of winter with two deputies. She was here before anyone died. I figure she's given us a secret task. We have to find out who the killer is."

Concerned, Julie worried her bottom lip. "I don't think so."

"I do." April Perkins moved closer. "Those three people are linked. Anyone who has been at the conference knows Kitty Pandora's and Jedidiah Longfellow's agent was Dakota Storm. Dakota mentioned their books *Frizzled* and *Nailed It*."

"So that's the first clue. The second and third would be in their bestsellers. We'll need to buy copies and hunt through them."

Jenny grinned. "And what was the book Dakota Storm mentioned during the agents' roundtable?"

Julie swallowed hard as realization dawned on her. "It was the *Frozen in Time* series. The first book is titled *Body in a Frozen Lake*."

"Oh, how intriguing." April made notes on a pad. "Soon as this forum has finished, we'll grab a book each and head for my room. We can work together. It will be fun. We have time before the next reading."

I must go and find Jenna. Julie smiled at her friends. "I'll be back soon. I'm going to the bathroom." She took off through the crowd.

With everyone involved with the conference, very few people moved through the ski lodge. The staff acted like ghosts and seemed to drift in and out getting things done when no one was around. As Julie headed through the walkways from one part of the conference area to the next, her neck prickled with an awful feeling that someone was behind her. She heard a slight squeaking like leather shoes on the tile and turned to look over one shoulder, but found the passageway empty. Swallowing the rising panic, she peered into the shadowed doorways along each wall. Each of them offered a place for someone to hide. Heart thumping, she gripped the stun gun in her pocket and quickened her pace. The corridors had no windows and when one of the lights flickered and went out, fear had her by the throat. Someone was following her and they must have ducked into the recessed doorways each time she stopped to look behind her. The terror of seeing a man in her room charged into her mind. It had been a stupid mistake to move around the lodge alone. She took her hand off the stun gun and went to depress the stone in the tracker ring when she heard someone clearing their throat. She spun around, ready to fight for her life, but recognized the person coming along behind her.

"Julie, isn't it?" The person smiled. "Mind if I walk with you? After hearing the sheriff's warning, I feel a little worried about walking alone."

Julie smiled. "Me too." She fell into step beside them.

"Where are you headed?" The acquaintance strolled along beside her.

Not wanting to discuss her need to find Jenna, Julie indicated with her chin toward the elevator. "I left my iPad in my room. I want to make notes at the forum."

"I'm heading that way too." The person smiled broadly and pressed the button for the elevator. "How wonderfully convenient."

Before she could reply, the elevator doors opened and Zac Rio appeared wearing a scowl. Julie looked at him in astonishment.

"What are you doing out of the conference hall?" Rio looked from one to the other. "Who's your friend?"

"Just someone wanting to use the elevator." They pushed past him, stepped inside and the doors closed.

"Who was that and why are you wandering around the lodge on your own?" Rio glared down at her. "Didn't you listen to Jenna?"

Embarrassed, Julie's face grew hot. Rio made her feel like his little sister, and unlike her, she'd never gotten into trouble. "Yes, I listened and I wasn't alone, was I? I met that person at the conference yesterday and they offered to walk with me to the elevator, so stop acting like my father." She sighed. "I don't recall their name. I needed to see Jenna urgently." She took in his disgruntled expression. "Is something wrong? You look angry."

"You could say that." Rio turned back to the elevator and pressed the button. "First, Kane roughs me up because I tried to protect you, and now he's moved into my room." He rolled his eyes. "Look, I'm not easily intimidated, but right now, I'm a red flag and he's a mad bull. I figure he's had a fight with Jenna. They're at each other's throats." He swung his gaze back to her. "Unless they're like this all the time?"

"No, they're usually great." Julie frowned. "Uncle Dave only gets mad if someone tries to hurt one of us, but then it's a cool calculated mad. I've never seen him yell at anyone, not ever." She thought for a beat. "We all assumed they were in a relationship."

"Well, that would make sense." Rio rubbed the back of his neck. "A lovers' spat maybe."

The elevator stopped at the interview room floor and Julie looked at him. "Talk to him, maybe he needs a man-to-man chat with someone."

"Me?" Rio snorted with laughter. "No way. I'm keeping my head down."

Julie led the way through the open door of the suite and headed for where Jenna was working on her laptop. "Jenna, I think I might have a clue to the killer."

THIRTY-FIVE

So close her hair brushed my cheek. I could smell her fear, and her eyes, so wide with terror, made the temptation almost irresistible, but only a fool would take such a risk. I'm in complete control and it would've been foolish to extinguish her in the elevator. The cameras are everywhere, and although I'd love to share my skills with the world, alas, to finish my story I'm compelled to keep my hoodie up and my head down. I take the elevator to the next floor, move quickly to the stairs, and make my way back down to the conference. I need to be seen in the crowd with hundreds of witnesses and will be the social butterfly this afternoon. My plans are set and I have everything I need waiting for me in the forest. I'm salivating at the thought of my next kill. I enjoy brutality, feed on pain and suffering, but the thrill will be dismembering someone right under the sheriff's nose and then presenting my kill as an offering.

I'm smiling at the thought of the delights to come. The next will be a confection of my skills, one that will make all who love writing about crime sit up and take notice. There will be fear but also kudos for my ingenuity, something that has been sadly overlooked by the publishing industry. Will the guests run screaming from the ski lodge, demanding the sheriff allow them to leave and damn the risk of dying on the road down the mountain? Or will the fools continue to believe my kills are just part of an elaborate charade? After this, I can turn my attention to a burning need, I refuse to deny myself: Julie. One thing is for sure, when my hands close around her slender neck, I won't be playing games.

THIRTY-SIX

On hearing Julie's voice, Jenna shut her laptop on the crime scene photographs she was scanning for clues. She'd had the unfortunate task of having to speak with Kitty Pandora's husband. The distraught man had informed her Kitty never removed the missing ring from her finger. It was her engagement ring and he'd send Jenna a photograph of Kitty wearing the distinctive diamond and sapphire ring. She smiled at Julie. "Okay, sit down and tell us what you've discovered. Rio, close the door. We don't want anyone listening in."

After everyone had drawn close, Jenna leaned back in her chair, listening intently to the link between the murder victims. She made fast notes and looked up at Kane. "So what's the deal with this killer?"

"Well, if it had been all agents, I'd say he was an author who'd been rejected, but why would he kill the authors?" Kane stared at the ceiling for a few seconds and then lowered his gaze to Jenna. "The fact he's using the authors' methods of killing in the three murders is significant. How I'm not entirely sure. Jealousy that they're published and he isn't, perhaps?"

Intrigued, Jenna stared at him, her mind rushing to work out all the implications. "When we talked to the Black Rock Falls series author on the day we arrived, she mentioned Dakota Storm was a great agent, but that she was blunt, let's say, to authors she rejected, and from what she said, that could be hundreds a week."

"That's true." Julie's eyes widened. "From what I hear, she's the agent all the authors want to represent them. She makes incredible deals and her clients are bestsellers but she only considers the very best. So, I would say, she very rarely takes on new clients."

As the possible motive of the murders slotted into place, Jenna nodded. "Okay, so we need theories. Why is the suspect killing authors, and if they wanted to be represented by Dakota Storm, why kill her?"

"That would depend on how deep she wounded the killer when she rejected them." Kane rested one boot on his knee and leaned back in his chair. "Say, the killer and the other two victims all submitted pitches at the same time. They're all friends and Dakota took two of them and rejected the killer. That alone would be enough to trigger resentment in a psychopath, especially a sleeping one, like Jo suggested, and might be enough to trigger a revenge episode."

"So where does the frozen-lake scenario fit in?" Emily stood and went to make coffee. "Dakota Storm only represented that book. She didn't write it."

"And that author isn't at the conference." Julie pushed her hands through her long hair. "Although, the book is all over Dakota's promotion. Her biggest deal yet. She would have made a ton of money out of her commission; she sold the film rights as well."

Mind working overtime, Jenna stared at her. "So, she was killed before she could enjoy the benefits of her deal?" She looked at Kane. "Now all we need to do is connect the three victims to someone at the conference."

"Not everyone." Kane raised both eyebrows. "We've narrowed the possible suspects down to four: August Bradford, Murphy Finnian, Bexley Grayson, and Parker Rain. The first thing I'd suggest is hunting down what connects our suspects to the victims.

Perhaps Dakota rejected one of them and triggered the killing spree. Remember, it only takes someone to trigger a psychopathic killer and it has a domino effect. It lights up their memories as if they happened yesterday and feeds their urge to kill. At this time, an organized psychopath can become a frenzied killer." He sighed. "Look at Bundy. He killed women, but one at a time, and then something triggered him to go on a killing spree at the sorority house. To anyone looking at him, he seemed like a nice guy and hid the truth in a mask of clever deceptions." He shrugged. "If you want my take on this, I figure we have a similar profile and the fact he went to Julie's room and did nothing suggests he is planning his next move. He's trying to prove a point... something that only he understands—one thing's for sure, we'll never be able to see the logic in what he's doing."

Jenna nodded. "Agents must keep records. We should start there."

"That theory only takes into account the motive for Dakota Storm's murder." Rio stood and went to help Emily carry cups of coffee to the table. "We have two constants in our puzzle. One is Dakota Storm. The second is the conference. We just have to discover who pitched to Dakota Storm and was rejected at the same time as the other two gained representation—and then match the list to our suspects."

"If it is one of our suspects." Rubbing her temples, Jenna looked at him. "If they come up clean, it will be like finding a needle in a haystack. We'll need a search warrant from a different county to start with, and then a ton of people to check."

"If that happens, we can start by asking the agency." Kane took a cup of coffee from Emily with a smile. "They might cooperate as it's a murder investigation. I'm more inclined to speak to the suspects again and ask them if they've ever pitched to Dakota Storm."

Jenna shrugged. "Okay. Get at it." She reached for her cup. "Although, you're assuming they'll tell you the truth."

"I know how to interview a psychopath." Kane sipped his

beverage. "I'll play to their ego and just slip the question in under the radar."

After mulling over the next step to take, Jenna looked at Rio. "Okay, Rio. I'll put you in charge of rounding up our suspects. Do it surreptitiously so it isn't noticed." She swung her attention to Kane. "Dave, you can do your thing and I'll go with Julie to search her room again. So far, the killer has left two earrings at crime scenes and taken a trophy from Julie and Kitty Pandora. I'm wondering if the intruder left anything in Julie's room. We haven't done a forensic sweep and maybe we need to look a little closer."

"As the person was covered from head to foot and no doubt wearing gloves, it would've been a waste of time." Kane leaned back in his chair. "There's unknown trace DNA and fingerprints in hotel rooms and anything we found would be inadmissible in court. Unless it was tissue or blood, or bloody finger- or footprints."

"It would be impossible to know if the killer left anything at Kitty Pandora's crime scene too." Rio stirred cream into his cup. "There's no way of telling what things belong to her. As she travels all the time and no doubt buys things along the way, I doubt her husband would know either."

Jenna finished her coffee and pushed to her feet. "Agreed." She turned to go and then looked back at Kane. "We'll take a break for lunch at noon. Do you want me to walk Duke while you're busy?"

"Nope." Kane didn't lift his gaze from his screen. "I'll make time to take him out before lunch. I need to stretch my legs too."

"Okay." Jenna smiled at Julie. "Ready to search your room?"

"Um..." Julie looked at Emily. "Can you do it? You're the expert and I'd like to get back to the conference. They're having a contest today. We team up in groups and try to solve a murder, so I'll be all over the place."

"Yeah, sure." Emily stood. "I'll grab my kit, just in case we find anything."

Jenna held up a hand to stop Julie leaving. "Wait here and go down with Rio I don't want you wandering around the conference alone. Promise me you'll stay with your group." She walked to the door and waited for Emily.

"Okay." Julie sat back down. "It will be perfectly safe. There'll be people all over. I'll be fine."

"And if I find you've been wandering around alone…" Emily narrowed her gaze at her sister. "I'll call Dad and he'll be taking you straight home. It's not worth the risk. If you can't find anyone to go places with you, call me and I'll come down." She followed Jenna to the door and lowered her voice to a whisper. "She doesn't seem to understand the danger."

Jenna pressed the elevator button. "After that creep got into her room. I think she does."

THIRTY-SEVEN

An icy blast, seared through Quentin Riggs's clothes and he buttoned up his coat as he stepped outside and surveyed the snowscape. Even the great pine forest hadn't shielded the ground from the blizzard. The branches of each tree bowed under the weight of the snow, and long icicles hung down like a million daggers as far as the eye could see. The scent of the forest in winter was unique—a blend of many flavors—but today the smell of freshly cut wood and gas engines lingered in the air. The sound of chainsaws disturbed the silence as the maintenance crew dashed out to do their daily clearing of the fallen branches. They returned dragging sleighs piled high with logs for the fires. He pulled out his pack of cigarettes, glad the manager at the lodge had conceded his guests needed the alarm on one of the emergency exit doors disabled to allow the smokers to escape outside to enjoy their addiction in peace. He lit up and inhaled, sighing as the smoke mixed with the steam from his breath and dissipated into the air. The door opened and another guest stepped out to indulge. He offered them a nod. "We must be crazy to be out here. My feet haven't thawed since I came out before. I must try and cut down. The cold will kill me before the cancer."

"I doubt the cold will kill you." A smile creased the guest's face.

Riggs held their gaze for a moment. "You look familiar. Have we met before?"

"Yeah, I pitched my novel to you at the last conference and you asked for the full. It was called *Revenge Is Sweet*." The acquaintance leaned against the wall and shrugged. "But you rejected me."

Searching his mind, Riggs took a long drag on his cigarette. "I do recall reading your submission. You write well, but your stories are without substance. Your murders lacked imagination and I knew who the killer was from the second chapter."

"If I write well, don't you think a good agent would have been able to guide me to becoming great?"

Riggs shook his head. "No. Agents often don't make good authors. You know as well as I do, if I represented you, I'd read your work and perhaps make a few suggestions, but I don't have the time to nurse potential authors along. I have to make a living too, you know."

"If you could indulge me for a moment." The guest moved a little closer. "What makes the murders in the book you talked about earlier more imaginative than mine?"

Biting back a laugh, Riggs grinned at him. "*Body Parts* is terrifying. It's a thriller that teases the edge of a horror story. The stalking, disabling, and dismembering of a person while they're alive kept me awake at night trying to get to the end of the book to find out what had happened."

"But wasn't that taken from true crime?" The acquaintance looked bemused. "I mean, to me it was almost a copy of the notorious murders that happened right here in this forest."

"I guess." Riggs pulled on his cigarette again, growing tired of the conversation. "There are so many stories out there and they'd have to cross over with real crimes by coincidence or intent. There are only so many ways you can kill a person and only so many plots to explore."

"No, there are unlimited ways to kill and I'd say if I allowed my imagination to run wild, I'd find a million plots to explore." The acquaintance moved a little closer. "I believe the Stanton Forest Killer's idea of injuring the spinal cord was unique, although the most productive way to damage the spinal cord to cause paralysis would be from the neck down—not the waist. Now that would take skill, or the victim would die at once and then the thrill of the kill would be lost. Don't you agree?"

Intrigued, Riggs smiled. "Go on, now you're interesting me."

"Well, if you take the notorious James Stone. He went for the waist and used a knife." The acquaintance moved closer. "I would go for the cervical spine area and use a stun gun. No blood, and the victim is immobilized at once. It would be so easy; the victim would never see it coming. Let me demonstrate."

The shock hit him hard in a blinding wall of pain. He fell into the snow twitching and his arms and legs refused to respond. Was this some kind of a sick joke? Riggs couldn't control his eyes or lift his head from the freezing snow. He tried to speak but nothing came from his mouth. Close by, the roar of an engine and the smell of fuel crawled up his nose as a snowmobile came from around the side of the building. Trapped in his own body, he tried to swivel his eyes. Was someone there to help him? The abductor leaned over him, wrapped a rope around his feet, climbed aboard the snowmobile and dragged him into the forest. Terror gripped him as his head bumped along behind his inert body, snow and pine branches catching in his hair and scratching his face. The forest closed in around them and they came to a stop. His eyes moved and he croaked out a whisper. "Okay, you made your point. Now take me back to the lodge."

A scarf was stuffed into his mouth. The woolen material pressed down on his tongue, making it hard to breathe. His tormentor walked away, leaving him petrified and alone. Some moments later, he heard shuffling and the person returning in coveralls, latex gloves, and a face mask with a Perspex shield. Without saying a word, they bent over him with a hunting knife to cut away his clothes, slicing through them like butter. No coldness penetrated Riggs's bare flesh. His head was raised onto a pile of snow so he could watch as the author tied cord around his thighs and the top of each arm using a stick from a fallen branch to tighten the binding into torniquets.

"Now we wait." His assailant smiled. "With the windchill factor and the fact it's about twenty degrees Fahrenheit right now, I figure what I'm planning will work better if your limbs are frozen. I don't want my saw to get clogged or kick back and cut me. I've read about the Ice Man, and he sliced up his victims after he froze them."

Riggs screamed through the scarf in his mouth but it was like a whisper on the wind. It was like a terrible nightmare. His vision blurred and he closed his eyes. The slap across his face brought back the terrible reality.

"Now, don't pass out on me." The crazy person slapped him again and then moved around him prodding his blue flesh. "You'll miss all the fun."

Satisfied, the acquaintance lifted a chainsaw from behind a tree and brushed away the snow before turning back to him. Trapped and helpless Riggs could only follow the person's moments by swiveling his eyes.

Panic had him by the throat when a dark unemotional gaze settled on him, and the ice-cold blade of the chainsaw ran down the side of his cheek in almost a caress. Riggs wanted to scream, fight back—do something—but he couldn't move. All he could do was stare into unforgiving blank eyes. It was like peering through the gates of hell.

"Do you still figure I lack imagination?" His abductor started up the chainsaw and smiled. "Let me change your mind."

THIRTY-EIGHT

Bored with waiting for Rio to round up the suspects, Kane scanned the files, trying to find a connection between the kills. It was all very well finding items the killer had left behind, but that proved nothing. Sure, the killer could have been involved in the Tate murder and the deaths of the men in the local forest all those years ago, but unless the serial killer was ten years old then, it couldn't have been any of their suspects. It wasn't easy to kill and from what he could find about the brutality of the series of murders, a kid would find it difficult to hide his involvement. The blood spatter in each case would have been significant and the kid had turned up to school each day and carried on as normal. In an adult psychopath he'd expect it, but not a ten-year-old. The idea seemed too remote to consider. He reached for his phone and called Jo. "Hey, Jo, can I bend your ear again?"

"*Sure, what's up?*" Jo sounded interested.

Kane leaned back and stared at the ceiling, his best position to center his thoughts. "Have you ever heard of a serial killer sharing his trophies?"

"*Hmm... not that I recall. I'd doubt they'd share something so precious to them.*"

"That's what I figured." Kane thought for a beat. "How would our current killer have trophies from a historical kill in his possession if he wasn't the killer?"

"Unless he met the historical killer in jail, and he told him about his kills." Jo tapped her fingernails on the desk. *"They do talk about their kills. Maybe the historical killer was dying and disclosed where he'd hidden his trophies, allowing the younger guy to live through the stories."* She sighed. *"I can't think of another reason... ah... unless the killer is the kid and he witnessed the original murders. These men's mutilations are signals of being guilty of a sex crime. Perhaps they were pedophiles?"*

Kane straightened. "And the mother was allowing it to happen?" He stared at the wall thinking. "Perhaps the kid told someone he was being abused and they did something about it, maybe someone who was abused as a kid himself? Maybe the kid took the trophies?"

"Oh yeah, that makes sense." Jo chuckled. *"You think like me—out of the box. Now all you need to do is find the link between the Tate murder and your suspects. I'll ask Kalo to hunt down where little Paul Tate is nowadays. He went into the system, so it might take a while."*

Kane smiled. "Thanks. I'll look forward to hearing from you. Bye for now." He disconnected.

The door opened and Jenna walked in with Emily. He'd do his job as if nothing had happened between them and hope like hell everything would go back to normal.

"We found Kitty Pandora's ring." Emily waved an evidence bag.

"It was just under the foot of Julie's bed, dropped and kicked under." Jenna smiled. "Now we know for sure, whoever killed Kitty was in Julie's room."

The hairs on the back of Kane's neck stood up. This was bad news, but from the smiling faces before him, neither of them had considered the ramifications. "I called Jo before and ran through a few ideas. I wanted her take on how the trophies from a historical case ended up here." He gave them the details of the call to

Jo. "So, if we consider ten-year-old Paul Tate witnessed the kills and took the earrings from a mother who'd allowed him to be abused, it would be enough to turn a susceptible kid into a killer. Now we have Julie, who has triggered the memory of his mother."

"The kid wasn't there. Paul Tate discovered his mother's body after school the following day." Jenna dropped into a chair. "And why Julie and not Emily? They are almost identical, apart from age."

Kane pulled up the image of Diane Tate and looked at the cigarette held between fingers with long red nails. "The blonde hair maybe but look at the fingernails. The combination of hair and red fingernails might have been enough to trigger him or at least make him desire to get closer. His full recollection of his mother would be diminished by time."

"And Julie does have a habit of holding a pen like a cigarette and twirling it in her fingers." Jenna nodded in agreement. "It could be enough, but it doesn't account for how the kid got the earrings."

"He could've taken the earrings from the body when he found her." Emily scanned her files. "It says he told the cops he checked to see if she was alive, so if he had blood on him, they would have discounted it." She looked slowly up at Kane. "Just how much danger is my sister in right now? Maybe we should call Dad to come get her?"

"If she remains in a crowd and we make sure she's never alone, it's safer than trying to negotiate the mountain road." Jenna glanced out the window. "The snow has been relentless and there's another blizzard due to arrive later today. When that blows through, the weather forecast said we'd have freezing temperatures and blue skies for a week or so." She sighed. "As soon as they clear and salt the mountain road, she is out of here. You should leave as well, just in case."

"Then you'd have no forensics team here." Emily gave her a determined stare. "I'm staying. You need me."

Kane's phone buzzed. It was Rio using the landline. "You've been gone over two hours. Couldn't you find our suspects?"

"Not yet. They're all in different places and move around. It's organized chaos down here, but I figure I've located August Bradford, and Bexley Grayson. The girl on the desk said she saw two people heading for the elevator fitting their descriptions not long ago, so I'm guessing they went back to their rooms. Finnian and Rain are in different conference rooms as far as I know. The person on the door doesn't know everyone by sight and people are coming and going all the time to change rooms, use the bathroom, or go outside to smoke." He sighed. *"Do you want me to wait until the current session is finished to grab Finnian and Rain or head up to the rooms, for Grayson and Bradford?"*

Alarm bells went off in Kane's head. "What do you mean by them "going outside to smoke"? Is there a separate balcony area or what?"

"Nope, the manager disabled the alarm on one of the fire doors on the ground floor so they could step outside. There's no smoking inside the lodge."

Kane shook his head in disbelief. "You're saying, we have an unmonitored exit for our killer to move around as he pleases?"

"Seems so." Rio cleared his throat. *"If I go and tell him to reinstate the alarm, and to inform the guests they must go out the front door to smoke, can you clear it with the boss?"*

Annoyed the manager made a significant security change without informing them, Kane sucked in a breath. "Yeah, do it now. He can announce it over the speaker system. Then go and collect Grayson or Bradford. They'll break for lunch soon, and we'll grab the others before the next session. Have you seen Julie?"

"Yeah, I escorted her to one of the halls. She'll be tied up there until lunch."

"Great. Thanks." He replaced the receiver and brought Jenna up to date.

"So, the killer hasn't been using the staff door as we thought. He's just been walking in and out of an unmonitored door. You'd have thought Mr. Brightway would've mentioned it—the idiot." Jenna rolled her eyes. "Going back to Julie being a possible trigger, I figure we have Emily here during the interviews, in sight at least." She collected documents scattered around the desk and sorted them into neat piles. She looked at Emily. "Sit just out of the direct line of their sight and we'll see if you attract any interest."

"You want to use me as bait?" Emily smiled. "Cool." She looked at Kane. "Do I get my own stun gun now?"

"Here." Jenna pulled one out of her jacket pocket. "Take mine. Do you know how to use it?"

"Oh yeah." Emily turned the weapon over on her palms. "I was there when Dave made sure we both knew how to use it, but I hope whoever is killing people doesn't come close enough for me to zap them. What setting is this on?" She peered at the controls. "High looks good to me."

"Be careful. High can kill." Jenna frowned.

"It's kill or be killed if he comes for me." Emily gave her a long unblinking stare. "My dad says if someone attacks me, to show no mercy, for as sure as the sun rises in the morning, they won't be giving me any."

The door opened and Rio walked in with Bexley Grayson. Jenna stood and looked at Kane.

"I'll speak to Mr. Grayson." She waved Grayson toward a desk across the room.

Kane stood and followed her. He had some questions of his own he wanted to ask and sat down. He placed his notebook on the table and pulled out his pen and turned his attention to Jenna. "I'll take notes."

"Thank you for dropping by, Mr. Grayson. Sorry to drag you up here again, but we're speaking to everyone concerning the death of Dakota Storm." Jenna leaned back in her chair. "Have you ever pitched a manuscript to her?"

"You called me away from the conference to ask me if I'd pitched to Miss Storm?" Grayson raised both eyebrows. "If you'd bothered to read my statement, I already told Deputy Rio she rejected me. She wasn't a very nice person, but I didn't kill her."

"Ah yes, so I see." Jenna scanned her files. "But we needed to speak to you again as you were the last person to see Jedidiah Longfellow, alive. Two of your acquaintances, dead within a week. Don't you think that's a little strange?"

"Ha, I can't believe this is your idea of an investigation, or a relevant way to select suspects, Sheriff." Grayson shook his head. "This is a crime writers' convention. Ask anyone of us how to hunt down clues, if you need help. Honestly, Sheriff, there must be at least fifty authors here who have pitched to Miss Storm and just as many knew Jed. He is a bestselling author and has been signing books since he arrived. He suggested I join his critique group. That's a group of authors who help each other by critiquing each other's work. He was a friend and opened doors for me. Why would I kill him?" He leaned back and raised both eyebrows. "I can't think of a single reason anyone would kill him." He looked at his hands and picked at his nails. "Miss Storm maybe, but Jed never."

"Do you know Kitty Pandora?" Jenna's gaze never left his face. "She's an author."

"And was in my critique group, but she left when Miss Storm signed her." Grayson frowned. "I went to her book reading and spoke to her afterward. I offered my congratulations, although she is such a self-centered woman, she looks down her nose at everyone."

"Maybe, but she drowned in her bathtub." Jenna's expression remained neutral. "We have you on CCTV footage heading toward your room when the lights went out. You couldn't have gotten inside your room, so where did you go, Mr. Grayson?"

"I used my phone light and went down the fire escape to the lobby and waited there until the lights went back on." Grayson cleared his throat. "Can I tell you who was there? No, not exactly. It was dark and most people congregated around the fires to keep warm. The heating went off as well, you know."

"So, you knew everyone who was murdered?" Jenna folded her hands on the table. "That's a little more complicated than just a coincidence."

"Like I said, there would be at least thirty people at the conference who knew them all as well." Grayson looked amused. "Why pick me? I'm a small fry in a big pond. There are so many other people here with an ax to grind with most of these people... maybe not Jed. Everyone just loved Jed."

Kane lifted his head from his notes. "Does the name Paul Tate, sound familiar?"

"Tate... Paul Tate... No, I can't recall an author by that name." Grayson shrugged. "Is he dead too?"

"Not that I'm aware." Jenna glanced at her notes. "Do you own a laser pointer?"

"No." Grayson narrowed his gaze. "I've seen them used during the conference. Has one been stolen?"

"I can't say at this time." Jenna glanced at Kane and raised one eyebrow.

After observing Grayson's body language throughout the interview, Kane closed his notebook and looked at Jenna. "I don't have any more questions."

"Okay, sorry to keep you, Mr. Grayson." Jenna stood and offered her hand. "Deputy Rio will see you out."

Kane waited until Grayson had left the room. "He didn't once look over at Em. His overall body language told me he was bored. We annoyed him, that's for sure, but what he said is true. There'd be a ton of people here who have been involved with the victims at one time or another."

"Yet he hasn't got anyone to verify his whereabouts, same as the other three." Jenna stood and went to the coffee maker. "Out of all the people here, those four seem to move around like ghosts." She wrinkled her nose. "Grayson is over the top—heavy fake tan, too white teeth, enough cologne to drown in, and from his face I'd say he has so much Botox pumped into him his expression is frozen. He has no emotion in his eyes at all. Like he didn't care any of those people were victims of horrible crimes."

Nodding, Kane stood and went to her side, pulling clean cups from a tray on the bench. "We didn't faze him. He sure didn't act guilty, but I've seen psychopaths who could convince a cop they were innocent as they were stabbing their next victim. I figure he's still on our watch list." He leaned on the counter as Jenna popped coffee pods into the machine.

"He didn't as much as look at me." Emily opened a box of cookies and looked around with one held in her fingers. "Where's Duke?"

Kane chuckled. "The walk outside in the cold was too much for him. He's in front of the fire in my room." He smiled at her. "Don't worry, he sleeps most of the day. He'll be fine. I'll go and drag him outside again before we have lunch."

"Why don't you take your break now?" Jenna sipped her coffee. "I can handle the interviews."

As they hadn't missed a meal when working together for as long as he could remember, Kane shrugged. If Jenna wanted to play hardball, well he could too. "I'd rather be here so I can observe the body language of the suspects. We're not filming the interviews and this will be a onetime deal." He added cream and sugar to his coffee and snagged a few cookies. "If that's okay with you, ma'am?"

"Okay." Jenna gave him a sideways glance. "I am capable of reading body language, but I know the FBI have one agent watching and one asking questions. I'm guessing we're throwing away gut instinct and doing it by the book now?"

Kane looked up as Rio walked in with August Bradford. The man gave them all a disinterested stare and sat down at the interview table. He turned to Jenna. "He's all yours."

THIRTY-NINE

Jenna took her coffee to the interview table and sat down. "Can I get you a hot beverage, Mr. Bradford?"

"No, just get this over with." August Bradford drummed his fingers on the table. "In case you don't know, we purchase tickets to various events here. I was just heading down to listen to a panel discussing forensics in crime novels. It's an opportunity I didn't want to miss."

Taking her time to open her notebook and find a page, Jenna nodded. "Yes, and I'm aware we have someone in the lodge murdering people." She gave him a hard stare. "I figure my investigation takes priority. You mentioned in your interview that you disliked Dakota Storm. Is that because she rejected your novel?"

"That's *Miss* Storm." Bradford's lip curled at the corner. "Nobody gets to call her Dakota. She is above all us slush pile people, don't you know?"

Bemused, Jenna glanced at Kane. "Slush pile people?" She leaned back. "What does that imply? Is that a derogatory word for the rejected?"

"The unsolicited manuscripts go into what they call a 'slush pile,' and sometimes, authors who've been in the pile actually get a contract, but usually by that time they've gotten themselves an agent or they've given up completely." Bradford steepled his fingers. "Such is the life of an author. We're only as good as the sales of the last book."

"Where were you when the lights went out?" Kane hadn't taken his eyes off Bradford.

"Locked in my room." Bradford rolled his eyes. "Alone." He sighed. "I was in the shower but I managed by my phone light to dry off and get into bed. I slept until the lights came on again, but I just turned them off and went back to sleep. These conventions are exhausting. I was resting in my room before. I broke my toe and only came out of the moon boot last week."

"How well do you know Jedediah Longfellow and Kitty Pandora?" Kane raised one eyebrow.

"They autographed books for me but we didn't say much to each other." Bradford shrugged. "I wouldn't say I knew them."

Jenna checked her notes. "Would those books be their recent releases by any chance? Do you recall the titles?"

"Sure, that would be *Nailed It* and *Frizzled*." Bradford's lips turned up at the edges. "I guess now as both are autographed, they'll be worth more seeing both authors are dead. I'll be sure to wrap them in plastic."

"What about Paul Tate?" Kane looked disinterested. "Know him?"

"Can't say that I do." Bradford's gaze slid across to where Emily was sitting and then moved back to Kane. "What does he write?"

Jenna ignored him. "Just one more thing. Do you own a laser pointer?"

"Yeah, but I don't have it with me. Do you need to borrow one?" Bradford looked amused. "Most of the people on the panels have them. I'd speak to them if you need one."

"Okay, Mr. Bradford, we've held you up long enough." She stood. "Thank you for coming by." She nodded to Rio, who came over and ushered Bradford to the elevator.

After waiting for Rio to return, she looked at Kane. "Get

anything?"

"Yeah, he has an underlying resentment. He steepled his fingers, which is something a person does if they believe they are superior and have the upper hand." Kane rolled his shoulders. "He looked straight at Em when you mentioned Paul Tate."

"He doesn't have an alibi for any of the TODs, same as Grayson." Rio shrugged. "Both seem suspicious to me, but Bradford more so. He might have tipped his hand when he looked at Em. Do you think he might be Paul Tate? He'd be the right age."

Jenna chewed on her pen and, staring into space, gathered her thoughts. "All the male suspects are around thirty but I'm not discounting these murders could've been committed by a woman. None of them took great strength—the victims died where they lay. They're spiteful kills and, trust me, a woman getting even wouldn't hold back. The trouble with this theory is how would she have Diana Tate's earrings in her possession from twenty years ago? Paul had no sisters or aunts and she'd be too old to be his child. I'll talk to Parker Rain after lunch, but the chances of the killer being female is remote." She sighed. "I'm ready to eat as soon as I've updated the files."

"I'll help." Rio sat down at the table.

"As there's nothing left to do here. When you're done, I figure we grab Julie and head down to lunch together." Kane pushed to his feet and pulled on a thick woolen cap with the Black Rock Falls Sheriff's Office logo on the front. "But first, I'm going to walk Duke. When I have him settled, I'll go find Julie. How about I meet you outside the Roasting Hog? We haven't tried that place yet."

"Sure." Jenna stared at him. "Don't let Julie out of your sight."

"Yes, ma'am." Kane touched his hat and headed out the door.

Running a hand through her hair, Jenna caught Rio's strained expression. She cleared her throat. "Don't even think about it." She gave him a sideways glance. "It's taken me years to stop Kane and Rowley from calling me ma'am. He's just doing it to annoy me." She let out a long sigh. "It makes me feel like Whistler's Mother."

FORTY

Cold still lingers in my hands and feet, but the scent of blood has regrettably gone from my nostrils and is replaced with the aroma of gastronomical delights as I line up to enter the Roasting Hog Restaurant for lunch. My heart still races, the effort of dismembering a person harder than I imagined. Even frozen flesh caught in the blade and the kickback when I cut through bone was nothing like sawing through a tree branch. I'm glad my plan was well executed. I chuckle to myself for making a play on words.

The hole in the snow I'd dug made a perfect workplace and, once I'd removed the limbs, I'd covered everything in snow ready for retrieval later. I also used snow to wipe down the chainsaw and then took my time sawing up fallen logs to remove the grease before returning it to the shed. The old man I'd disabled earlier, still lay there, out cold but breathing and the small heater he kept inside his shed would keep him from freezing to death. I had no need to kill him and soon he'd regain consciousness believing he'd had a fall. The bruise on his head from where he hit the floor will convince him.

I still have plans for Riggs. I must admit I gave him the best experience of them all. I had to because he did show interest in me toward the end. Pity the die was cast or I may have forgiven him, but it's not my place to forgive, and when I decide on a path, I never take a step back. Not as a kid, not now. I'll never forget the look in his eyes when I held up one of his feet and then the other. Did he know he was living a scene from the novel he crowed about and went the extra mile to promote for the best deal? Did he understand why he must die? You see, the story had a major flaw. The author concentrated on the cop's angle the entire story, and I couldn't believe the killer's enjoyment wasn't even a consideration. To me, that makes a boring crime story, and it only came close to the truth when the cop had to face down the psychopath. Now that part excited me.

I listen with interest to the announcements. They mention the times of the afternoon sessions and the closure of the emergency exit door for smokers. My fingers close around the passkey in my pocket. I don't need the door open any longer. When everyone is asleep, I'll be on the move again, setting up a wonderful surprise. I must finish the story, and then take time to indulge myself in a fantasy that haunts my dreams. The cravings are becoming over-powering, but I smile as I'm ushered to a seat. I join a group of people from my critique group. They understand me and, apart from Jed, not one of them made my list. This alone proves I can control my urges, as most like me would kill them all and this alone makes me special. My gaze scans the room and rests on a blonde head. My hand trembles as her long red nails comb through her white-blonde glossy hair. She will be my ultimate reward and I must concentrate hard on keeping control, but seeing her so close makes my heart race. Right now, nothing else matters but Julie.

FORTY-ONE

It was like eating in the middle of a flock of geese. Jenna winced as a woman sitting at the next table screamed with laughter and almost spilled her glass of wine. It seemed the convention was two weeks of continuous celebration. She rolled her eyes at Kane. "They sure know how to party."

"The ball on the last day is on my 'not to be missed' list that's for sure, and I have a ticket." Julie grinned. "I hope you're coming."

Jenna leaned back in her seat and sighed. "The ball is the last thing on my mind right now."

"I hope we find the killer before the convention ends." Rio eyed her over the rim of a glass of soda. "You'll have one hell of a time keeping people locked up here once their stay is over. Do you figure the mayor will meet the costs of all these people if you insist they stay? The forecast is for clear skies after the next blizzard. They won't believe the roads are blocked."

Shaking her head, Jenna attacked her slice of Black Forest cake. Her appetite was ferocious of late. "If we can't catch this killer in the next ten days, when he is locked up right under our noses, I'm quitting." She glanced around the table. "I called Bobby Kalo before and he has nothing on Paul Tate after he left foster care. He is checking other states, but unless he has priors, we'll never find him."

"He could have changed his name." Kane added cream to his cherry pie. "Has Kalo looked into that angle?"

Jenna swallowed and nodded. "Yeah, but there are a ton of men by that name in the States."

"What if he didn't change his name... as in legally." Julie's eyes twinkled with excitement. "We're at an author's conference. What if he's using a pen name? Many of the authors here are using their pen names. Kitty Pandora's real name is Doris Slaughter. She's married to an IT company director by the name of Ed Slaughter."

Jenna stared long and hard at Kane and then moved her attention to Rio. "I have two of the most intelligent deputies in the state, and you didn't think about checking out people's pen names? Really? What's happening here?"

"I was concentrating on the crimes and trying to link them to the suspects." Rio looked taken aback. "I'm doing my best. I've never seen such diversity in crime scenes before—what we're dealing with here is one of a kind."

"They're all one-of-a-kind murders in Black Rock Falls." Kane continued to eat. "We're constantly having to look outside the box to catch a killer." He slid his attention to Jenna. "I'm aware some of the authors here are under pen names. That is why I made a point of asking the suspects if they knew Paul Tate. I'd expect some kind of reaction if it was their real name. I also asked Mr. Brightway to check for the name in his records. If anyone is using a credit card under that name, he'll let us know."

Jenna raised both eyebrows. "And you decided not to inform me about this part of the investigation?"

"It was a fail-safe, Jenna." Kane pushed his plate away. "Paul Tate isn't a suspect in the homicides here as far as we're aware. The cops had no reason to believe he was involved in the deaths of his mom and the two men twenty years ago. They have him staying with a friend around the times of all the murders. From what I read from the files, he often spent the entire weekend at his friend Peter

Burrows's home, going there after school and not returning home until the following Monday. From the report, Mrs. Burrows believed Paul's homelife with a single mother wasn't very nice and welcomed him to her home." He shrugged. "It's all in the files, if you get time to read them." He held up his hand as the waitress walked by and ordered a pot of coffee.

"I've read the files, but I was searching for a clue to link him to one of our suspects." Jenna pushed both hands through her hair. "I'll leave you and Rio to handle the last two interviews. I'm going to hunt down Peter Burrows and his parents and see if he can shed any light on Paul Tate."

"Sure, but Burrows doesn't know where Paul is. Kalo already called him to find out Paul Tate's last known address." Kane refilled his cup from the pot the waitress had placed on the table and added cream and sugar. "Kalo has Burrows's details. Do you want me to call him?"

Jenna pulled out her phone. "No, I'll send him a message."

The reply came back in seconds and Jenna glanced at Kane. "I'll call Mr. Burrows soon. He'll be at work and he's an accountant. With luck, he might have time to speak to me."

"Sounds like a plan." Kane sipped his coffee.

"Now you two have stopped bickering." Emily rolled her eyes at Jenna. "When this is all over, the killer is behind bars, and the blizzard is a bad memory, I hope you'll come shopping for a ballgown with me and Julie." She grinned. "Now dad has a chopper, he said if the weather was clear, he'd fly us to Helena for the day. He has business there next Friday... something about a medical examiners' meeting or something. Come on, Jenna, live a little. You wear jeans all year round. It will be fun to get our hair styled and dress up for a change."

Unable to stop smiling at Emily's infectious giggle, she nodded. "Okay, but so far we don't have a clue who is murdering people. We could be still chasing him down at Easter."

After lunch, Jenna sent the others on their way and went back to her room. She needed a quiet place to speak to Peter Burrows.

She made the call and after stating her business had the usual obligatory wait as the receptionist kept her on hold for fifteen minutes. When Burrows came on the line, he seemed to be pleased to speak to her. "Good afternoon, Mr. Burrows. I'm sure you're wondering why I'm contacting you after so many years about the murders out of Black Ridge."

"At the time, nobody listened to me." Burrows's concern came through the tone in his voice. *"I was just a kid. I'm a little younger than Paul. I was nine at the time his mom died."*

Jenna made notes. "Did he stay at your home often?"

"Yeah, as often as his mom would allow him." Burrows sighed. *"At the time, I didn't understand what was going on, but now I look back on it, all the signs were there."*

Intrigued, Jenna grabbed the recording device out of her kit and put her phone on speaker. "Signs of what exactly?"

"Abuse. Paul was a choirboy, he had the voice of an angel. He loved to sing and then suddenly he didn't. He went from being excited about choir practice to running and hiding in the woods to avoid going." Burrows cleared his throat. *"I was at his house one time and his mother had a friend around. She'd been drinking. She sent me home and the man dragged Paul to his room. I figured at the time Paul was getting a whooping for misbehaving. He never said a word to me about anything, but looking back I'm convinced his mother allowed men to abuse him, including the local clergy."*

Appalled, Jenna sucked in a breath, the question hovering on her lips. "Do you think he was capable of killing his mom?"

"I really can't say." Burrows cleared his throat. *"It's something that has played on my mind for years. I never knew what happened to Paul after the cops took him away. He never contacted me."*

"Okay." Jenna chewed on her bottom lip. "How well do you recall the night his mom died?"

"Like it was yesterday." Burrows lowered his voice. *"I recall he was staying with us. He was sleeping in my room when the cops found the priest and the other guy in the woods as well. This is where I get confused. He was just a kid, so at first it never entered*

my mind he might have killed them. At the time, I was never sure if I was dreaming or had made a mistake about things but the more I think on it, the more I'm sure he was somehow involved."

Heart thundering with excitement, Jenna leaned closer to listen. "How so?"

"Well, the cops spoke to his mom because they'd seen her in a bar with the first guy. He's the one I saw taking Paul upstairs to his room. The next time Paul slept over, he told me he'd told the cops he'd seen a scruffy guy hanging around the woods, a biker maybe. He was super excited, like he was playing a game or something—like he'd tricked them." Burrows paused a beat. *"This is where things get muddled in my head. You see, I'm not sure if I was dreaming, but I remember waking on three occasions and seeing his bed empty. At the time, I figured Paul was using the bathroom, but at one time, he went to bed in green PJs and the next morning woke up in yellow ones. That was the night his mom died, and when I think back, the reason I remember the nights he wasn't there is because the cops came to our house the next day to find out if Paul was staying with us."*

Mind spinning, Jenna checked to make sure the recorder was still working. "So, what do you think happened?"

"I figure Paul could have murdered them all." Burrows's voice sounded strained. *"There's something else. My mom had one of those knives with the sheath that sharpens them when you push it in and out... know the kind? Well, she yelled at me for touching it because it went missing and showed up in the wrong drawer. I think he used the knife to kill them all."* He blew out a long breath. *"Think about it... if those guys were pedophiles and Paul wanted to lure them into the woods, trust me, he was smart enough to do it. He had this way about him that made everyone believe he was an angel, but in truth he manipulated people. I can see it as clear as day the way he used to talk to my folks to allow him to stay all weekend."*

Jenna rubbed her temples. "The autopsy report says his mom was murdered in her bed. I guess a kid of that age was more than capable of slitting her throat. But two grown men? How is this possible?"

"I heard they were mutilated." Burrows' voice seemed to faulter. *"Maybe you should read the autopsy reports and seriously consider what could have been happening to a ten-year-old in the woods. I figure he went home and cleaned up after he killed them, showered, changed. He probably tossed his bloody clothes into a dumpster along the way and then crept back into my house."*

Jenna nodded to herself. "And you've never heard from him or seen him since?"

"Nope." Burrows's chair creaked. *"Not a word. He could be dead for all I know."*

"Okay." Jenna stared at the red blinking light on the recorder. "That's very interesting. I'll send you photos of a few men. Could you see if you recognize any of them as Paul?" She sent the images of her male suspects.

"It's been a long time." Burrows sighed. *"Sorry, none of them look like Paul."*

Jenna chewed on her bottom lip thinking. "Just one more thing. Did you ever see Paul with any of his mother's jewelry?"

"Funny you should say that." Burrows brightened. *"The morning the cops came around to tell him she'd died. He didn't cry or anything. He just stared into space. When they informed him he couldn't go back to the house, they asked him if he wanted anything of his mother's. He shook his head, but when they left, he said he had a remembrance of her and showed me a pair of earrings."*

"Hang on." Jenna sent him the image of the earrings they'd found at two crime scenes. "Did they look like this?"

"They sure did." Burrows sounded intrigued. *"That's them. Where did they show up?"*

Staring at her phone, Jenna shook her head. "I wish I could tell you. Right now, they're evidence in an ongoing investigation. I really appreciate your help. Would you sign a statement, if I write this up?"

"Sure, but it's only recollections of a kid. I'm not sure it will hold up in court." Burrows sounded confused.

Jenna couldn't believe her luck. "It's just for the record. Thank you so much for your time. I'll be in touch."

"Anytime." Burrows disconnected.

Jenna stood, her mind swimming with the implications of the conversation. "Well, Paul Tate, whoever you are now, you're a walking time bomb and you just became my prime suspect." She hurried out the door and headed for the elevator.

FORTY-TWO

Kane listened with interest to the recording. "That's the making of a psychopath if what he says is true, but none of this proves Paul Tate is our guy. We're going on the recollections of a nine-year-old."

"Kids do remember things. I sure do, but then I do have a different type of memory than most." Rio chewed on his pen. "Do you remember significant things?"

Too many things. Kane nodded. "Yeah, my memory is real good. I can remember learning how to walk and sitting in my highchair trying to push food into my mouth."

"Good for you." Jenna leaned on her hand. "I remember falling off a swing, but that's not helping the investigation. Is Paul Tate one of our suspects?"

Kane shrugged. "It's impossible to know, if he's been living under an alias for years."

When a knock came on the door, Kane stood and headed to answer it. "That will be Parker Rain. She's a literary agent, so if she's the killer, then it shoots all our theories to hell. She's not Tate, is not related to him, that's her real name, and she doesn't fit any of our revenge or jealousy motives." He turned to look at Jenna walking backward. "Em didn't get a vibe from her, so we might be able to remove her from our list."

"Emily does a fine job, but she doesn't have your experience, Dave." Jenna looked up from her notes. "Dig deep and see what shows."

"Do you still want me to stay over here during the interviews?" Emily took her coffee back to her seat.

"Yeah." Kane smiled at her. "We have Finnian next."

After showing Parker Rain to a chair, Kane sat down beside Rio opposite her. He'd found Rio to be an astute interviewer and he had the ability to keep everyone's answers in his head for comparison, which came in useful. "Thanks for coming by. There're just a few things we need to ask you. From the previous interview you mentioned an animosity toward Dakota Storm. Could you please expand on the reasons?"

"Do you mean, was it reason enough to kill her?" Rain smiled broadly. "If I was a psychopath, yeah, I think that would trigger me into an episode of destruction, but I'm a businesswoman and I have to accept that I lose out on some deals. It's just with Miss Storm, well, she was a piece of work. Now she's dead, I figure the author she snapped up from under my nose will find his way back to me."

Kane narrowed his gaze on her. "So, you had a motive to kill her?"

"Yeah, well I suppose I did... but I didn't." Rain shrugged. "Although I admit it does look suspicious. Hell, it would make a great plot for a story. Agent kills agent over a client."

"Okay." Kane exchanged a meaningful glance with Jenna. "Do you think the ending would be the same? Miss Storm drowned in the pool outside her chalet."

"More like, did she slip or was she pushed?" Rain's full lips curled into a satisfied smile. "Rumor has it there was a pen involved? Do tell me where they shoved it?"

On full alert, Kane leaned back and observed her for a beat. Had he read this woman all wrong? Not a soul outside their team knew about the pen. "What pen is that?"

"Oh, I overheard it on my travels. Someone mentioned something about her favorite gold pen being involved." Rain examined her nails. "I don't recall who said it. Do you have any idea how many people speak to me at a conference? Hundreds." She rolled her eyes dramatically. "Every one of them wants to pitch a story to me, insisting their story is the next bestseller." She threw both hands in the air. "Do you have any idea how many actually have an idea that will sell? Less than one percent. Honestly, I know how long people labor over writing stories and I appreciate the time they take, but if they don't have the ability to write, nothing I can do will sell it."

The woman was doing a classic time-wasting ploy and she was darn good at it. Kane leaned forward on the desk and eyeballed her. "Can we cut to the chase? What exactly did Dakota Storm do to outmaneuver you in the deal with Joel Stanley. I already know he is the author of the novel in question."

"I'd already informed him that I'd like him to sign with me." Rain picked imaginary fluff from her sweater. "I sent him a contract. Next thing I know, she has his novel in an auction. Joel called me and told me she'd offered to take a lower commission, and as she has such a great reputation for making deals, he went with her."

Kane cleared his throat. "At least he told you."

"Yeah, and that's why I've already called him about signing with me now that she's dead." Rain smiled. "I'm not giving anyone else a chance."

"Have you heard of a person by the name of Paul Tate?" Rio looked up from taking notes.

"Paul Tate?" Rain blinked a few times and then shrugged. "Maybe. I do recall an author who pitched to me by that name... he used a pen name but I can't remember what that was. His name was Paul Tate. Why?"

Interested Kane leaned forward and examined her reaction. "Would you be able to find his details in your records?"

"I have no idea." Rain gave him an appalled look. "It could

have been at any of the conventions. I only keep the details of the people I'm interested in reading their work. I'm sure if he impressed me, I'd have read his manuscript and remembered his name. I could give my PA a call and ask her to look through my files, but I don't like your chances."

"If you wouldn't mind and then get back to me if you find anything, I'd appreciate it." Rio handed her his card with a smile. "Call me anytime."

Not quite finished, Kane smiled at her. "Just one more question. Do you own a laser pointer?"

"Yeah." Rain shrugged. "I need it for the discussions." She stared at him. "They're not weapons... well, unless you point them at aircraft. Now that would make an interesting plot, wouldn't it?"

"I think it's been done before." Kane pushed to his feet. "We've held you up long enough. Thanks for your help." He walked to the door and waited for Parker Rain to follow him. "Just one more thing. Do you know Jedidiah Longfellow and Kitty Pandora?"

"I've met them, yes." Rain leaned against the wall, her eyes flitting in all directions but refusing to meet his gaze. "I often speak to the bestselling authors and hand them my card. It's good business." She raised both eyebrows. "Every day is a competition in my world."

The cab arrived and Kane waited for her to step into the elevator and then walked back into the suite. He leaned both hands on the table and sighed. "Wow!"

"Yeah, she'd score high on the Hare Psychopathy Checklist." Jenna was scrolling through her notes. "I'm not discounting her yet. She's young and strong and quite capable of killing in my opinion."

Emily's phone buzzed and she frowned at the text. "Julie's bored, and once she's done this session, she's skipping the next forum." She stood and looked at Kane. "I need some fresh air. I'll take Julie with me. Do you want me to take Duke out for a run?"

"Sure." Kane fished his keycard out of his pocket and handed it to her. "He'll need his coat. Why don't you bring him up here when you're done? He'd enjoy the company."

"I'll ride down with her." Rio stood and grabbed his coat. "It will be safer."

"Then go with them but don't go too far." Jenna looked up from her screen. "We can handle Murphy Finnian."

FORTY-THREE

It had been a really weird day for Julie. She had the prickly feeling of being watched, and after heading for a quiet place, she'd called Emily, all the while feeling someone's eyes following her every move. She'd returned reluctantly to the hall, but it seemed she'd grown a second sense for danger since moving to Black Rock Falls. She thought she'd gotten used to living in a crazy world, but obviously she hadn't. It seemed that day-to-day life changed so swiftly she never really knew for sure what would happen next. Would life ever return to normal? Could she reach her goal of becoming a pediatrician? It seemed such a long way off and with so many obstacles in the way. As she'd grown older, the harder life became and being an adult wasn't what she'd thought it would be at all. If it wasn't for her dad, going the extra mile and keeping her interested in her studies, she might have fallen by the wayside. Pushing her worries aside, she glanced around the hall. It was nice being with her friends at the conference, but the hairs on the back of her neck rose again, followed by the need to turn around. When she did, she saw people, smiling faces most times—so what was spooking her?

She tried to immerse herself in the lecture but the awful feeling someone was watching her just wouldn't go away. Apologizing to her friends, she stood and made her way to the door.

Waiting inside the entrance, she scrolled through the selfies she'd taken with her friends and various authors. Her stomach dropped as she scanned six or seven images and then noticed the same person photobombing each shot. She went back to the previous day and there in the background was the figure again. It was as if the person had pulled up their hoodie and turned their back when she'd taken the image. It seemed too much of a coincidence the person was in every shot. She lifted her gaze from the screen and scanned the room. There must have been twenty or so people wearing sweaters with hoods. It was warm in the conference rooms but not warm enough to go without a sweater. She shivered. Was the person who'd broken into her room stalking her? Did he want her to know he was close by, close enough to touch her?

Fingers trembling, she slid the phone into her pocket and pushed her iPad into her backpack. She'd been buying a new book almost every day, having it autographed and collecting all the handouts from the authors and booksellers. Her backpack was filled to the brim. Her heart lifted at the sight of Emily and Zac at the door. She hurried to them and after bending to greet Duke, thrust her phone at Emily. "Look, the same person in each shot. Do you think that's a stalker?"

"Maybe, or someone having a joke." Emily frowned. "This is why you can't risk being alone. Dave doesn't think that person in your room is the killer or you'd be dead. There's no motive to kill you. All the murders are aimed toward people in the publishing business and you're a student."

"I hope the creepy guy or whoever in your room was just a peeping Tom." Rio walked beside her. "If he is this person in your pictures, yeah, you should be worried, but I very much doubt either of them would risk attacking you when you're surrounded by people. You also have your stun gun, but if you see anyone following you, run into a crowd. If you get left behind in the bathroom, wait and call Emily rather than risk walking through the passages alone during the sessions."

"You're coming upstairs with us as soon as we've walked

Duke." Emily's mouth had turned down. "I figure you need to show these images to Jenna. She'll know what to do."

FORTY-FOUR

After updating her files, Jenna called the office. As she was
expecting Maggie to pick up, Rowley's voice surprised her. "Hi,
Jake. It's Jenna. Is anything wrong? I thought you'd be taking a few
personal days to get the twins settled."

*"No need. Sandy's parents have moved into the ranch to help
out. I came in to relieve Walters."* Rowley sighed. *"Everything is
under control here, just the usual fender benders in the snow. Most
folks are staying home, apart from dashing into town for supplies
when the snowplows go through."*

Jenna stood and paced the room, stopping to peer out the
window at the relentless snowfall. "How is Sandy? Are the twins
doing, okay?"

"She's exhausted." Rowley cleared his throat. *"She insists on
feeding them herself and it's a ton of work. They're hungry all the
time, and Doc Brown suggested we supplement them with a bottle,
but they won't take it and get so upset."* He sighed. *"This is why I'm
at work. I can manage the diaper thing just fine, but I can't help
feeding them. Her mom has this knack of getting them back to sleep,
and once the chores are done, I'm just getting in the way."*

Having no experience with babies, Jenna sucked in a breath.
"I'm sure Sandy appreciates you being there, Jake. I know it's

stressful, but they'll settle soon." She thought for a beat. Maggie the receptionist was very capable and lived within walking distance to the office. "As it's quiet in town, why don't you leave the office to Maggie? She has Walters, Webber, and even Wolfe close by to call in an emergency."

"*I guess.*" Rowley sounded reluctant. "*The snowplow has been keeping the road out my way clear. So, I could get here if needs be.*"

Jenna nodded to herself. "That's good. Did they clear the road to the hospital?"

"*Yeah, the main problem was a snowplow was blocking the road. It had gotten stuck in a drift. It was so high the snowplow was completely hidden. It took some time but they cleared the road. The snowplows are running twenty-four hours a day. Plus, we have locals using their own to help clear some of the side roads.*" Rowley cleared his throat. "*It's a friendly town, apart from the serial killers. Do you have any suspects yet?*"

"Four, but whoever is doing this changes their MO for each kill." Jenna went back to her desk and sat down. "They are trapped here right under our noses and it's like trying to catch smoke." She turned as Kane's phone buzzed and he moved away to take the call. "I have another interview to do. You get on home and I'll call again when we get things sorted here."

"*You'll catch the killer.*" Rowley chuckled. "*You can catch smoke but you just need to think about it some more.*"

Jenna smiled. "Okay, I will. Chat soon." She disconnected and looked at Kane.

"Thanks, Bobby." Kane closed his phone and turned to Jenna. "It may be nothing but August Bradford and Bexley Grayson were adopted. The records for their real parents are sealed and even Kalo can't hack the files. This would tell me they came from a family involved in a crime. Either of them could be the son of a psychopath or witnessed horrendous crimes as a child. They're using the names their adoptive parents gave them on their driver's licenses and taxes. One of them could be Paul Tate, but being ten-years-old at the time, they'd still remember their real name and that they'd been adopted. These things don't happen overnight. They could've spent some years in foster care before their adoption. This being the case, we should've got a reaction from them when the name was mentioned. It would have triggered an instant recollection and they didn't as much as blink."

Jenna considered his words for a few moments. "What if they're suffering from traumatic amnesia? Chances are they don't remember their old life at all and it would account for why Paul Tate never contacted his best friend."

"Normally I'd say this was a possibility but it doesn't add up on three counts." Kane rested one hip on the edge of the desk. "The killer might have been traumatized after the first kill, but he killed twice more. He took trophies and he remembers his mother—because why else would he stalk Julie?" He rolled his shoulders and cricked his neck. "Why would he risk speaking to his friend? That's the one person he wouldn't want remembering details. Tate would know his old friend had seen things that could bring him down. He'd be hoping everything from that time would've been long forgotten."

Jenna rubbed her temples. "So, if Murphy Finnian isn't Paul Tate, we're back to square one."

"Only if we're making the assumption that Paul Tate is the killer." Kane scratched his chin. "He stabbed and mutilated his victims and not one of our current murders fits his MO. I think as Tate's is a historical case, we should keep him as an alternative killer until we have more evidence. Yeah, we have earrings belonging to his mom, but that's all. Like Jo said, our killer might have known Paul Tate at one time."

Thinking of every possible angle, Jenna moved her attention slowly back to Kane. "Unless the killer planted the evidence? Think about it. What if the killer did know that Paul Tate murdered his mother and used the earrings to confuse us? If they did, they sure put up a massive smokescreen."

A loud knock came on the door.

"Maybe." Kane glanced toward the noise. "And if it isn't Paul

Tate, then taking your theory into account, it could just as easily be Parker Rain." He walked over to see who was there. "Ah, Mr. Finnian, thanks for dropping by. Take a seat."

"I thought we'd been through all this before." Finnian sat down with an exasperated expression on his face and placed his briefcase at his feet. "What on earth do you want with me now?"

Jenna smoothed the pages of her notebook and met Finnian's gaze. "Three people have died, Mr. Finnian, and you are one of four people who can't verify their whereabouts at the time of the deaths. Four people out of everyone here, so you see we need to eliminate possible suspects."

"Do I need my lawyer?" Finnian leaned back in the chair, elbows resting on the arms and hands clenched as if he were praying.

"You're not under arrest." Kane sat relaxed in an unthreatening pose, his face almost expressionless. "We're trying to establish a timeline for each of the deceased and we need to know if you crossed paths is all. We're gathering all the information we can find."

"Honestly, if this is part of an elaborate hoax, I'll be sending you a bill for my time." Finnian shook his head. "This is a business trip for me, this is where I find new clients."

Jenna nodded. "I wish it were a game, but it's not." She lifted her pen and looked at him. "I'm sure you're aware of the names of the people involved by now. We've been tracking their whereabouts before their deaths and it seems all of them were in plain sight almost up to the time they died. This is very unusual, which leads us to believe they all knew their killers. So, Mr. Finnian, let's take this one at a time. Did you know Kitty Pandora?"

"I've never actually met her, but she pitched to me at one time." Finnian bent and fished a tablet from his briefcase. "I only remember her name because when her book was published, I recalled the title. I rejected her submission." He scrolled through his tablet. "Ah yes, I liked her story but she had nothing else to offer. I don't work with one-hit wonders; I prefer to represent someone with a ton of ideas."

"Are you sure you didn't run into her here? She did do a reading of her book, I believe." Kane made a few notes.

"Very sure. Like I said, I've never met her." Finnian sighed. "Next."

The aggravation poured off Finnian like a thick fog. "Dakota Storm?"

"Everyone in this business knows Miss Storm." He drummed his fingers on the desk. "In fact, most of the agents at the conference know each other. Many of us move from one agency to the next as we learn the business."

Interested more by the insights of the publishing business by the day, Jenna lifted her chin. "Has she ever undercut you in a deal?"

"Trust me, she's undercut everyone." Finnian barked a laugh. "She is the queen of the deal. I've lost clients to her. Everyone has. It wasn't worth killing her for. There are hidden gems everywhere, but admittedly, with her out of the picture it will level the playing field a little."

"Okay." Kane looked up from his notes. "While you have your files open. Do you recall anyone by the name of Paul Tate?"

Finnian gave a slight shake of his head but his eyes remained fixed on the screen. Jenna chewed on her bottom lip. Was this a tell? She exchanged a glance with Kane but couldn't read his expression. After some moments had passed without Finnian saying a word, she leaned forward. "Well, Mr. Finnian. Have you had any contact with Paul Tate?"

"No, I have not." Finnian straightened. "At least he's not in my current records. He could have pitched to me. I have thousands of authors pitching to me by email each week, not to mention the current conventions around the country. I do represent a variety of genres not just crime."

"I see." Jenna sighed. They weren't getting much information from him. "What about Jedidiah Longfellow?"

"Yes, I've met Jed." Finnian placed his tablet on the desk and leaned back in the chair. "He was one of the clients Miss Storm managed to tear from my clutches, but he did have a ton of offers." He stared at the wall and shook his head slowly. "We could have made a great team. I would have guided him to a greatness Miss Storm could have only imagined." His attention shifted back to Jenna. "To think that talent is gone. Such a waste, such a waste."

A sudden thought grasped Jenna. "Do you know August Bradford, Parker Rain, or Bexley Grayson?"

"Parker, yes. I know her quite well. She's an agent, and August Bradford and Bexley Grayson pitched to me here at the conference." Finnian opened his hands wide. "Have I made them an offer? No, not as yet. I gave them my card and they'll be forwarding the first three chapters of their manuscripts. They sounded reasonably interesting, but talking the talk isn't walking the walk, is it?"

Unable to think of any more questions to ask, Jenna looked at Kane. "Do you have any further questions?"

"I've seen some of the presentations and noted with interest that many of the presenters use laser pointers during their sessions." Kane was scrutinizing Finnian and had his combat face front and center. "Do you own one?"

"Yeah, most of us do if we're using the screen with examples." Finnian shrugged. "It's nothing unusual. Why?"

"No reason." Kane made a note and then closed his book. "That's all we need for now. Thank you for your time." He stood and walked Finnian to the door and out to the elevator.

The elevator doors opened, Jenna heard Julie's voice and she looked up to see Rio, Emily, and Julie spill into the hallway. They came inside and Julie rushed over to her. The girl looked wide-eyed and concerned. "Is something wrong?"

"Yeah, I think someone is stalking me." Julie dropped into the chair Finnian had vacated and explained.

Concerned, Jenna listened with interest. "Show me the selfies."

She flicked through the image files and handed the phone to Kane. "That's creepy."

"Yeah." Kane's eyes narrowed as he looked at the screen. "Maybe I should sleep on the sofa in your room until we catch this guy."

"I will." Rio leaned on the table. "You'll never fit on that sofa. Don't worry, I'll keep them safe."

Anxiety gripped Jenna's stomach. "As soon as we can get you down the mountain, we will." She held a hand up to stop the protest she could see forming on Julie's lips. "In the meantime, one of us will be with you at all times."

"That's crazy." Julie's eyes blazed. "Okay to and from the conference like now, but please don't make me look like a kid in front of my friends. Come on, I have to go to school with these guys." She looked from Jenna to Kane. "Do you honestly think the killer will try and hurt me in a crowd of people? Look I'll even sit between my friends—okay? If I see anyone with a hoodie close by, I'll move away."

Jenna shook her head. "I don't like it, but as you're legally an adult, I can't make you do anything. But we all just want to keep you safe." She looked at Julie's distraught expression. "Okay, inside the halls, we'll leave you be, but one of us will be there to walk you to your next session. We'll try not to be noticeable but will be close by just in case. It's not just you. Emily isn't going anywhere alone either."

"Thank you." Julie gave her a hug and then hugged Kane. "You're the best."

Jenna shook her head. "I hope I don't live to regret this."

"So do I." Kane grimaced. "In case it slipped your mind, all of our suspects were wearing hoodies."

FORTY-FIVE

Excitement grips me as I check the digital readout on the bedside clock radio. It's a little after three and I haven't been able to sleep as my mind plans the next move. The fact the sheriff is aware I'm using a laser pointer to disable the cameras is challenging, but with so many of them being used at the conference, she'll never suspect me. I've dressed in black, a woolen cap pulled down low to cover my hair, a hoodie arranged over the top, to make a shadow fall across my face. I wear leather gloves but will snag a pair of the big rubber gloves from the kitchen supplies to cover them as before. They're so accommodating here and seem to supply everything I need. My room is off the main corridor, away from the CCTV camera beside the elevator, and another bonus is the hotel doors are recessed. The resulting shadow offers me protection as I head for the stairs, out of sight of anyone passing by. Once I reach the lobby, I'll use the door to conceal me, when I aim the laser pointer at the camera. Then I'll be free to move around undetected for at least two hours before returning to my room by retracing my steps.

I'm breathing heavily as I push the release on the fire door and peek into the lobby. The lights are dimmed and only small down-lights add a soft glow to the passageways. I aim my laser, watch the flash in the camera and, making sure my hood is pulled well down, ease out into the shadows. The myriad of human smells congeals in the heat from the ever-present log fires. I stop as the flames lure me closer, bringing back vivid memories of sins as a child. I enjoyed lighting fires and watching hunting cabins crackle, flames licking the sky and igniting the forest but I paid my penance after confessing my sins. My mom made sure of it but I must never tell.

All is quiet. With so much snow, everything is silent once night descends; the guests go back to their rooms and then the mad rush of cleaners come out like elves to work from midnight until three, but all are gone by now. The next shift will be the bakers, who arrive at four each morning. I've watched and learned their shifts. I've a short time to do what I must for the maximum effect. I'm through the door to the kitchens and drop my passkey into the box and select another before making a mental note of the new security code on the blackboard by the door. I smile to myself—1 3 1 3 would be funny if I were superstitious. After helping myself to a pair of thick black rubber gloves and changing my shoes for one of the pairs of rubber boots in the mudroom, I head for the door. My thick socks will protect me from the cold. As I reach the exit, I hear someone cough and pull the knife from my belt. This wasn't part of my plan. There's no time to think. I step inside the broom closet, ease in beside the buckets and brooms, and then pull the door closed just enough so I can peek through a crack.

Outside I hear voices, a man and a woman speaking in hushed tones. They shuffle past me, bringing the smell of the outdoors with them and trailing snow from outside, leaving wet footprints on the clean floor. How marvelously convenient. My heart pounds as they enter the kitchen but I wait and watch. Disposing of them would be a distraction and spreading their entrails across the kitchen floor an amusing idea, but it wouldn't further my cause. I let out a silent sigh as they hurry past me, their arms laden with food supplies. They slip out the back door blissfully unaware how close they came to death. If they'd seen me, I'd have killed them and not given them a second thought, but then my plans would've been spoiled. I give them time to move away before I grab a potato sack from the pile beside the door and head outside. I'm smiling as my flashlight bobs through the forest. I have all I need to collect a few of the better chapters of Quentin Riggs and drag them back to the lodge.

As I inhale, the cold hits my lungs in a bolt of pain, but the smell of the tall pines is fresh and invigorates me. Snowflakes touch my cheeks like angel's kisses in a welcome. I am one with the snow. It protects me, covers my tracks, and has kept all my adversaries from leaving before I'd taken my revenge. It will be a memorable night's work and I won't need an alibi, for not a soul has even noticed Riggs is missing. I chuckle. "Well, Sheriff, good luck at working out the time of death. It will be next March before you find the rest of him, unless the bears find him first."

FORTY-SIX

Hammering on the door shocked Jenna awake. Grabbing her Glock and leaping out of bed, she checked the peephole. Mr. Brightway, his face ashen, was out in the hallway wearing a dressing gown. She threw open the door the same time as Kane burst out of the next room and Rio appeared in the doorway of the girl's room. "What's wrong?" Jenna lowered her weapon.

"There's a head in the kitchen freezer." Brightway leaned on the wall and dry-retched.

Horrified but drawing on her professional calm, Jenna sucked in a breath. "Okay, Mr. Brightway. Who found the body?"

"The baker, Jeromy Eton." Brightway visibly tried to keep control. "He called me and I went to look. I thought it must have been a prank."

Jenna frowned. "Where are the rest of your staff?"

"The bakers arrive early, make the dough and leave it to rise, and then have breakfast before they return to bake the loaves." Brightway rubbed both hands down his face. "They're in the dining room. I told them to leave at once and go there."

"Does it look like the victim was killed in the kitchen?" Kane gave Brightway's arm a shake. "There would be blood everywhere, signs of a struggle."

"N- no." Brightway straightened, gathering himself. "Someone tracked snow into the kitchen, there are footprints to the storeroom but nothing else. The baker just thought it was people stealing again. We've had food going missing for weeks. We believe it's staff members, but we've not worried too much. I do supply their meals, after all." He shuddered. "Oh, Jesus help me, I can't stop seeing it. The eyes are wide open... just staring." He heaved again and covered his mouth.

Swallowing the bile creeping up the back of her throat, Jenna looked at Rio. "Stay here with Julie and go tell Em we need her." She looked at Kane. "Get dressed and we'll go take a look."

"It's four in the morning." Emily stepped into the hallway. "What on earth is happening now?"

Jenna explained. "Wait here, Mr. Brightway. We'll be with you in a few minutes." She hurried inside to dress.

Pleased to see Emily had rallied to the call in an instant, she touched her arm as they stepped into the elevator. "This sounds brutal. Will you be okay? You're not fully qualified to take this on. I'll understand if you refuse."

"After what I saw in the James Stone case, I can handle a severed frozen head." Emily rolled her eyes. "If I were squeamish, I wouldn't want to be a medical examiner. This sort of thing doesn't upset me. I just want to find out what happened to them. I can process the scene as well as Dad, but you'll need to keep the body on ice, preferably in situ, so he can examine it firsthand. I'm not qualified to make the determination of cause of death."

"Oh, my God. How am I going to feed everyone?" Mr. Brightway covered his face with his hands. "I can't legally run a kitchen with human body parts in the freezer."

"I assume you have more than one freezer?" Kane pulled on latex gloves.

"Of course, we do." Brightway gripped the handrail in the elevator with white knuckles.

"So, we'll move the freezer to another location. You have a fork-lift here. We'll move it to an unoccupied chalet or one of the maintenance sheds." Kane shrugged. "I'll move it. You'll have to dump any food in with the body, but apart from that, unless the murder occurred in the kitchen, there'll be no problem with contamination."

Taking into consideration Kane's conclusions, Jenna chewed on her bottom lip. "Due to the unusual circumstances, if the murder occurred elsewhere, once we've done a forensic sweep and cleared the crime scene, I'll allow you to send in a crew to do a thorough cleaning, and then you'll be able to reopen the kitchen." She glanced at Kane and wrinkled her nose. "Although I suggest you swear your staff to secrecy. I don't think the guests will be too happy if they find out, no matter how many times you clean it."

"We'll be ruined." Brightway, looked at her, his eyes wide. "What will you tell the media?"

"We don't release details of crimes." Kane raised an eyebrow at Jenna. "Come morning, we'll have moved the body and any press lurking around will see us working outside. I suggest you come up with another excuse for the kitchen closure."

"I can't help you move the remains." Brightway swayed a little. "I can't go near the body again."

Jenna exchanged an exasperated look with Kane. "Don't worry, Mr. Brightway, we'll handle all that. We'll even make an inventory of everything we remove from the freezer. You'll have to replace the freezer, I'm afraid. It will be taken into evidence."

"I don't think my insurance covers damage by murder." Brightway looked horrified. "I'll have to contact the owner. They live in Florida."

Jenna nodded. "I suggest you do that a little later, when they're awake."

The doors whooshed open and they walked into the foyer. Jenna turned to Brightway. "We can take it from here. Please go and bring up the CCTV footage from last night. It would help us a great deal if you could look through it and see if anyone was moving around between say eleven and now."

"The staff finish cleaning at three, so he couldn't have dumped the body before then." Brightway stood staring at them. "The baking crew come on at four, so whoever did this did it between three and four." He swallowed hard and his Adam's apple moved up and down. "I should go and speak to the staff."

"No." Jenna touched his arm. "Check the CCTV footage for us. I'll speak to the staff, and when it's okay to return to the kitchen, I'll let them know. Breakfast will be canceled and maybe lunch too, I'm afraid."

"You'll need these. They open everything." Brightway handed her and Kane passkeys. "To get through the staff entrance."

"Thanks." Jenna followed Kane to the kitchen doors and used the passkey to get inside. "So, the killer has an all-access passkey. There must be one missing if the staff leave them in the kitchen before they leave."

"Yeah, but Brightway doesn't have an exact number. He said twenty or so. I asked him when I handed back the master keys after the blackout." Kane moved inside the brightly lit area. "Ah, foot-prints, as mentioned by Brightway. The staff usually change their shoes in the mudroom before entering the kitchens."

"Looks that way." Emily dropped her kit onto a bench and pulled out booties. "Better suit up. Can you capture the scene, Dave?"

"Sure." Kane took the booties from her and pulled them over his boots. "We'll clear the area first. I doubt anyone is lurking about, but we'll need to check. Wait here."

After suiting up, Jenna pushed open the door to the kitchen. The fresh air was tainted with the smell of fresh meat, making her stomach clench. The freezer stood wide open and, heart hammer-ing, she stared into the unseeing eyes of a dead man, his blue lips stretched out around Julie's distinctive blue and orange scarf, the fringed ends stiff with frozen blood.

FORTY-SEVEN

Sickened by the decapitated head, Jenna steeled herself to look closer. It was male for sure by the stubble covering the cheeks. Melted snow had plastered dark hair to his head, and water dripped off his nose. A pool of watery blood had collected in a large plate. On each side, two hands, and beside them the soles of two feet rested on a shelf. Dread shivered through her as she slipped silently through the kitchen doors, weapon drawn, and systematically cleared every walk-in storeroom. Kane followed close behind her, calling out as he cleared each area. She turned to look at him. "Go help Emily. I'll speak to the staff." She glanced around the spotless kitchen. "Nothing happened here. I could eat off this floor. Do you figure you can move the freezer?"

"Yeah, but I'll need Rio's help. They bring in supplies through the staff entrance using a forklift. I recall seeing it when we arrived. It will mess up the floor but I should be able to use it to move the freezer. With Rio's help, I'll take it to a more suitable location. I was thinking maybe a maintenance shed as there's one close by. They have power, so we'll have plenty of light to do a forensic examination."

Jenna nodded. "When I'm through here, I'll go upstairs and swap with Rio. Once you have the body secured off-site, we'll call in Wolfe and get to the bottom of this. There must be more of this victim out there and we'll need to find it." She tapped her bottom lip. "Okay, process the scene. I'll go take some statements. Head up to the suite with Julie when you're done and we'll work out a plan of action."

She walked into the dining room. "I'm Sheriff Alton. Who found the body?"

"That was me. The door wasn't closing properly or I'd have walked right past it." A man in his fifties came forward. "I'm Jeromy Eton, the head baker."

Jenna nodded. "What time was this?"

"A little after four." Eton frowned. "It was a shock, seeing it staring at me."

Glancing at the stunned people sitting at the tables, Jenna kept her tone even. "Did you see anyone here when you arrived? Anyone outside?"

"Nope, we all arrive at four. We walk down as a group every morning and come in the back door. We usually change in the mudroom and then get on with our chores. I came in first and straight away noticed the freezer door. When I saw what was inside, I kept everyone waiting in the mudroom and called Mr. Brightway. He told us to remove our shoes and come in here." Eton shrugged. "Apart from the freezer door, the only thing I noticed was the footprints tracked to the storeroom. It's where we keep the hams, cans of fruit, things like that, and someone has been taking food every week or so. They don't usually leave body parts behind."

Jenna had checked the other fridges and freezers when she'd arrived. "Well, there's nothing in the kitchen. It seems they only used the smaller freezer outside in the hallway. Why is that outside the kitchen?"

"It's just an overflow freezer, is all." Eton rubbed his chin. "What happens now?"

"We'll be processing the scene." Jenna handed him her statement book. "I'll need you to write down everything that happened with times if you have them."

"Okay." Eton pulled a pen from his top pocket and began to write.

Jenna looked around the staff members. "Anyone else notice anything unusual this morning?"

Most shook their heads but the others had fixed startled stares like a deer caught in the headlights. She glanced over her shoulder as the door opened and Kane walked into the room.

"No sign of forced entry." Kane led her away from the others and lowered his voice. "There are tracks outside from the staff coming in this morning, but I couldn't find anything else of significance. The maintenance crews are all over the complex daily with snowmobiles, collecting firewood, so there are tracks everywhere." He sucked in a breath. "There's a maintenance shed close by and I looked inside. There's blood in there but only a few spots. I spoke to Brightway and he said one of his crew had a fall in there yesterday and banged his head. He's taking a few days off with concussion. I'm moving the freezer into that shed once Em has finished a preliminary examination. I sure don't want the media coming out and stamping all over the evidence. We'll need to keep this on the downlow for now."

Jenna nodded. "How long will you need to clear the area? I figure they'll want to start cleaning the kitchen as soon as possible."

"Hours. I'll need daylight to search for the rest of the body and the murder weapon." Kane pulled his woolen cap down over his ears. "It's bitterly cold out there and we won't be able to stay outside indefinitely. Once we're set up, I'll contact Wolfe in a video call. There's power and a bench in the shed we can use for the examination. I'll grab a few rolls of plastic wrap from the storeroom to cover the bench." He blew out a long sigh. "From the mangled way the body is cut up, I figure he used a chainsaw. It must be around here somewhere, it's not something you can carry around inside a hotel without being noticed." He indicated with his chin to the staff. "You might as well send these people away.

Tell Brightway we'll contact him once we've finished and he can send in a cleaning crew."

"Okay." Jenna headed back to the sea of expectant faces and pulled her notebook and pen out of her pocket. "I'll need a list of the names of everyone here and then you can leave. The restaurant will be closed for most of the day."

"If nothing was touched inside the kitchen, why close the restaurant?" Eton stared at her. "How will they feed the guests?"

Jenna shrugged. "The other eateries will have to cope for one day. We'll need time to process the scene and then the kitchen will need to be cleaned."

"What about your team?" Eton frowned. "You won't have time to line up for hours for food."

Jenna stared at him, surprised by his obvious concern. "What do you suggest? We have a coffee machine and a microwave upstairs in our suite, and plates and silverware, but no food."

"There's bread left over from yesterday, butter and fixings in the refrigerator in the staff break room." Eton scratched his head. "There's a ton of pies in the refrigerator, and plenty of milk if you want cereal. Everything you need to keep you going for today, and we have spare toasters in the store cupboard. They use them in the chalets. Take what you need to your suite to feed your team. The food is left for our breakfast, but after we've eaten, everything is thrown away before the next shift arrives."

Jenna nodded. "Okay, so you usually eat here during your shift?"

"Yeah." Eton glanced at the others. "Once we've prepared the bread, there's an hour before we bake it, so we eat breakfast. The food will go to waste unless you take it. We have food at home." He smiled and pointed to an aluminum room service cart. "There's a cart over there you can use."

"Thanks that's very kind of you." She collected the list of names and counted them off. "Okay but before I let you go. Please, don't mention a word of this to anyone. The future of the ski lodge and your jobs are at stake. I must find who did this and the smallest leaked details will hamper our investigation. Don't worry, Mr. Brightway will keep you up to date. Use the front entrance on your way out, please."

Confident Kane had things under control, Jenna grabbed the cart and headed through the kitchen to the staff area. She found the refrigerator and the toasters and then loaded up the cart. Before she left the kitchen, she drew her weapon and moved in silence through the corridors. A deranged serial killer was here somewhere, maybe lurking close by watching her every move. Which one of her suspects had committed such heinous crimes? Shadows leaped out at her like gargoyles on ancient buildings as she moved along the passageways increasing the pounding of her heart. The killer was escalating rapidly and no one was safe.

FORTY-EIGHT

Black Rock Falls

After listening to Kane's matter-of-fact details of yet another homicide at Glacial Heights Ski Resort, Wolfe seriously considered driving up the mountain and taking his chances. Anger rode on his shoulders at the thought of his precious daughters being isolated on a mountain with a homicidal maniac on the rampage. He'd not been able to sleep, waiting for the next call from Jenna or Kane to inform him of another murder. Containing his anger, he set up his equipment to receive a video feed from Kane's phone. "Do you have eyes on my girls?"

"*All the time.*" Kane's phone rustled as if he'd handed it to someone.

"*Hi, Dad. It's Emily. We're fine. I'm here with Dave, and Rio is guarding Julie. During the day, Julie is surrounded by her friends. We don't allow her even to walk back and forth to the sessions alone. Trust me, the moment the weather clears we'll be coming home.*" Emily passed the phone back to Kane.

"*The weather forecast says we'll have clear weather from this afternoon with more snow forecast next week.*" Kane sounded optimistic. "*As soon as we've located the rest of the body and the murder weapon, if the weather holds, I'll bring the body down and the girls. No one else has wanted to leave. This is the strangest group of people I've ever encountered. Most would be running for the hills. It seems crime writers and all those who work with them figure having a psychopath in their midst is all part of the fun."*

Shaking his head in disbelief, Wolfe adjusted his webcam and an image of Kane popped up on his screen. As he was about to examine body parts, he needed a wide screen and not his phone. "Until one of them is murdered."

"They seem to think it's an elaborate hoax, a game the convention has organized. We have groups trying to figure out the killers. It's unbelievable." Kane narrowed his gaze. *"Okay, what do you need first?"*

Wolfe cleared his throat. "The overall image. I want to see the remains in situ."

An image appeared on the screen and Wolfe captured what he needed. He swallowed hard at a very familiar scarf. "Don't tell me that's Julie's scarf stuffed in the mouth."

"Yeah." Kane's eyes flashed with anger. *"It went missing from her room after she saw the guy at the end of her bed."*

Squashing the need to swear, Wolfe nodded. "Okay, Em, I gather you did a preliminary examination. Did you remove the limbs from the shelves?"

"Yes, I slid one to the edge to examine the cut and then replaced it." Emily's face looked pale and drawn. *"It was pretty chewed up, the bone splintered. We've wrapped the bench in plastic. Do you want us to take them out so you can look at them?"*

"Yeah, we'll examine each piece at a time—feet, legs, hands, arms, and head last." Wolfe leaned on his desk. "How many pieces apart from the head do you see?"

"Six. The torso is missing." Kane held a foot and calf in front of the camera. *"Hold the phone steady, Em."*

Wolfe ran his gaze over the masticated end of the stump. "Hmm, I've seen this before. This is a chainsaw used on frozen flesh. You'll have to check all the chainsaws on the premises for human blood or tissue traces. The management will have a record of how many they own. It must be one from the resort, likely taken from one of the maintenance crew. Em, you'll have to take swabs and test them as you go. Push the swab deep into the chain, look for places that might have collected blood spatter or tissue. A chainsaw tears up flesh, even frozen, so you'll find traces on the tool even if he tried to clean it." He made a note and looked back. "Now show me the thigh."

What he saw surprised him. "The main problem here is the blood clot on the severed end and, look, above the knee, there's a tourniquet mark. This person was dissected alive."

"Oh, now that's darn right nasty." Kane's voice came through the speaker. *"A psychopath with masochistic tendencies, that's all we need."*

"I see the same mark on the other thigh and both upper arms, Dad." Emily stared into the screen. *"How do you get someone to just lie there and let someone dissect them? Even if they were knocked out, the pain would bring them around. This doesn't make sense."*

In his experience in battle, Wolfe had seen indescribable atrocities. He thought back, seeking comparisons, and stared into the camera. "Now the head. Forget the face and show me what's left of the back of the neck."

As luck would have it, Kane had no problem displaying the head, and there it was, the two little red dots right at the base of the skull. "Okay, I've seen enough. This person, presumably male by the features and size was hit with a stun gun. On high, the shock would have caused paralysis from the neck down. From what I'm seeing, this is torture. This killer gets off on fear. I've given the cases a great deal of thought and that's what connects them all. Dakota Storm, bludgeoned, half strangled, stabbed in the eye, and tossed into a freezing lake. Kitty Pandora, was likely forced into the bathtub and the killer used a hairdryer dangling over the water to scare her, the same motive for Jedidiah Longfellow. He died slowly, stalked by his killer—he was actually scared to death—and now this one. Which of your suspects knew the victims well enough to be trusted? These murders are all very personal."

"I'll discuss it with the team." Kane returned the body parts to the freezer and closed the door. *"The problem is we have two hundred people here and as most of them believe we're playing a mystery game, no one is coming forward at all. I'd expect people to be banging our door down with information but no one is saying anything. I figure they're concerned that if they've found a clue, they'll miss out on a prize or something. It's bizarre. Most of the suspects have been involved with each other and the victims at one time. Identifying the killer is like finding the odd strand in a plate of spaghetti."*

FORTY-NINE

I've been waiting for Julie, hanging around a display of books, on constant alert. The mood is different today, the long wait to buy food making everyone jumpy. I lined up at one of the eateries, hoping to see Julie, but she didn't show. People around me sniff the air, concern over their faces. The announcement of a gas leak in the main restaurant being the main topic of conversation. I smile to myself, knowing the reason the place is closed, and I try to imagine the expression on the person's face who'd found what I'd left of Riggs. I'd set his final scene to the book, right down to the placement of his hands and feet. I'd made his client rich overnight. Publicity, no matter how gruesome, was always good for sales. No doubt, within the year I'll be seeing *Body Parts* made into a movie... of course, with my added touch of flavor. How incredibly amusing, I can hardly refrain from bursting into laughter.

Ah, I see her now, blonde hair flying and with the sheriff strolling along beside her. As Julie greets her friends, the sheriff does a sweeping scan of the immediate area. Casually, I lift a book from the table and peruse the pages. She has interviewed me, but I'm confident I outwitted her. She has no evidence against me and

I can see, as her eyes sweep past me, I'm no one of interest to her. I blend in, just a normal person enjoying the conference. But I will take extra precautions, especially after overhearing Julie mention someone photobombing her selfies wearing a hoodie. For now, I've kept mine tied around my waist. A cunning move as Julie constantly moves away from anyone wearing one, and that isn't in my best interest. Later, after the session ends and the rush for the elevators begins, I'll need to be close by. I've made plans to encourage her to take the stairs. People are so effortlessly controlled. With one suggestion, they'll follow like sheep, and my little lamb can so easily get lost in a crowd.

I leave the bookstand as Julie joins the line into the last session of the day. A panel of experts titled "Forensics Procedures You Should Know."

As I move in behind her, she peeks over one shoulder and gives me the sweetest smile. Red nails rake through her bangs, and as her perfume fills my nostrils, I move closer. My hands are trembling so hard that I push them deep into my pockets among the discarded candy wrappers. A toss of her head sends silver-blonde hair cascading down her back like wet silk. I open my palm and allow the glossy ends to brush my flesh. My heart pounds. Beads of sweat run down my forehead, tickle across my cheek on the way to my collar. So close, my fingers ache to touch her white flesh. I so need to watch her eyes widen and bulge as I squeeze the life from her. I bite down hard on my cheek and lift my gaze, fixing it anywhere but on her. I feel my control sliding into the abyss. I must remain strong for a few more hours. My job is done here. Now it's time for fun.

FIFTY

In the interview room, Jenna stared at the information she'd correlated from all sources on each of her suspects. The report from Bobby Kalo hadn't given any more clues on how the suspects and victims were connected, but he'd been able to identify the victim in the freezer using facial recognition software against all the males staying at the ski resort. The victim was a literary agent from New York, Quentin Riggs. The man hadn't been missed, and Jenna had spent most of the afternoon checking CCTV footage to determine a timeline between the last time Riggs was seen alive, during a session in one of the halls, and the time the baker discovered his body. She looked up as Kane and Emily came into the room with Duke close on their heels. "Ah, good. Find anything?"

"Yeah, we discovered where the killer stored the body parts overnight." Kane went straight to the coffee machine and poured two cups. "By the look of things, he buried them in the snow just outside the staff entrance to the lodge. We searched all around, even took Duke out with us, but found no trace of the torso. No doubt that will show up in the melt. The killer left nothing behind, no evidence we can use. Em collected the blood evidence on scene, but as sure as hell, he wasn't killed there."

"The chainsaws were a wipeout." Emily's lips were blue and

her nose bright red. "I checked them all, but there's one missing. Mr. Brightway is checking the numbers on them to find out who was issued the missing one. It must be close by somewhere. I figure the killer buried it with the torso." She took the coffee Kane handed her. "Any pie left? I'm famished. It was freezing out there."

"Did you establish a timeline for Riggs?" Kane searched the fridge and pulled out a pie, cut it into sections, slid it onto a plate, and handed it across the table to Julie. "That man suffered. This killer is on a personal revenge murder spree. There must be something to link the victims together."

"I've looked over the suspects' statements so many times my head is spinning." Rio leaned back in his chair and stretched. "I went and spoke to all of them again today. We need to take out Bradford and concentrate on the two literary agents: Finnian and Rain. We know they've both had axes to grind with at least two of our victims. I'm keeping Grayson on the list because apart from the two agents, he's the only author on the list who can't account for his whereabouts between three and four this morning. Bradford spent the entire night with a woman, and Jenna verified his arriving and leaving on the CCTV feed. His woman friend's door is in plain sight of the camera. It can't have been him. The other three spent the night alone and inconveniently all have rooms in corridors with shielded access to the fire stairs. We can track them to their rooms and leaving this morning, but any one of them could've sneaked out overnight and used the stairs."

"I figure you can take Parker Rain off the list, as well." Emily sipped her coffee and sighed. "I'm fit and I work out every day, but I couldn't hold up the chainsaws they have here for more than a few minutes. They're boy's toys and so heavy, plus they run on gas and trying to start them is a nightmare. I tried many times and failed. Add the cold and the difficulty of sawing up a body. Rain is my size. There's just no way she could've used one of the chainsaws. They're too darn heavy."

Listening with interest, Jenna nodded. "I agree. This cuts our suspects down to three possible."

"Why can't you lock them up?" Emily pushed her empty plate away. "If you'd locked them up at the get-go, we'd have had three fewer murders."

Pushing both hands through her hair, Jenna sighed. "I wish we had that power, but we need probable cause to detain someone, and we have no physical evidence. All of them have cooperated. In fact, we could have this all wrong and it's a member of the staff." She pressed her palms flat on the table. "We don't have anywhere to detain people, no surveillance gear, trackers, or anything else. If we locked them up until the road is cleared, we'd be charged with deprivation of liberty. These people have no access to a lawyer to protect their legal rights. The problems go on and on."

"Oh, yes, I see." Emily shook out her long hair from its pony-tail, gathered it back up, and secured it. "Isn't there anything we can do?"

A plan had already been forming in Jenna's head. "Yeah, it will cause problems, but it's the only option I can find." She sighed. "We'll ask guests to move rooms, so we have the three suspects in rooms under the surveillance of the CCTV camera at the elevator. I'll explain things to Brightway and insist he places them all in adjoining rooms." She smiled. "Then we take shifts watching them."

"I figure as there's only three of us armed and we have to sleep sometime, we should use the conference's people to assist us during the day." Kane eyed her over the rim of his cup. "If one or two of the suspects are in a session, we show the people on the door a photograph of them and ask them to call us if they leave the hall."

Jenna nodded. "Do you think they'd do that for us? I mean, one of these could be a serial killer."

"They won't need to be involved with them at all." Kane put down his cup and twirled it in his fingers. "Just a simple phone call is all. I figure they'll find it thrilling, and probably believe it's all part of an elaborate game... just like everyone else here."

"Okay." Jenna nodded. "Rio, print the images of the suspects and get that set up now."

"I'm on it." Rio turned to his laptop and moments later the printer whirred into action.

Jenna's phone buzzed. It was Mr. Brightway. She listened and then explained her plan. The man wasn't happy but complied and the changeover would happen after dinner. She disconnected before turning to Kane. "Okay, I've organized the suspects' rooms and Brightway has the possible location of the missing chainsaw. Would you believe it should be inside the maintenance shed where you stored the freezer?"

"You have to be joking?" Emily stood wearily and grabbed her coat. "After you catch this lunatic, I'm sleeping for a week."

FIFTY-ONE

It had been an amazing day, so good that Julie contemplated ditching the idea of becoming a pediatrician and trying her hand at becoming an author. The intriguing masterclasses on the different techniques used to tell a story had been compelling. During the three sessions, she'd kept her friends around her due to Jenna's team being involved in an emergency. Meals from the main restaurant had been suspended and an announcement made of a gas leak, but Jenna had secretly informed her it was another murder. The other eateries had been inundated with people lining up for ages, and a shortage of bread had made things worse. Lunch had been staggered as usual and three choices of hot food were available. She'd heard from Uncle Dave that the kitchen was being cleaned, and dinner looked like a possibility. As her friends drifted toward the elevators, she overheard someone speaking close behind her.

"I'm sick of lining up today. I'm taking the stairs." It was a man's voice.

"Yeah, good idea. It's only one flight." A woman pushed past her and her red coat vanished in the crowd.

"I'm taking the stairs too. Wait for me." Another woman hurried away.

Julie looked over at her two friends in deep conversation with a couple of boys and pulled out her phone. "Uncle Dave, do you still have the CCTV app on your phone? Can you see me in the foyer?"

"Hold on." Kane covered the mouthpiece and she heard a mumbling and then he sighed. *"Why didn't you tell us you'd finished the session?"*

Annoyed, Julie moved a few steps closer to the elevators, but she still had a long wait. "Because I know you're all busy and I'm with friends. They're going to ride up in the elevator with me. There are at least a hundred people waiting down here. I'm perfectly safe."

"There's no such thing right now." Kane cleared his throat. *"Jenna headed upstairs just before and I'll call her to meet you at the elevator. In the meantime, wave so I can see you."*

Feeling stupid, Julie waved pretending she'd seen someone she knew. "Can you see me?"

"Yeah. Zac is going to watch you. I'm helping Em bag the victim."

Shuddering, Julie nodded. "Okay, see you later." She disconnected and looked around.

Her friends had moved forward in the line and she couldn't make them out. Up on her toes, she searched the crowd and then glanced at the man beside her. He wasn't wearing a hoodie and looked harmless enough, and a woman wearing strong perfume stood on her other side. Zac was watching her, she'd be safe.

A voice came from behind her. "Julie, your friends headed for the fire stairs. They just went through the door. If you hurry, you'll catch them."

Julie half turned but there was a sea of faces behind her. It could have been any one of them speaking to her. "Thanks." She pushed her way through the people waiting for the elevator and headed toward the fire stairs.

As the heavy door clanged shut behind her and cool damp air surrounded her, Julie stared up the stairs, listening intently for footsteps but heard nothing but a slow drip of water. She stepped around a puddle on the floor and started up the stairs. Her friends couldn't have got far and, after hoisting on her backpack, she took the steps two at a time to catch up. The door clanked shut below her and the sound reverberated in the confined space, followed by footsteps and then an unusual metallic whine. She looked up the stairwell but saw no one above her. Panic gripped her. Had the information about her friends been a lie? She tried to increase her pace, but under the weight of the heavy backpack, it was like climbing a mountain. Heart pounding, Julie made out the red lights above the first-floor exit beaming like a lifebuoy and hurried toward them.

Without warning, darkness surrounded her in a cloud of black. She stumbled, falling to her knees. Was the lodge suffering another blackout? As she searched for her phone, footsteps came from behind her, moving up the stairs in slow deliberation. Unhurried and steady, and getting closer by the second. Grasping the handrail, she peered over the edge and looked down. Most people would use their phone light to guide them in a power cut. Why hadn't this person? *Because he doesn't want to be seen.* Terror hit her in a wave of nausea, and she pushed her phone back inside her pocket. She could hide in the dark as well. She grasped the handrail and climbed the stairs. Ahead had to be the first-floor exit and safety. Breathing heavily as she reached the landing, she ran her hands along the door searching for the long metal release. She pressed down and pushed. Nothing happened. The door refused to open. Pushing down on the bar and franticly shouldering the door, she glanced behind her. A wall of unforgiving darkness surrounded her. From the gloom, the sound of heavy breathing had joined the footsteps and then came a low chuckle. Julie's bottom lip trembled. He was coming for her.

FIFTY-TWO

After searching the maintenance shed, Kane found the chainsaw in a closet with shovels and brooms. It didn't take too much time to find the evidence to prove it was the murder weapon. Although the killer had tried hard to remove the gore, Emily had found numerous pieces of flesh and blood spatter. When she looked up at him and nodded, Kane slid the chainsaw into the freezer to preserve the evidence. He helped Emily collect the evidence bags. After storing them inside the freezer, he closed and locked the shed door. "Okay, it's been a long day. Let's get cleaned up."

"The camera in the lobby is down." Rio stared at him through the staff entrance door to the kitchens. "I rewound the feed. There was a flash and then nothing."

On full alert, Kane pulled off his gloves and grabbed his phone from Rio. He rewound the footage and swore under his breath. "Laser pointer. The camera has been disabled. Something is going down." He looked at Rio. "Call Jenna and see if Julie is upstairs. If she's not, head for the lobby. I'll be right behind you." He grabbed Emily's arm and they hurried inside the lodge. "I'll find a safe place for you."

"I want to come with you." Emily pulled back.

"It's not safe." Kane pushed into the kitchen, startling the staff, and located the chef. "This woman's life is in danger. Don't let her out of your sight until I come back and get her. Understand?"

"Yes, of course." The chef ushered Emily to a corner of the kitchen and produced a chair for her. He waved to a young man. "Peter, get the young lady a cup of coffee and some of the cake." He turned back to Kane. "I won't let her out of my sight."

Just as Kane stepped out of the kitchen, a buzzer went off on his phone. His stomach tightened when he stared at the screen. Julie had triggered her personal alarm. The tracker rings were used only in an extreme emergency, as in being attacked or kidnapped. He pressed the phone to his ear, listening intently. Like Jenna, Wolfe's girls and Sandy had a one-way tracker in their rings. They transmitted an emergency call to the team's phones. The idea being that if the wearers were in danger, the rings could give an undetectable commentary of where they were and who was involved. Kane moved swiftly out of the kitchen and ran toward the lobby. "Come on, Julie, tell me where you are."

As if she'd heard him, a breathless voice came through the earpiece and Kane pushed a finger in his other ear to hear her.

"I'm in the stairwell leading from the lobby. I'm just going past the first floor. Someone is following me. I can't see who it is. The lights went out and it's pitch black in here. I'll keep moving up the stairs, but I'm not using my phone light. I'm hiding in the dark. Hurry. The first-floor exit is locked. I'm stuck in here."

Kane ran as he hit Jenna's number. "Did you get Julie's message?"

"Yeah, I'm heading for the stairs now." Jenna's footsteps thundered through the earpiece. *"Tell Rio to get the lights back on. Someone must have turned them off."*

"Copy." Kane pushed people out of his way and saw Rio heading toward the stairs. "I see Rio. Jenna, I'll come in silent from below and we'll trap him between us."

"Copy. I'm at the fire door. Dammit, it's locked."

Kane rushed to Rio's side. "Jenna, I'm at the stairs now."

"I got the call from Julie as well." Rio rushed toward the fire door and yanked on it. "It's locked."

Recalling what the maintenance staff had told him about the doors, Kane pulled out his passkey and swiped it through the reader beside the door. It clicked open and Rio yanked the door wide. "Jenna, use your passkey in the reader beside the door."

"*Copy.*" Jenna disconnected.

Pushing his phone into his pocket and pulling out his weapon, Kane peered into the darkness and lowered his voice to just above a whisper. He thrust the passkey into Rio's hands. "There's a panel here somewhere. You'll need the passkey to open it. Try and get the lights back on. Jenna is heading down from above. Follow me in silence, I want to get the jump on him."

Moving in the dark was second nature to Kane and he headed up the stairs in absolute silence, taking them three at a time. He heard scuffling from above and increased his speed, biting back the need to call out and tell Julie help was on the way. He dropped into combat mode, pushing away the anger he had for someone daring to hurt one of his family. Overreacting never helped in a situation. He needed stealth and cunning. His only objective was to save Julie, take down this killer alive, and dissect his twisted mind.

FIFTY-THREE

Gasping for breath, Julie rounded the top of the next flight of stairs. One hand gripped the stun gun, but in the dark she had no idea if she could safely turn it on. Her fingers moved frantically along the grip. A switch on one side of the handle turned it on and the other side had a safety switch that also worked the flashlight. But if she turned on the flashlight, she'd give away her position. She kept on moving, her heavy breathing almost blocking the sound of the relentless footsteps behind her. It was as if he had all day. She let out a little sob. How had he locked all the doors? She'd seen people heading for the stairs and yet there was nobody trapped in the dark like her. What was happening?

She paused to catch her breath and listen. The footsteps echoed in the stairwell and now the man was humming. Trembling with terror, Julie pushed on, feeling her way in the pitch black. Uncle Dave would be coming soon, she just had to keep moving.

"Why don't you take a rest, Julie?" It was a man's voice and he was close by. "No one can get in here. It's just you and me. No one knows where you are. I was right behind you when you told the sheriff or maybe her deputy that you'd be taking the elevator. Won't they be surprised when you go missing and they find you in here?"

Chest tightening with fear, Julie struggled to the next landing. As she moved across the smooth floor, she tried the door. Locked. She followed the handrail and continued upward but behind her the footsteps quickened. The next moment, a door opened high above her and a beam of light flooded the stairwell. Julie stared at the stun gun in her hand and hit the switch. The flashlight lit up the face of a man, dressed in black and wearing a hoodie. She screamed as he lunged at her, her fingers desperately trying to find the correct switch on the stun gun. She gasped as his gloved hands slid around her neck and squeezed.

"Sheriff's department, step away from the girl now." It was Jenna's voice coming from above her.

As Julie went for the man's eyes, fighting for her life, she made out a bobbing flashlight. Jenna was coming down the stairs. The man's hands slackened a little. Frantic to get away, Julie smashed the man in the face with the stun gun and scratched at his eyes, but it was useless. His hands closed around her throat again and squeezed. As red spots danced across her vision, over his shoulder Julie could see Jenna rounding the top of the landing and, without breaking stride, she flung herself from the top of the stairs. Her scream echoing through the stairwell like a war cry.

"Let her go."

The impact as Jenna collided with the man hit Julie like a ton of bricks. The stun gun slipped from her fingers as they all tumbled like ninepins across the landing. All the air had left Julie's lungs, but the man was staggering to his knees.

"Run, Julie, run." Jenna pointed her flashlight toward the stairs.

Julie rolled onto her back and kicked out at the man, aiming for his face. The man grabbed her foot and twisted. She kicked with the other foot and then jumped to her feet and sprinted up the stairs. She heard Jenna grunt and the flashlight beam faltered. Darkness closed in around her. She stumbled but kept on going, as heavy footsteps and raspy breathing closed in behind her. Gasping for air, she hit the landing and burst through the door, looking for a place to hide or someone to help her, but the hallway was empty. The door opened behind her and the man's hands reached out to grab her, but she ducked and weaved out of his grasp. Lungs bursting, she hurtled along the passageway. She had to get away. The lights at the end of the hallway shone red over the other fire door with an invitation of escape. With no time to wait for an elevator, Julie ran for the exit. She pulled open the heavy door and headed down the stairs, jumping the last six or so, rounding the corner and barreling down the stairs again.

Behind her, the relentless pursuer's rasping breath and heavy steps rung out in the confined space. Terror pushed her on and she burst through the door at the bottom of the next flight of stairs. The freezing chill hit her like a wall of ice as she ran up to her knees in snow. She looked frantically around. The locked pull-down doors to the delivery area were the only break in the back wall of the building. She turned and, leaping over bushes to hide her tracks, headed into the forest. Using the dark shadows to conceal her, she crouched down behind a snow-laden bush as the door to the stairs slowly opened.

FIFTY-FOUR

The lights came on as Kane rounded the top of the steps. His attention snapped to Jenna. He'd seen her leap down the stairs, giving a warrior's cry so fierce she'd startled Julie's attacker into dropping her, and they'd all crashed into the wall. Jenna had rolled on impact and the fall had stunned her, but she'd managed to send Julie running for her life.

"Up there, he's still after her. It's Bexley Grayson." Jenna was sitting against the wall, holding her wrist. "I've busted my wrist. Go!"

Kane headed up the stairs and burst into the hallway. It was as silent as a church. He grabbed his phone, hoping to hear Julie's voice, and peered at the pulsating dot on the map. It wasn't moving. The GPS signal gave no indication of Julie's position inside the building but somehow, she'd gotten outside. Mind spinning, he bolted for the opposite fire exit. He called Rio as he ran and gave him the location. "If he's planning on strangling her, we have two maybe three minutes."

Stuffing the phone inside his pocket, he jumped over the railing to the next floor, landing and rolling before crashing through the exit and out into the snow. Grayson hadn't bothered to disguise his trail into the forest and, drawing his Glock, Kane charged into the frozen tundra after him. The silence was deafening, which could mean Julie was hiding or dead. As he pushed his way through the snow-laden branches, ice flicked into his cheeks. The cold bit into his unprotected skull, freezing the metal plate he'd received courtesy of a car bombing and sending crippling agony across his eyes. He shook his head, scanning the forest for any movement.

A scream cut through the silence like a knife. Digging deep, he blocked out the pain and ran. He burst through the trees as Julie's scream sent birds flying into the air. Julie was fighting for her life, clawing at Grayson's face as he choked her. Kane grabbed him by the arm and tossed him against a tree. As the man staggered to gain his feet, Kane aimed his weapon at him. "Sheriff's department. Facedown on the ground, hands on your head." He flicked a glance at Julie. "You okay?"

Julie nodded and rubbed her sore neck, backing away from Grayson. "Shoot him. He tried to kill me."

"Don't you see? I must kill her." Grayson refused to comply and his eyes swiveled toward Kane. "Then I'll have peace for a time. Just one more. Look, I'm not armed. You can't shoot an unarmed man, can you, Deputy?" He staggered to his feet. "That's against the law."

Kane wanted to laugh. Grayson honestly believed he could take him. He stared at the shivering man. "Who'd tell anyone if I did? And who would care? It would save the county a ton of money if I finished this now. But I don't need a weapon to deal with the likes of you. Bare hands are so much more satisfying, don't you agree?" He holstered his weapon and narrowed his gaze. "Hands on your head. Now!"

"I'm not finished yet." Grayson pulled something from his pocket and lunged at Kane.

FIFTY-FIVE

Terrified, Julie screamed as the sound of a stun gun clicked and Grayson lunged toward Uncle Dave. "Watch out!"

The punch came so fast Julie almost missed it. The man's head snapped back and he fell sliding into the snow, coming to rest under a tree, the stun gun slipping from his hands. Shivering, she stared after him and then noticed Rio bounding through the trees. Behind him, she made out Jenna, walking slow, gripping her arm. Holding back a sob, Julie pointed at Jenna. "Jenna's hurt!"

"I know." Kane held out his arms. "Come here." He slid one arm around her shoulder and hugged her trembling body. "Are you okay? Did he hurt you?"

"Not really." Julie burrowed into him, her teeth sounding like castanets. "I have his DNA under my fingernails, but it was so dark I couldn't see to power up the stun gun. I bashed him with it though."

"You did everything right. Your dad will be very proud of you. I'm just sorry I didn't get here sooner." Kane smoothed her hair and pushed her gently away. He turned to Rio. "Cuff him, pat him down, and when he regains consciousness read him his rights."

"Sure, but tell me one thing." Rio secured the prisoner and

looked up at him. "He could've had a knife. Why did you holster your weapon?"

"Kane is a weapon." Jenna walked into the clearing, her teeth chattering. "I've seen him take down six men in a fight. That piece of shit was never a threat to him, with or without a weapon." Her mouth turned down and she looked at Kane. "It's hard to believe that flamboyant, over-tanned, self-confident egomaniac murdered all those people. I can't wait to hear his story."

"Me either." Rio dragged Grayson to his feet and read him his rights.

Freezing, Julie rubbed her arms. "Why didn't you kill him, Uncle Dave? A man like him doesn't deserve to live."

"Oh, I sure wanted to, but he'll suffer in jail for the rest of his life." A nerve ticked in Kane's cheek and it was as if he'd turned to stone. "Bexley Grayson, I'm arresting you for the attempted murder of Julie Wolfe."

FIFTY-SIX

Head throbbing fit to burst, Kane pushed Grayson toward Rio, and they trudged back through the snow to the front entrance of the ski lodge. He shielded Jenna and Julie with his body as the hovering press that frequented the lobby bombarded them with questions. He glared at them. "No comment." He followed everyone into the elevator.

"You don't have any evidence against me." Grayson gave him a bloodstained grin. "It will be my word against the cops. Look at me. This is police brutality."

"Dream on." Rio snorted. "This isn't a novel. You're going to rot in jail."

"Nah, I'm special." Grayson smiled and winced, the scratches down his cheek and his swollen eye showing how well Julie had defended herself. "You won't be able to prove a thing."

"Have you ever heard of DNA?" Jenna lifted her chin and her lips twitched into a smile. "The earrings you left at the crime scenes belong to Diane Tate. If you're a match, then we know you're Paul Tate. You killed your own mother, didn't you, Paul?"

"I killed a demon." Grayson's lips curled. "You know nothing about me." He changed from anger to amusement in a blink of an eye and chuckled. "I'll walk away from this... and you'll never know when I'm coming back... to get you."

"Good luck with that." Jenna stared at him and turned back to Kane. "I'll speak to the DA. He confessed to killing his mother in front of us. I want him held until Jo can get here. Between the two of you, you'll be able to get the truth out of him. He has a story. Something turned him into a monster and I figure his mother had something to do with it."

"Yeah, I blame my mom." Grayson grinned at her. "I'll tell the judge she drove me to insanity. I'll have the old women on the jury crying for me."

Anger bubbling just under the surface, Kane fixed him with a stare that shut his mouth. "You planned your murders, and revenge isn't a defense. Don't worry, I'm sure the judge will give you the same consideration you gave your victims."

Cold and dripping with melting snow, they reached the interview room and Kane opened the door. He turned to Rio. "Secure the prisoner. Cuff him to a pipe under the sink for now. Use flexicuffs on his legs as well. We'll head down the mountain as soon as the road is cleared." He looked at Grayson. "One more word from you and I'll gaffer-tape your mouth."

He waited for Rio to secure Grayson and, shutting the door behind him, went back to the other room. Taking in Jenna's ashen face, Kane went to her side and examined her arm with care. "I'm pretty sure it's broken. We need to get that looked at." He smiled at her. "You're the bravest woman I've ever met. You saved Julie's life."

"We both did." She eyed him critically. "You're as pale as a ghost." Her eyes widened. "Oh, no. You went outside without a hat. Your head must be killing you. Do you have your meds with you?"

Kane rubbed his head and rummaged inside his pockets. His fingers closed around a bottle. "Yeah. I'll be fine. Forget about me. Sit down before you fall down." He grabbed some blankets from a cupboard and wrapped them around Jenna and Julie. "You need to get warm. I'll make us a hot drink and then you need to change into dry clothes."

"I hope they have a doctor here." Jenna swayed a little and sat down hard in a chair, holding her arm protectively. "I want someone to look at Julie."

"The hotel has paramedics." Rio walked back into the room. "I've already called them for our prisoner. Duty of care and all that."

"Good." Kane nodded and prepared hot chocolate. "Jenna, we'll get the paramedics here to triage you, and then you're going to the ER and so is Julie. I want Grayson out of here and locked up in a cell. I'll call out snowplows to cut a path through the back road. That's the most logical way to go. It has some cover from the forest and it hasn't snowed since lunchtime. I'll get through with the Beast, and Rio can follow us with the prisoner." He looked at Julie. "I'll call Em and tell her what's happened. She'll be able to help you pack. I'm sorry about cutting your time here short, but leaving with us is nonnegotiable."

"It's okay. I miss my dad." Julie rubbed her neck. "He'll be so angry. I placed every one of you in danger."

"No, you didn't." Jenna took a cup from Kane and blew across the steaming beverage. "In fact, you helped us catch him. We didn't have enough people to watch the suspects twenty-four/seven. This guy is an anomaly. We may never have caught him."

* * *

After calling the ski resort's paramedic team to Jenna's room, Kane arranged for the snowplows and then called Wolfe and explained. "We had Julie covered. Rio was watching her on the CCTV camera, in a crowd."

"I'm seriously wondering if I should move the girls to Helena. I

could still work on your cases, but they wouldn't be in constant danger." Wolfe sounded calm, but Kane could hear the anger just below the surface. *"Have you asked her why she took the stairs?"*

Kane reeled at the idea of Wolfe moving but refused to comment. "No." Kane headed toward the front desk. "She's traumatized enough as it is without me badgering her with questions. She fought well, and if she'd flipped the switch on the stun gun, she'd have taken him down unaided." He sighed. "I'm arranging for the freezer to be loaded on a trailer. I'll bring it down the mountain and drop it at your office. You'll need a forklift to unload it."

"Nothing is going to defrost in this weather. Drop the trailer and get the girls to the hospital. Delay with a fracture could be life-threatening."

Fully aware of the problem, Kane cleared his throat. "The ski lodge does have a team here for emergencies. I'd figure broken limbs would be the most common. I'm sure they can stabilize Jenna for transporting and check Julie, but she seems to be okay." He sighed. "I'm getting the road cleared as fast as possible. I'll get back to you when we leave. Call Julie, she needs her dad right now."

"I wish her mother was still with us. She'd know what to do." Wolfe paused for a beat. *"I want to wrap them up and prevent things happening, but in truth I'm powerless to do anything. It is so much easier with Anna, but when kids become adults, it's sure hard to protect them."*

Unable to keep his concern from spilling out, Kane bit the bullet. "Maybe, but here you have Jenna and me. In fact, you have the entire darn team to protect them." He dashed a hand through his hair. He'd had Wolfe around for so many years, it would be like losing a brother. "Trouble can come from anywhere and we're a family. I don't figure moving away is the answer. Staying and facing the problems together is the key."

"Yeah, maybe it is." Wolfe suddenly chuckled. *"Good advice. Maybe you should take some of it for yourself."*

Kane frowned. "What do you mean by that?"

"*Oh, nothing. I just remember the best part of arguing with my wife was the making up. I'll see you in a couple of hours. Drive safe.*" Wolfe disconnected.

FIFTY-SEVEN

Traveling down the mountain at a snail's pace behind the snow-plow in the dark, with her arm throbbing, was an experience Jenna never wanted to go through again. She'd refused pain meds from the paramedics as she needed to have her head in the game. With one arm in a sling, she could feel every bump on the uneven service road. They had Julie and Emily with Duke between them in the back seat and gave Rio the responsibility of transporting their prisoner. In a convoy with Kane following behind Rio, she kept a vigilant eye on the back of Rio's vehicle. Although his vehicle was equipped to carry prisoners, Kane had insisted on securing Grayson in the back seat, behind the bullet proof divider, by tethering him hand and foot to metal rings. Due to the frequent occurrence of serial killers to their quiet town, all the sheriff's department vehicles had been similarly equipped. Only Kane's Beast, being his private vehicle, was not able to carry prisoners. His was more a team survival vehicle, built for speed and protection.

Jenna handed her phone to Emily in the back seat. "Can you get Jo on the phone for me, please?"

"Here you go. It's ringing." Emily handed back the phone.

Jenna waited. It was after office hours and she had called

Special Agent Jo Wells on her cellphone. "Hi, Jo. What's the weather like there? We have a situation."

"The snow is thick on the ground, but we've had clear skies all day, no snow forecast." Jo sounded enthusiastic. *"I'll call Carter, but he was out in the chopper this afternoon. I'm pretty sure we can get to you. What's been happening? Did you arrest the killer?"*

After explaining, Jenna sighed. "Kane's dropping the girls and me to the hospital and then following Rio to the office. Wolfe will meet us there. Grayson is dangerous. He needs guarding around the clock, and shipping him off to county before we get the chance to interview him will depend on his lawyer. We have him dead to rights for the attempted murder of Julie. Three law enforcement officers as witnesses means he won't walk."

"What else do you have?" Jo sounded interested.

Jenna glanced at Kane. "He admitted to killing his mother... well, when I confronted him with it, he said he'd killed a demon. If the DNA is a match, he's the missing kid Paul Tate. If he killed his mother, there's reason to believe he murdered the men in the forest as well."

"Hmm. He could have been a victim of abuse. If you call us in officially, as you have at least four homicides and one attempted, over two states, he is a suspected serial killer. It's obvious from reliable witnesses that a crime was committed and a suspect identified. In this case, we can hold the prisoner for seventy-two hours and delay moving him to county in order to obtain additional evidence proving the suspect's guilt." Jo paused a beat. *"I'll confront him with his crimes and, as he's been Mirandized, he'll either call for a lawyer or not. In either case, there's no doubt he's guilty of at least one crime, and likely the four at the ski lodge. He is a danger to society. I'm sure his lawyer will allow us to question him. It's essential we gather as much information from him during his heightened state. As they calm down, they become more cunning."*

Relieved, Jenna leaned back in her seat. "Okay, yes, please, come and help us. You'll have to use one of the helipads at the hospital. Wolfe keeps his chopper on top of the ME's office now. We'll meet you there."

"Not a problem. I'll call Ty and get right back to you with an ETA." Jo disconnected.

"They'll probably arrive before us the time this is taking." Kane flicked her a glance. "How are you holding up?" He glanced in his mirror at Julie. "Julie, you okay back there?"

"I'm okay. My throat is sore is all and I have a headache." Julie snuggled with Duke under a blanket.

Jenna smiled at her. "We'll both be fine although I'm not too excited about seeing your dad. He won't be too happy with me."

To her surprise, Wolfe was the opposite of mad. He thanked Jenna for saving Julie. It was a relief when the ER doctor sent Julie home after a few tests and a surprise when Wolfe returned to check on her. She glanced up and smiled at him, as a nurse adjusted a sling on her arm. "It's a clean break. Six weeks in plaster. I'm just happy it's my left hand."

"Carter and Jo have arrived." Wolfe indicated with a thumb behind him. "They're loading their bags into my truck. The roads are clear to Louan, and Kane has organized deputies to watch over the prisoner tonight." He frowned. "Grayson lawyered up and called in Sam Cross, but Kane has already spoken to him and he's willing to allow Jo to speak to his client. Kane suggested letting her and Carter handle him—Sam Cross, I mean."

Hackles up, Jenna shook her head. "No way. It's my collar. I should be doing the interview."

"It's your call, but you know as well as I do that having a behavioral analyst like Jo asking the questions and Kane as her wingman, would make more sense. Grayson has a violent history and they need to find the underlying cause of it." Wolfe sighed. "Kane obtained a DNA sample from him as well. Grayson wanted a soda, so Kane gave him one and bagged the can. I'm running it against Diane Tate's DNA now."

Jenna took the bottle of pain meds the nurse gave her and pushed them inside her pocket. "Trust Kane. He doesn't miss a trick." She gave the wheelchair a grimace but sat down. It was pointless arguing with hospital policy. "Shouldn't you be home with Julie? Surely Webber can wait on the DNA results?"

"Julie was asleep before we arrived home." Wolfe pushed the wheelchair out the door. "She's bruised and shook up but okay. The doctor gave her something to sleep. Emily is sitting with her. I have a bag of body parts to take care of and you'll need answers ASAP."

It was good to see Jo and Carter sitting in the back seat of Wolfe's truck. Jenna climbed in the front and turned to look at them. "Thank you so much for coming. My cruiser is at the office if you need it, and you're welcome to stay in the cottage."

"Thanks. We'll move our gear into the trunk when we get to the office." Carter looked her over and frowned. "You look like you need some rest. Nasty bruise you have on your head, and your arm must be painful."

Jenna shook her head. "They gave me something for the pain, but I'm not missing the interview with Grayson. This guy is one of a kind."

"If the DNA comes back a match, I have a way of getting through to him." Jo leaned forward in her seat. "I'll need to speak to the DA, but as he was ten at the time of his mother's murder, I might have a way to get inside his head and convince him to admit to the ski lodge murders."

FIFTY-EIGHT

The smell of fresh coffee greeted Jenna when she arrived at the office. In her absence, Kane had fed the prisoner, arranged his legal counsel, and ordered in a ton of food from Aunt Betty's Café. He was currently waiting outside the interview room, to make sure the secured Grayson didn't cause a problem for his lawyer, Samuel J. Cross. Maggie had returned to the office and informed her that Rio had written his statement and Kane had sent him home. He'd be back first thing in the morning to assist Rowley.

Jenna led Jo and Carter into her office and went to the coffee machine. "We might as well grab something to eat while Grayson is talking to his lawyer. There's a ton of food here. Help yourself. It's going to be a long night." She poured coffee, grabbed some sandwiches, and looked at Jo as they returned to her desk. "So how do you want to do this?"

"I guess it all depends on how much Sam Cross allows him to say." Jo sat down and placed her food and coffee on the desk. "A psychopath, and I've little doubt he is one, isn't easily intimidated. They like to believe they have the upper hand. Reasoning with them never works, so we have to make it appear that we are offering him a way out of trouble."

"He must know he's facing serious jail time." Carter collapsed into a chair and let out a long weary sigh before tossing his Dober-man, Zorro, a few cold sausages and adding a few more to Duke's plate. "I figure we suggest making a deal with the DA to take the death penalty off the table if he cooperates with us."

Intrigued, Jenna sipped her coffee, allowing the rich brew to spill over her tongue. Kane had insisted on supplying the office with his special blend of coffee and she'd missed it being away for so long. She nodded. "Maybe suggest he'll be immortalized in the FBI's ongoing research into psychopathic behavior. It worked for James Stone, one of our other cases. He lapped it up."

"Yeah, they sure like to be famous." Jo smiled. "Grayson is particularly of interest mainly because he switched his MO for each victim and none of them resembled the slash, kill, mutilate cycle he had as a kid." She nibbled at a sandwich. "We can use that fact... that interest in him to make him talk." She looked at Jenna. "Kane should be involved. His insight is an asset and so is Ty's."

"Why thank you, ma'am." Carter grinned. "I have interviewed a few psychopaths in my time, but I've learned a whole lot from you."

"Sam Cross is waiting outside." Kane walked into the office, closing the door behind him. He wore an exhausted expression and nodded to Carter and Jo. "He didn't specify what he wanted. I guess he needs to discuss something with you, Jenna."

Why would the defense lawyer, Sam Cross, want to consult with her about anything? They'd never gotten along, and had crossed swords many a time. Concerned, she nodded. "Send him in. He'll be talking to all of us as Jo and Carter are officially involved now."

"Okay." He grabbed two chairs from alongside the wall and placed them in front of Jenna's desk and then pulled open the door. "Come in and take a seat. You know special agents Jo Wells and Ty Carter. They're involved in the case."

Jenna waited for Cross to sit down and rested her aching arm on the desk. "What can I do for you?"

"My client is prepared to speak with you." Cross drummed his fingers on the arm of his chair. "I gather that in the rage of battle he said a few things. Eyewitness accounts of three law enforcement officers and Julie Wolfe's testimony to prove attempted murder is all you have. I will fight to defend him against the other charges and have told him so."

"He won't be getting bail." Carter pushed back the brim of his Stetson. "We're prepared to hold him pending further evidence for a time, so he won't be fronting a judge for a while."

"And I'll be determining if I consider him a risk." Jo leaned back in her chair.

Jenna met the lawyer's gaze. "Wolfe is running tests as we speak that will tie Grayson into the death of his mother." She shook her head slowly. "I honestly can't believe you want to defend this guy. He tried to strangle Julie right in front of us. He begged us to allow him to kill one more time."

"I'm a defense attorney." Sam Cross stood and leaned on the table, eyeballing her. "I'm here to keep you honest. It wouldn't be the first time you arrested the wrong man." He checked his watch. "Are you ready to interview my client? It's getting late."

"You know the way." Kane got to his feet and brushed past him on his way to the coffee machine. "The sheriff will be right along."

Jenna's phone buzzed as the door closed. It was Wolfe. She listened and smiled. "Thanks, that's going to change things. I'll tell the team. We haven't interviewed Grayson yet." She disconnected and looked at Kane. "The DNA is a match. The suspect is without doubt Paul Tate, our missing kid." She looked at Jo. "Ready? Let's do this."

"Sure." Jo stood. "May I suggest you start in and then I'll take over the questioning with Kane? Once I've established a rapport, you and Carter can ask questions." She smiled. "I have an idea. Kane, can I have a word?"

"Sure." Kane pushed away from the counter and followed her into the hallway.

Jenna stared after them. "I wonder what Jo has up her sleeve?"

"Whatever it is"—Carter smiled and stood slowly—"you can be assured she knows exactly how to handle psychopaths. I just sit back and watch her play them like a fiddle."

FIFTY-NINE

Thinking on Carter's advice, Jenna paused to speak to Jo and Kane outside the interview room. "Would it be better for me to remain outside with Carter? We don't want to crowd the suspect. He might get defensive."

"No, I think it will work to our advantage." Jo opened her notebook and scanned the pages. "If he thinks he intimidates us, I can use it against him. Just give me a chance to crack him open and then you can move in with your questions. But remember, play to his cunning side. We don't want the monster coming out. If that happens, he'll shut down—or try to kill us all."

"Fat chance of that." Kane slid his weapon into the drawer along with everyone else's and locked it. "He might be crazy but he's not going to hurt anyone. Not on my watch."

They moved inside, leaving the dogs in the hallway and took seats opposite Grayson. Jenna set the video recorder, gave the date and time, and let everyone in the room identify themselves. She looked at Bexley Grayson and indicated to Jo. "Mr. Grayson, we tested your DNA against a woman by the name of Diane Tate and you came up a match. We have reason to believe you are her son, Paul Tate. Is that correct?"

"So what?" Grayson shrugged. "I was adopted after my mom died. I'm sure that is on the record somewhere."

Realizing at once she'd already put Grayson on the offensive, Jenna pulled back and gave Jo a nod.

"But you kept it a secret, didn't you? When Deputy Kane asked you if you knew Paul Tate? I can understand why you lied." Jo looked up from her notes and smiled. "I'm conducting research on early childhood behavior patterns following a traumatic event. You may have blocked that period of time from your mind."

"I remember everything." Grayson stared at Jo with cold eyes and an expression that chilled Jenna to the bone.

"I do know something about your life in Black Ridge." Jo's expression was guileless. "We've spoken to your old friend Peter Burrows. He explained to us how you loved to sing in the choir, never missed mass, and spent many weekends sleeping over at his house. He was concerned for you and wondered why you've never contacted him."

"Peter was the means to an end." Grayson made a dismissive gesture with one of his secured hands. "I needed to get away from my mom at the weekends and he was a convenience is all. When I left, I forgot he existed."

So, the classic lack of empathy had started at a young age. Jenna exchanged a meaningful look with Kane. It was unusual for psychopaths to admit they didn't care or had no feelings for the people they'd hurt. He'd explained only recently how although the lack of empathy was the primary trait of many underlying psychoses in a psychopath, but, being so smart, faking empathy was quite usual. It hid them in plain sight and many, even with the most antisocial behavior, could charm and cajole people.

"I see." Jo turned to Kane. "Can we have Mr. Grayson's restraints removed? It's difficult speaking to him when he's hunched up over the table."

"Sure." Kane stepped forward and removed the cuffs.

A prickle of apprehension raised the hairs on Jenna's arms and, as if he'd felt her concern, Carter stood and went to lean against the wall closest to the prisoner. She held her broken arm and waited with bated breath for Kane and Jo's plan to unfold.

"I understand where you're coming from." Kane sat down and looked at Grayson. "No father in the picture, a kid looks to a priest or other male figure for guidance. They trust and love them as a father figure. Sometimes things happen and when you tell your mom they get mad. I've been there. You're not alone in this problem."

Trying not to gape at the crock of lies falling from Kane's lips, Jenna opened her notebook and smoothed the pages. Her attention moved to Grayson, who blinked a few times and inclined his head as if assessing the man before him.

"You're like me, aren't you?" Grayson's forehead creased into a frown. "Yet, how come you're on that side of the table and I'm chained to the darn floor?"

"Yeah, I've killed." Kane shrugged. "I figure everyone in this room has killed apart from your lawyer. We just have different reasons to kill, don't we, Paul? What happened to the choirboy that made him kill? Tell us what happened way back then and you'll be immortalized in Agent Wells's book."

"Why should I do that?" Grayson opened his hands wide. "I'll walk free."

Jenna looked up from making unnecessary notes. "No, you'll go to jail. Ask your lawyer. At this point in time, you should be considering if we're going to suggest or oppose the death penalty. We have enough evidence to charge you with the murder of your mother, and as it occurred in this state, if you were over the age of seven, you knew you were committing a crime." She shrugged. "All this crap"—Jenna waved a hand to encompass the room—"is to give you the chance to tell your side of the story, for as sure as hell, once you get to court it will be lost in the process."

"Paul..." Jo glanced around the room and everyone went quiet. "That is your name, isn't it? Look, we understand how lonely kids are tricked into trusting adults. They're young and vulnerable, but soon they come to realize something isn't right. They confide in their moms or friends and are ridiculed. Then bad things happen. No one would blame you, a kid of ten, for wanting it to stop."

"Tell them what happened, when you were a kid." Sam Cross stared at his client. "We'd have the jurors on our side if you suffered abuse as a child."

"This is what we call grooming." Kane flicked a glance at Jo and then stared at Grayson. "You see, the adult lies to the kid, tells them they love them, and the kid believes them. They enjoy the attention until it becomes abuse."

"Yeah, it was like that at first." Grayson clasped his hands before him on the table and stared at them. "I loved being in the choir and the priest told me I had the voice of an angel. When he asked me to stay back and help him, I thought I was special. Later, I told my mom what he'd asked me to do to him and she thrashed me for speaking about such things." He rubbed both hands down his face. "I refused to go back to church, but then the priest would visit my home and it all started again."

"How did the other man become involved?" Jo placed her notebook on the table and folded her hands in her lap.

"Uncle Bob would visit as well on the weekends." Grayson looked wildly around. "I fought and screamed so much that Mom had Uncle Bob take me into the woods. From then on, I went to stay with Pete to avoid them. I knew Mom would put a stop to it soon and I needed to do something." He suddenly smiled as if recalling a sweet memory. "I made plans to meet Uncle Bob in the woods. I snuck out of Pete's house late one night to meet him. I knew what he wanted, but this time I had the knife I'd stolen from Pete's house on my belt." He chuckled. "The moment he dropped his pants, it was easy. The knife was so sharp, it was like cutting off the head of a chicken. Uncle Bob ran about like a crazy man, clutching his groin, and then just died. I covered him with leaves and branches. They didn't find him for weeks."

"That's self-defense." Sam Cross was making copious notes. "Did your mom invite these men to abuse you?"

"She told me I must keep the secret because they put food on our table." Grayson's expression changed, going like stone, unemotional soulless eyes moved around the table. "I heard talk about her being a prostitute and didn't know what it was for some time, but when I did, I realized I was just an added attraction. I did the same to the priest. It was easy to lure him to Uncle Bob's cabin. I left him there in a pool of blood."

"Killing your abusers is a defense." Jo appeared so relaxed as if he'd just told her a fairy story. "Did your mom know you'd killed them?"

"Not until I stabbed her in the throat." Grayson didn't as much as blink. "I can still see her face, but I didn't care. I cleaned up, burned my clothes, and went back to Pete's house. They didn't even know I'd gone missing."

"You were just a little boy in an untenable position." Jo shook her head. "I've seen a picture of your mother. Did seeing Julie, trigger a memory of her?"

"It was the red nails and the way she played with her hair." Grayson leaned back in his chair and smiled. "All I could see in my head was my mother bleeding out. Watching her die was the best thing in my life. I was free."

"So, after killing the people at the ski lodge, you figured killing Julie would purge you again?" Jo's pen hovered a few inches above her notebook.

"Yeah." Grayson chuckled. "I really enjoyed those."

Jenna held her breath. Jo had extracted a confession of guilt from Grayson, but Sam Cross dashed her hopes when he jumped to his feet.

"I think that's enough questions." Sam Cross stared at his client both eyebrows raised in disbelief.

"Nah, I'll tell them. I might as well go to jail and be respected." Grayson smiled at Jo. "If she immortalizes me in her book and agrees to take the death penalty off the table, I'll be the King of County."

"Just wait one darn minute." Sam Cross glared at Grayson. "I make the deals."

"Not this time." Grayson smiled. "I'll have the recognition I deserve."

"Okay, that's a deal." Jo lifted her chin. "What was the reason behind the ski lodge murders?"

"Revenge." Grayson steepled his fingers, loving the attention. "They're all responsible for the rejection of my book in one way or another. Not one of them or the authors they represented had my flare for the written word. So, I demonstrated the flaws in the murder scenes by re-creating them. I showed them how they could've been written through the eyes of the victim or the killer." His gaze moved over Jenna and then settled on Jo. "Those idiots were nothing, a mere inconvenience. I have so many stories to tell you, Agent Wells. I hope you'll be a frequent visitor and we'll become friends."

"Oh, I'll be speaking to you in the future, but I'm not finished here yet." Jo narrowed her gaze at him. "Why didn't you kill Julie the night you broke into her room?"

"It wasn't time and I wanted to play with her some more. Mind games, Agent Wells. Building up the fear before the kill makes it so much better." Grayson wet his lips. "She was going to be my reward for a job well done."

There was one thing Jenna had to know. She kept her voice conversational. "What was the significance of the pen?"

"Miss Storm bought that pen after earning her first million in commissions. She used it to sign all the contracts, so I used it in her final contract with death." Grayson grinned. "A nice twist, don't you agree?"

"Just one more question: Why leave your mom's earrings at the first two murder scenes?" Jo leaned forward. "You did remove them from your mother's body post-mortem, didn't you?"

"Yeah, I ripped them out of her ears. You see, when it's really good—the killing—I keep things to recall what I was feeling at the time." Grayson giggled almost childlike. "You want to know why I left the earrings, the ring, and the scarf behind? That's so easy. I bet most of the authors at the convention could've given you the answer. I'm a crime writer. Don't you know only the very best of us leave a ton of red herrings?"

* * *

It took hours to complete the statements and it was three in the morning before Jenna had everything squared away. She'd dragged the DA out of bed to explain everything and he'd arrived at the office to discuss the case with Sam Cross. The deliberations led to Grayson deciding on a guilty plea to all the ski lodge murders and to manslaughter for the cold-case murders in Black Ridge. He would face a judge in the morning and be transferred to county. Jenna's broken arm throbbed but, exhilarated, she looked round at her exhausted team. "We did it. A full confession." She hugged Jo. "You are amazing."

"I'm convinced he's killed more people." Jo rubbed her forehead. "I'll need to delve into his background more closely. Maybe investigate some cold cases in California and I believe he was in Florida for a time too. I'll get Kalo onto it when we get home."

After Jenna checked that the deputies from Louan were ready to take over guarding the prisoner overnight, she grabbed the others and they headed for the front door. She looked at her team. "I'm sure looking forward to taking something for my arm and crawling into bed. We don't have to be in the office until ten. The hearing isn't until eleven and I have people to cover for us."

"Hallelujah." Carter opened the door for her and waved her through. "Tomorrow night we'll celebrate."

EPILOGUE

Over the next day or so, and after saying goodbye to Jo and Carter, it seemed life had returned to normal, apart from the awkwardness between Jenna and Kane. They worked together as smoothly as ever, but being so busy tying up the case, their breakup hadn't been a priority. But now that the dust had settled, Jenna really hoped they could talk. One thing, Kane hadn't moved his belongings back to the cottage, made her a little optimistic, but although they'd eat together, like civilized people, the topic of their relationship never came up. Kane would do the chores as usual, but after dinner would go to his room. He'd set up a TV in there and virtually ignored her. They didn't work out together since she'd broken her arm, and he spent his time pummeling the punching bag, lifting weights, and skipping. They didn't talk much and, without another case, she had no excuse to disturb him. He always had his head in a book, reading. This worried her as they were becoming like strangers. She'd had a chat with Jo and bared her soul. From what Jo said, some men didn't like confrontation with women about such things. Her telling him she didn't want to wait would be enough for Kane to back off—some men just didn't feel comfortable about being where they weren't wanted. She considered Kane to be just that type of man. If Jenna wanted to make things right, then she'd have to make the first move.

As the organizers of the crime writers' convention had invited her, Kane, and Wolfe's team to the ball at the ski lodge on the weekend, she'd spent a wonderful time the previous afternoon in Helena with Emily and Julie shopping for ballgowns. Jenna smiled to herself. She'd gained a deep respect for crime writers. Not one of them had left the convention, even after they'd been informed about the murders. It seemed the fact the killer had been arrested had made the experience more exciting for them. Many wanted to know the gory details she couldn't provide, but she had encouraged them to follow the trial for more information.

Jenna worked around Kane, trying to help as he cooked dinner. He'd elected to do just about everything since her injury, but he'd always preferred to prepare the meals and did so with efficiency. She took a deep breath and looked at him as he grilled the steaks. "I thought you would've moved back into the cottage when we returned home."

"I would have, but moving twice is a pain in the middle of winter." Kane stared at the steaks. "I'm planning on getting a place of my own in town after the melt, but if being here is a problem, I'll move out tonight. I can get a room at The Cattleman's Hotel and then come by for my stuff later."

Heartbroken, Jenna stared at him. "I don't want you to move, Dave. I like having you here in the house with me. I had to ask. You've hardly said two words to me outside of work."

"I think in the circumstances it's for the best, but as you'll need help around the ranch, I'll still drop by each day and do the chores until you're better. I won't leave you to fend for yourself." Kane served the food and, after cutting up her steak for her, placed the plates on the table. "If you're looking for a husband, no guy will set foot in the place with me living here, and I'm not sure I could cope seeing you bringing men home either."

Heart thundering, Jenna stared at him. "I'm not husband hunting."

"Really?" Kane sat down and cut into his steak. "Your words are kinda burned into my head, Jenna. What did you say? Ah yeah: 'From now on, with or without you, I'm going to enjoy every single day.' That might as well have been a declaration of war to me."

Swallowing hard, Jenna bit her bottom lip. "What do you mean by that? You know I care for you, Dave. We argued, so what? All couples argue."

"I'm an old-fashioned guy and I take threats personal." Kane stared into her eyes. "When I commit, I commit. If by that comment you meant you're planning on stepping out with other men while I'm in the picture, I'm moving out. Unless you want a bloodbath, because if you're my woman—which you seemed to imply—then I'll defend what's mine." He chewed his steak, his eyes never leaving her face. "You know what kind of man I am, Jenna. If we married, I'd be possessive. It's in my genetic makeup, and if another guy touched you, I'd want to kill him. I'm not saying I would, but I'd want to." He sighed.

Surprised by his candidness, Jenna blinked. "I think I'd be disappointed if you didn't defend me... I just don't like to be treated like I'm incapable of looking after myself. You must admit that when you first arrived you tried to smother me. If I'd known about Annie at the time, I'd have understood you better."

"This is who I am, Jenna. I've become the man you wanted me to be, kept my overprotectiveness in check and respected your position at work. If you still want me in your life, I'll continue to be that man... but you're so not ready for the real Dave Kane. I already lost one wife and our baby. What about when you're pregnant? In here"—he poked at his chest—"I'll want to wrap you in cotton, but in here"—he tapped his head—"I know I'll be pushing you away. But it will happen. I'll be concerned something might happen to you. We live in murder central. It's not really conducive to happy families, is it? Could you cope with me in combat mode twenty-four/seven? This is what you need to think about—all of the above. It's what's been doing my head in for weeks." He sighed. "I should've explained better at the ski resort, but you didn't give me the chance."

Jenna ate and allowed his words to filter through her mind. She sipped her water and lifted her chin. "I never knew you thought of me as your woman."

"Really? I'm living in your house and I thought we were building a relationship." Kane shook his head as if in disbelief. "Being this size, I can be intimidating, so I was waiting for you to make the first move. Until you told me how you felt, I figured we were moving along just fine, one day at a time."

Jenna shook her head. "And I figured if you'd wanted me, you'd go all Neanderthal on me and throw me over one shoulder and carry me off into the sunset."

"Maybe I should have, but you're an independent woman, Jenna. Doing something like that might have had the opposite effect. See my point? I'm damned if I do and damned if I don't." Kane finished his meal, stood, cleaned his plate, and dropped it into the dishwasher.

Wanting to sort things out between them, Jenna touched his arm. "Can we talk some more? I don't want you to move out. I like being us. Maybe we can set ground rules that makes it easier for both of us?"

"Ground rules, huh?" Kane scratched his cheek. "That might take some time and you're going to a ball tonight. Don't forget, Wolfe said he'd be dropping by to collect you at eight. I've got things to do. We'll talk later." He stood and went to his room.

Jenna stared after him and then gasped when she checked her watch. She had to be ready for the ball in forty minutes. She had no idea if Kane was going. He hadn't offered to drive her and although the roads were clear now, snow could come again anytime. She hadn't wanted to risk driving up the mountain with a broken wrist, and when Wolfe offered to drive her, she'd jumped at the chance. It didn't take her too long to dress, although wearing a ball gown under her thick coat, seemed a little surreal. She pulled on her boots and picked up her purse and shoes. She'd change them when she arrived, rather than freezing her feet.

The sky was surprisingly clear and when she climbed out of Wolfe's truck she could see every star in the sky. The snow reflected the flashing yellow lights around the ski lodge entrance and the wind made the icicles on the trees jangle together. It was a beautiful but freezing night. Inside, the lodge was warm and the smell of woodsmoke and perfume filled the air. Women and men moved around dressed in their finest and music drifted out from the ballroom. Beside her, Julie was bouncing with excitement as they removed their coats and stowed away their boots.

"I can't believe Em is on a date with Zac." Julie giggled. "She likes him. You know, Dad didn't say a word. Yet when she mentioned liking Ty Carter, he kinda growled, like an old teddy bear."

Jenna smiled. "Don't place too much into it. It's just a ball and I doubt either of them wanted to come alone. I came with your dad and we certainly aren't romantically inclined."

"I guess." Julie led the way into the ballroom. "Oh, look at Uncle Dave over there dancing. Doesn't he look handsome? I thought he'd be bringing you to the ball. Didn't you want to go with him? Em mentioned you'd had an argument."

Jenna sighed. "He didn't ask me." She noticed Wolfe standing next to the buffet and headed in his direction. "Look there's your dad. Let's go and keep him company."

She nodded to the people who smiled at her and made her way to Wolfe and stood on the edge of the dancefloor watching. Her gaze kept moving to Kane. He danced so well and seemed to have a ton of admirers. When Wolfe suddenly asked her to dance, she smiled at him. "I'll ruin your boots. I've never been able to dance to country music. I'm very much a jiggle-to-the-music type of dancer."

"Well, this Texan has three daughters and is used to having his boots stepped over." Wolfe bent his head and lowered his voice. "You'll have to save me. Crime writers seem to find a medical examiner fascinating. I don't get many invitations to balls and I really don't want to talk shop all night." He held out his hand.

Jenna went into his arms and they moved around the floor, Wolfe expertly avoiding her feet. When he danced her to where Kane was twirling Emily around, Wolfe stopped and smiled at her. She gave him a puzzled look. "Is this a set up?"

"Maybe, but one thing's for sure, you won't fight in front of all these people." Wolfe smiled at her. "He's a stubborn man. You'll have to make the first move, Jenna." He tapped Kane on the shoulder. "I want to dance with my daughter."

"Sure." Kane turned and looked down at Jenna. "I haven't had my boots trampled on all night and I kinda miss it." He took the hand in the cast and laid it gently on his chest. "Come on Jenna, live a little."

They danced in silence and for once in her life, Jenna didn't step all over his boots. When the song finished and a slow number came on, Kane didn't stop dancing. She rested her cheek on his chest and looked up at him. It was now or never. "It just so happens that I love your combat face. It's what makes you special and I like feeling safe with you around all the time watching out for me. I love *you*, Dave. You must know that by now, right?"

They danced right out of the ballroom and Jenna found herself in the hallway. She'd said the L-word and it was out there, waiting for a reply and she'd never felt so vulnerable. She swallowed hard and waited, not sure if Kane gave second chances. "Did you hear me?"

"Uh-huh." His lips curled into a slow smile.

The next moment he bent and tossed her over his shoulder and headed toward the foyer. Pressing her good hand into his back, Jenna gasped for air. "Dave, what are you doing?"

"I'm taking my woman home."

A LETTER FROM D.K. HOOD

Dear Reader,

Thank you so much for choosing my novel and coming with me on another exciting adventure with Kane and Alton in *Fallen Angel*.

If you'd like to keep up to date with all my latest releases, just sign up at the website link below. Your details will never be shared and you can unsubscribe at any time.

www.bookouture.com/dk-hood

Writing this story was great fun. I love writing about the different aspects of human nature and what drives them to murder. I hope I thrilled you with Jenna and Kane's hair-raising week at the Glacial Heights Ski Resort.

If you enjoyed reading my story, I would be very grateful if you could leave a review and recommend my book to your friends and family. I really enjoy hearing from readers, so feel free to ask me questions at any time. You can get in touch on my Facebook page or Twitter or through my blog.

Thank you so much for your support.

D.K. Hood

KEEP IN TOUCH WITH D.K. HOOD

http://www.dkhood.com
dkhood-author.blogspot.com.au

 facebook.com/dkhoodauthor
twitter.com/DKHood_Author

ACKNOWLEDGEMENTS

A huge thank you to my amazingly supportive editor, Helen, and the incredible Team Bookouture—you are the Olympians of the publishing business.

Many thanks to my wonderful Facebook friends, who support me with their delightful comments and share my promotions. I truly appreciate every one of you and wish I could add everyone here. This time, special mention goes to Wendy Steenblok, Lisa Philips, Rene Murphy, Linda Hocutt, Diane Dell'Aquila, Vicki Clouston, Christy Flynn, Kim Bradley Blalock, and Laura Croskey.

Printed in Great Britain
by Amazon

21676730R00171